FELICITY'S FOOL

FELICITY'S FOOL

by
François Gravel

translated from the French
by Sheila Fischman

Cormorant Books

The translator wishes to acknowledge the support of the Canada Council. Published with the assistance of the Canada Council and the Ontario Arts Council.

Felicity's Folly was originally published in French as *Bonheur fou* by Les Éditions du Boréal in Montreal, in 1990.

Cover illustration by Geneviève Côté.

Printed and bound in Canada.

Published by
Cormorant Books
RR 1, Dunvegan
Ontario, Canada K0C 10

Canadian Cataloguing in Publication Data

Gravel, François
(Bonheur fou. English)

Felicity's fool

ISBN 0-920953-72-7

I. Title.   II. Title: Bonheur fou. English.

PS8563.R388B6613   1992   C843' .54   C92-090083-6
PQ3919 .2 .G73B6613 1992

This translation is dedicated
to the memory of
Larry Shouldice

1

Bernard Dansereau had always been preoccupied by the question of happiness. Not that eternal happiness the priests promise to all those who accept suffering and who bow to authority, but earthly happiness, here and now. Not so much his own personal happiness, either, although he wouldn't have spurned a straightforward offer, but the happiness of all humanity, without which individual happiness is merely an illusion. He firmly believed that one day, thanks to a discovery still to be made, the secret of happiness would be found. Such ideas were not especially original during the nineteenth century, at least among scientists.

At the age of five, he had started badgering his parents on the subject. They were decent farmers from the Louiseville area, who would talk to him about good harvests, about unusually mild winters, about the satisfaction to be gained from a job well done, and about the graces that the Lord bestows as a reward for our virtuous deeds. Bernard was disappointed: did he really have nothing to look forward to except these fleeting joys? Why should happiness exist only in the plural? For happiness in the singular, replied his parents, you must wait for eternity. Why? Because it was God's will. And why was it

God's will? Because that was the way God wanted it. And why did God want it that way? Wait, they'll explain it in school.

Never had a Louiseville child been so eager for the first day of school. No sooner was he in the seat assigned to him than he asked the instructress, a sixteen-year-old terrified at the prospect of teaching fifty children, to explain to him, at once, the secret of happiness. The young girl stammered that first he'd have to learn to read and write, that it would be better to ask the curé about such matters, and that, above all, he must learn to put up his hand before talking. Meekly, Bernard acquiesced. All through elementary school he worked conscientiously. Because it had been impressed on him that reading, writing, and arithmetic were indispensable prerequisites for happiness, he did his utmost always to come first in class. And he succeeded.

When he had finished elementary school, he still had not found answers to his questions, but during those few years he had at least learned when to keep quiet. He already knew that it served no purpose to ask people whether they were happy; his experiments along those lines succeeded only in making adults squirm. For some obscure reason, the secret of happiness, along with the secret of where babies come from, seemed to be a topic that must not be discussed with children. If he wanted to learn something about these matters, there was nothing like observing nature, which Bernard did whenever he got the chance.

After spending hours watching hens, cows, and cats, he had been able without too much difficulty to determine the basic mechanism of procreation. Happiness, though, remained a total mystery. In an attempt to set matters straight in his own mind, he had performed several dissections on the cadavers of whatever animals he could get his hands on — particularly pigs, who were undoubtedly the happiest animals in creation. Perhaps happiness was secreted by some organ that he now simply had to track down?

Bernard's parents worried about his passion for dissection. One day when the curé came to call, they confided their fears. Was it normal for a twelve-year-old to spend days on end rummaging around in the brains of pigs? The curé reassured them: Bernard was a lively, curious child who got excellent marks in school, and they shouldn't hesitate to send him to a classical college. He had never seen anyone so obviously slated to become a doctor.

And so Bernard ended up at the seminary. During his first year, his spiritual adviser enjoined him in his most syrupy voice to tell what lay in the depths of his soul, to advise him of his slightest doubts, to confide in him utterly. Bernard, who had never been asked his opinion about his alleged medical vocation, was suspicious. But he tested the waters none the less.

"Father, I sometimes wonder if hens, even though they aren't endowed with much intelligence, can be happy."

"Hens cannot be happy, my child. Hens have no souls, thus they cannot have emotions. The reason why men have emotions is that they have a soul."

"But hens are alive. If they find food when they're hungry they can be happy, if they're cold they can be glad of a warm henhouse. . . ."

"Providence has given hens and all other animals an instinct that takes the place of intelligence and enables them to survive. When they are hungry, that instinct is what urges them to eat. They can satisfy their hunger, but they cannot experience happiness; true happiness comes from the Spirit, never from satisfying our instincts."

"Do all emotions come from the Spirit?"

"Righteous emotions most certainly do, but there are evil emotions too, that have their origin in our base instincts."

"And how does our brain know the difference between righteous sentiments and base instincts?"

These discussions went on and on. In time, Bernard discovered that priests were far more patient than laymen when it came time to talk about happiness: after a few hours they inevitably advised him to pray hard and to wait until he was studying philosophy, at which time he would most assuredly learn how to distinguish truth from error. If he wanted to take full advantage of his philosophy classes, however, he must start right now to apply himself to the study of Latin and Greek, otherwise he ran the risk of some cruel disappointments. Terrified at the thought that ignorance of some dead languages could have such dreadful consequences, Bernard threw himself into his studies.

In philosophy class he finally discovered the Greek thinkers. According to Socrates, man could accede to happiness here below to the extent that he was virtuous. But the teacher also had a warning for his pupils: the ideal was magnificent, but without the aid of grace it was impracticable. For Plato, happiness represented the supreme goal of existence. Pleasure alone could not cause happiness, because it could not bring about stability, purity, plenitude. Nor did happiness exist only in knowledge, for knowledge without pleasure was insignificant. Happiness was to be found in wisdom, to which, the professor reminded them, must be added grace.

Bernard wanted to intervene, but his classical education had taught him that it is better to keep one's thoughts to oneself. Perhaps man would not find happiness in scientific knowledge, but was it not conceivable that science would provide men with the necessary conditions for happiness? Could Plato have had an inkling that people would float across the sky in dirigibles, that steamships would crisscross the oceans of the world? Science, thought Bernard; only science would give satisfactory answers.

After the Greeks, they moved on to Saint Thomas. Happiness would be relegated to the next life, and for a thousand years philosophy would carry on as if it did not exist.

When he had terminated his classical studies, Bernard was somewhat disappointed, but not bereft of hope. Prayer and philosophy had not revealed to him the secret of happiness, but at least his long years of study had given him access to the great writers. He had revelled in the novels of Voltaire, which he had got his hands on through the complicity of a classmate whose father was a free-thinker, and even more in the works of Auguste Comte, whose ideas matched his own in every respect.

At night, he would read a few pages by his favourite author, then turn to dreaming: all over the world, scholars were multiplying discoveries at such a rapid pace that one could believe, without risk of error, that some day science would be able to solve every problem. After all, the elements had been identified and classified, and now all that remained was to find the right combinations to reconstitute the solids, liquids, and gases. Some day when microscopes were more powerful, physicists would isolate atoms, and then only insignificant mechanical problems would be left to solve. It would certainly take longer to penetrate all the mysteries of biology, but they'd get there, it was just a matter of time. How many years? Twenty, thirty, fifty?

Once the natural sciences were fully understood, they would tackle the human sciences: there would be no more poverty, conflicts, war. Now, it was likely that not all the countries in the world would advance from the religious to the scientific stage at the same time; a few primitive peoples would be left in Africa and Asia, but scientific missionaries would be sent there, replacing the religious ones. . . . By the middle of the twentieth century, the Indians would still be fighting a few minor wars, but Europe, land of the Enlightenment, would provide an example of peace and prosperity for the rest of the world.

Had Auguste Comte committed the sin of

excessive optimism? Absolutely not. Anyone who had eyes to see and ears to hear knew that the march of progress was irreversible: railways would cross the country, steam engines would multiply the strength of workers a thousand fold, the telegraph would make possible instantaneous communication with all the big cities in America, so what was there to prevent the triumph of science?

Not only had his education given him the opportunity to enrich himself with stimulating reading of this kind, but it had also opened the doors to the finest medical faculty on the continent. At McGill University, Bernard would finally have access to Science. Dissecting human brains would surely lead him to something.

* * *

It was September of the year 1850 when Bernard, quivering with enthusiasm and determined to penetrate all the secrets of life, first crossed the threshold of the acclaimed university.

As he had to learn English along with medicine, the first two years did not give him many opportunities for thinking about happiness, or even for exploring Montreal. During his third year, he could finally allow himself some recreation. Early on, he had discovered the marvellous library at the Institut Canadien, where he quickly became a regular visitor. He didn't miss a single scientific lecture: visiting European professors talked about astronomy, physics, or magnetism, and, in addition to new knowledge, they gave Bernard a deep sense of satisfaction. He was now a man of science and a participant in the grand march of progress. He admired these speakers so greatly that he copied their every move, their slightest intonations — so much so that, in only a few months, his voice had dropped a full octave. He had also grown a beard, a thick one, which he trimmed straight across. These two attributes would contribute greatly to his success.

Little by little, however, the scientific lectures became less frequent, and their place was taken by politics. The Liberals were proposing the annexation of Canada to the United States, an idea with which Bernard was in full agreement. If the French Canadians were condemned to live with the English, it would be better to choose those who were democrats. It was easy for Bernard to understand how people could become impassioned by politics: after all, the solution to the problem of happiness would be either biological or political, there was no getting around that. But, whether because of temperament (he didn't like crowds) or training (it seemed to him that politics had no scientific basis), fine speeches never stirred him. That the happiness of a people could depend upon a law, a constitution, or an annexation was certainly an appealing prospect, but it was necessarily incomplete: under the best of circumstances such changes could help to abolish obstacles to happiness, but they would not create it. Freedom was a necessary condition, but not a sufficient one. He remained a subscriber to the library for some time; the lectures, however, he attended only rarely.

* * *

During their third year, medical students had a serious problem: dissection was obligatory for obtaining one's diploma, but there were few cadavers available. Some of the wealthier students could get an unidentified body for fifty dollars, after dropping in on the regulars at a certain tavern on rue Saint-Denis, while others made do with black Americans, whose corpses were cheap and easily obtainable. They arrived by train, in bundles that looked like sacks of flour. The waiting period was so long, however, that when the time came to dissect them, it was hard to tell the liver from the spleen. Students who weren't wealthy and who wanted to get their hands on a suitable cadaver had to resign themselves to making nocturnal expeditions to the graveyards.

And so it was that, one November evening, Bernard was in the Côte-des-Neiges cemetery, holding a lantern, while three of his classmates dug into the freshly covered earth of the common grave. They had read in the newspaper that a Spanish sailor killed in a brawl had just been buried there. This was the perfect chance, especially because it was snowing: the cold would preserve the cadaver and the snow would cover their footprints.

They took turns digging, opened the grave, and dragged their burden to the entrance of the graveyard, where a cart stood waiting. When they were back at the university, they left the corpse in the autopsy room and spent the rest of the night drinking.

The next morning, they began the dissection. While Bernard was opening the skull with a metal-saw, eager to have his first look at the mass of grey matter which produced ideas, his colleagues made a priceless discovery: in the corpse's stomach were two gold coins. Bernard suggested telling the authorities, but his classmates proposed instead that they drink a few glasses of beer in the company of those young ladies who offered their services at the faculty's back door. They finished off the dissection and went to a little hotel where, far too briefly, Bernard forgot about the brain — the only human brain he'd ever seen. When they returned to the university a few hours later, the cadaver had vanished, probably stolen by some other students. Now they'd have to start all over.

For the rest of his life Bernard would dream of that expedition, and the pale light of a lantern dancing in the night would always remind him of his missed opportunity. At the very moment he had been discovering one of the delights of existence, someone had stolen his brain — the only human brain he had been able to observe at leisure.

* * *

When he completed his internship in 1853, Bernard's professors advised him to move to Hochelaga, a small village outside Montreal that was destined for rapid expansion. It was shrewd advice. The workers in the tanneries and slaughterhouses earned meagre wages; still, he soon built up a substantial practice among the rich landowners who were building luxurious second homes for themselves along the river, as far as Pointe-aux-Trembles, and among the wealthy farmers in Longue-Pointe who provided food for all of Montreal. With the thousand dollars he had inherited from his parents and another thousand borrowed from the bank, he had enough to buy a house on rue Sainte-Catherine, furniture, a horse and buggy, and office equipment, including an oak desk, a few chairs for the waiting room, prescription forms imprinted with his name, and big black ledgers for keeping accounts. At fifty cents a visit, one dollar for house-calls, and a dollar-fifty for deliveries, it would take him twenty years to repay his loan.

In time, however, his vision of science triumphant would fade. It seemed that none of the cases which turned up in his office bore any resemblance to what he had studied in books, and that his patients were going out of their way to invent new diseases he had neither the time nor the knowledge to treat properly. Equipped with only a wooden stethoscope, a thermometer, a reflex mallet, and a measuring tape, how could he diagnose and care for all the mysterious stomach-aches, discharges, and bloody sputum? It was painful to take stock of his ignorance, but, as one who had long since learned how to conceal his hand, he knew how to keep his helplessness to himself.

Like most doctors of his time, Bernard had learned early on to listen to his patients. Their words were sometimes most revealing. Bernard would palpate the patient at length in search of a swollen spleen or a vague tumour, then he would try to guess. Nine times out of ten he knew nothing about the disease. Once the examination was complete, he would nod his head and scrawl a prescription: hot compresses, mustard plasters, iodine solutions, country air.... When his patients didn't get better, at least Bernard could console himself with the thought that his perfectly harmless remedies had not aggravated their conditions. Fortunately, it happened fairly often that, through some mysterious process, a remedy prescribed by chance was effective beyond his wildest hopes. Such successes, even unmerited, were good for his morale: that was how he learned that he must count chance among his allies, and that effectiveness often exempts us from comprehension.

A little later, in discussions with his colleagues at the Hôtel-Dieu, he discovered the virtues of powders and liquids. Patients adored yellow powders, and green ones often worked miracles. The physician's art lay in varying mixtures of the same medicines through the use of different colourings, so that he could prescribe a green powder one week, a yellow one the next, then go back to the green, adding a little red now and then, just for a change. The same was true for liquids. The coloured ones always yielded better therapeutic results than the colourless, and he had to learn how to vary the doses: a few drops the first week, a teaspoonful the second, two tablespoons the third, always making sure that the concoctions tasted hideous: punishing themselves for being sick helped patients make quicker recoveries. Powder or liquid, what mattered was that the medicine have a Latin name, one that immediately set it apart from old wives' remedies, and that it be new: if a medicine is too well known it inevitably loses its power.

Just one year after his arrival in Hochelaga, Bernard's practice was big enough to guarantee his future. Disappointed by science but still preoccupied by happiness, Bernard decided to marry.

* * *

Early in the spring of 1855, he had donned his finest suit and introduced himself to the directress of the Hochelaga convent, which was renowned for training the finest doctors' wives in the province. The nun had come up with the ideal candidate right away: Viviane Gouin had stood first in domestic science and bookkeeping, her puff pastry was so delicious that her services were always requested when the archbishop came to call, she was a gifted singer, and her touch at the piano was divine. Moreover, she came from a good family of wealthy Longueuil farmers. Bernard was introduced to Viviane that very day and he was won over by her almond eyes, her white skin, and her slightly protruding teeth, which seemed to be involuntarily thrusting her lips towards him.

And so he took the ferry-boat to Longueuil the next week and introduced himself to Viviane's parents. Every Saturday that summer, and until the last days of autumn, he returned to her house. The sun on the river, the pike that swam in the clear water, the flights of Canada geese that traced his fiancée's initial in the sky, Viviane's puff pastry, her mother's fudge, the father's generously proffered gin ... it was a wonderful summer during which he didn't once dream about his expedition to the graveyard.

The beginning of autumn marked the time to

start thinking about the ice that would soon prevent the ferry-boat from crossing to Longueuil. Should they wait until spring, or marry in time for Christmas? The decision was quickly made. They were married at the end of October and, directly after the ceremony, they moved into Bernard's house.

Viviane fell in love at her first sight of the splendid, slate-roofed greystone house at the corner of the street, with its stained-glass windows and its broad white gallery. On the main floor were the office, library, kitchen, and dining room. Upstairs, the master bedroom opened onto a balcony overlooking the street, and there were also three smaller bedrooms, and a parlour dominated by a piano. When Viviane had moved in, Bernard had certainly thought about happiness: if only there were some way to erase everything else that was cluttering up his memory uselessly, and to keep only that moment. . . .

* * *

Bernard always treated Viviane with respect, asking his due only with the firm intention of procreating, or when he was driven by reasons of elementary hygiene, never out of boredom or for want of something better to do. Viviane, although tiny, was clearly in excellent health, and Bernard seemed to have all the qualities necessary for reproduction. Seven years later, however, the little bedrooms were still empty. Viviane was examined by Dr. Lacoste, who had studied in London. Her Fallopian tubes were obstructed, so that her ova never left their nest. One day, undoubtedly, medicine would discover a cure, but in the meantime. . . .

In the meantime, the little village of Hochelaga had become a town, Bernard's practice had continued to prosper, and Bernard himself had virtually puffed up before the townspeople's eyes: the excellent meals that Viviane prepared, along with the glasses of brandy he awarded himself at the end of his long working days, probably had something to do with it. When Viviane observed that he was gaining weight, he invariably replied that his abdominal appendix had always been an important factor in the prosperity of his practice. Had Hippocrates not said that the physician's first duty was always to be in excellent health, a kind of walking advertisement? The mere sight of his round belly, his prophet's beard, and his scholar's spectacles immediately made his patients feel better. If Viviane preferred skinny men, why hadn't she married a pharmacist? Members of that profession have a duty to stay thin, because they are part of the punishment inflicted on the sick. If that were not the case, how could they sell castor oil? Viviane smiled and resumed her knitting.

Bernard never had any reason to reproach Viviane. She had devoted herself to taking care of the office and house, serving as nurse, secretary, and housekeeper. In the evening she went to church to pray, performed good works, or played the piano. It was a quiet life, and a full one, despite the empty bedrooms. He had no reason to criticize her, but marriage had not brought the happiness he'd hoped for. The more brandy he drank, the more the images of his expedition to the graveyard came back to him.

One day just before Viviane's fortieth birthday, she was struck down by an apoplectic fit while she was sitting and petting the old grey cat. She remained paralysed for two months, then quietly passed away one morning in the spring of 1880. She was such a slip of a thing that she was buried in her wedding gown.

* * *

A few days after Viviane's death, Bernard hired a housekeeper, Mrs. Robinson, a poor Irishwoman who had watched her own parents die of typhus during the hard crossing that had brought them to Canada. As the unfortunate woman could neither read nor write, she could not perform secretarial tasks, but as Bernard's evenings were often free, he had no objection to keeping his own books. She was, however, an excellent housekeeper and a tolerable cook. Aside from the dreadful boiled chicken she fixed for him every Sunday night, her meals, while they could never erase the memory of Viviane's puff pastry, were acceptable.

He conscientiously observed mourning for a year, and then he found a lady friend, Florence, whom he visited on Sunday and who was prepared to take care of his hygiene. He had not had to look very long: there's no lack of opportunities for a doctor.

* * *

A glass of brandy, the bottle within reach, a comfortable chair, legs outstretched, a hassock for his feet, a Cuban cigar wrapped in its thin outer leaf, and silence. On Saturday night the stethoscope stays in the drawer, and patients are requested to submit with good grace. "I'm not in to anyone, I need to think." "Very good, Doctor," replies Mrs. Robinson, quietly closing the heavy padded door to the library and tiptoeing away. Since Viviane's death, Bernard spends his Saturday nights reading. He reads a few lines of Auguste Comte, just a few, and catches himself dreaming as he did when he was young.

Yes, Comte was right: the triumphal march of science is continuing. Mendeleev has succeeded in classifying all the elements found in nature. A Canadian has found a way to send the human voice along wires, and in a few years people will be able to telephone to Pointe-aux-Trembles. Soon — who knows? — it will be possible to transmit the voice to London, Paris, Rome. . . . Medicine has progressed so quickly in recent years that everything Bernard learned in university is out of date. A few more years and the germ that causes cancer will be identified, women will no longer die in childbirth, a way will be found to unblock Fallopian tubes, humans will live to a hundred, perhaps longer.

And when science has triumphed, will mankind finally be happy? Will madness still exist? Since it is obviously lodged in the brain, there is nothing to prevent discovering what causes it. If Koch could isolate the bacillus responsible for tuberculosis, why shouldn't someone find the ones that trigger hysteria and epilepsy? And if madness is lodged in the brain, is it absurd to assume that it is the seat of happiness as well?

Bernard has long since laid down his book.

Using surgical scissors, he snips the tip off his cigar, then moistens it, caresses it with the flame of a match so that it will retain only the salt of his saliva, strikes another match, waits until all the sulphur has burned off, then lights it. A grin appears on his lips. He is a widower with no ties, utterly free. Why should he remain on the sidelines while science makes its triumphal march, why not launch himself into research?

The clock shows twenty minutes to midnight. He must fast before Mass the next day: Bernard puts away his bottle, then walks to the window and throws open the shutters so the cool August air can pour into the library and drive away the cigar smoke.

Outside, the street is deserted. He can hear dogs calling to each other now and then, the neighing of insomniac horses, yowling cats.

Happiness, science, the brain. At the age of fifty-three, Bernard has his old dream restored, utterly intact. But where should he begin?

2

Bernard was very fond of Sundays. For one day, he would transform himself into a country doctor, taking advantage of his weekly rounds to visit his friend Florence, who lived in the village of Longue-Pointe.

He always attended early Mass, then spent a while on the front steps of the church, giving free consultations. After that he would go home, eat heartily, then hitch up his horse and buggy and set out on his Sunday circuit. He drove along rue Notre-Dame, which was always full of traffic, stopped in the Hudon mill district, where some patients were waiting to see him, and continued along to the last streets in Hochelaga.

When he reached the place where rue Notre-Dame became the Chemin du Roy, Bernard ordered his horse to slow down, while he breathed deeply and admired the scenery. On either side of the road lay fertile land where hops and barley grew. Here and there, along the banks of the river, shady lanes ran up to opulent houses that were barely visible from the road. In places the road ran parallel to the river, and you could see big ships leaving the harbour.

After trotting along for more than an hour, he

turned reluctantly onto the dirt road that went to the Limoilou house, former summer residence of George-Etienne Cartier, which had been bought up some years earlier by the owner of a soap-works. Just after moving into the house of his dreams, the man had suffered an unfortunate fall from a horse, an accident from which he had never recovered. Now confined to bed, he was afflicted with terrible headaches that made him irritable, and his bad moods infected the entire household. Although Bernard came to see him every Sunday, his condition did not improve.

Whenever Bernard went into a house with an oppressive atmosphere, he generally made his way directly to the patient and immediately took his temperature. The thermometer cut short any complaints; the gold watch he took from his jacket pocket to read the sick man's pulse had the same effect on the rest of the family.

Fifteen seconds would have been more than enough for him to determine whether the man's condition was stable, but he deliberately prolonged his examination for more than a minute. When all signs of agitation had vanished, he took a dose of morphine from his bag and gave it to his patient's wife: stir into a glass of milk, administer three times daily, four if the patient requests it, everything will be fine, that will be one dollar for the visit plus two dollars for the morphine. He also advised her to open all the windows to give the patient some fresh air, and to add another pillow to raise his head a few inches: his madness was heavy; perhaps — who knows — it might descend through gravity.

"He's not going to pull through, is he?"

"I couldn't say. I can see to it that he's comfortable, but as far as a cure is concerned, only God has that power. Is he violent?"

"More and more. Yesterday, he tried to set fire to his clothes again."

"In that case you should put him in Saint-Jean-de-Dieu. They'll take good care of him. Do you want me to look after the formalities? I have business in Longue-Pointe, I could see about admitting him while I'm there."

"I'd appreciate that, Doctor."

On his way out of the Limoilou house, Bernard could have kicked himself. Why had he taken pity on the lady? Why had he offered to go to the asylum? Couldn't he have just signed one of those forms he always carried with him? It would have been so simple to fill in the boxes as he'd done so often. What is the patient's trade or occupation, or, in the case of a woman, that of her father or husband? How much education does he have? Is this the first attack of mental alienation? What are the patient's eating, sleeping, and personal cleanliness habits? What family members, including grandparents and cousins, have been afflicted with madness? Has he been dealt any blows to the head? Twenty-seven boxes to fill in, then it was off your mind: the sick man would be admitted to the asylum.

When his horse stopped outside Florence's house without being told, Bernard's thoughts were still confused.

Florence was waiting for him on the gallery, as she had been doing since the start of their friendship. Four years already! At first he had resisted her advances. "I will abstain from every voluntary act of mischief and corruption; and, further, from the seduction of females . . ." in the words of the Hippocratic oath. But she was so beautiful, his Florence, round and pale as the full moon. . . . When she had undertaken to seduce him, Bernard had been a widower for a year and was beginning to worry about his personal hygiene. Was there a risk that he would go deaf? Would he have been wiser to copy some of his colleagues, who cared for women of easy virtue at home in exchange for payments in kind? Surely God would be merciful to a poor sinner who was subject to temptation every day because of the very nature of his calling? He had soon convinced himself that neither God nor Hippocrates would have seen anything wrong with his behaviour. But while God and Hippocrates were very remote, Viviane's memory was still green. Could she understand that it was, after all, simply a matter of hygiene? Would she have preferred that he remarry, that another woman move into her house, into her bed, quite openly and publicly?

Bernard's scruples had lasted only a week. After that, he stopped off at Florence's every Sunday, emerging a few hours later cheerful, relieved, and ready to face another long week of routine.

* * *

As he left Florence's house that day, he let his horse trot along peacefully while he did his best to make his mind go blank. He started by looking at the vast fields that bordered the river, and at the endless stone fence that surrounded the asylum. The mere sight of the fence made him shudder: he feared the asylum and he didn't trust nuns. He told himself, like Pinel, the great French alienist, that Catholicism was probably one of the causes of madness.

When he stopped before the iron gate at the main entrance, he experienced a shock: the long lane lined with elms and maples, the gardens where white-clad patients were bustling about, the two angels who had opened the gate to him, and the individuals all around him who, in the greatest innocence, were busy pushing wheelbarrows to the shed, leading horses into the stable, or carrying buckets of warm, foamy milk from the cowshed to the kitchen — all were evocative of paradise. Silent, angelic assistants, a setting that was lively but, all things considered, peaceful — town and countryside reconciled — the kind of healthy spot that Pinel wanted, where, in the absence of family and urban life, patients dressed in clean clothes would be healed while they breathed fresh air! Bernard rubbed his eyes: how could a lunatic asylum assume the nature of paradise?

In the distance he spied the building, inspired by Mount Hope in Baltimore, which the nuns had had constructed: in the centre was the huge main structure, its ground floor in freestone, the four upper storeys in brick; a long wing on either side led to two other structures. The whole resembled an enormous stone bird that had alighted in the middle of the countryside, and then lacked the courage to get up.

The chapel bell had rung just as he was step-

ping down from his buggy. All the angels doffed
their hats to pray. Bernard's horse snorted, and
Bernard too bared his head: what was he thinking
about? Four o'clock! He mustn't dawdle any longer.
He entered the building and went directly to the
admissions office, where he filled out the commit-
ment form.

After that he had some trouble finding his
way, and had to wander for a while through the
asylum's endless corridors. Procurator's office, dispensary, doctors' offices, everywhere a surprising
calm prevailed. While he was still looking for the
exit, he found himself by chance in front of the
morgue. He stopped there briefly, as if hypnotized.
When a passing nun asked what he was looking for,
rather than request directions for getting out of the
building, he asked her a series of questions about the
establishment. How many patients were there? How
were they cared for? Were there many deaths? Were
the cadavers returned to the family, or were they
buried at the asylum? The nun answered him as best
she could, but since there seemed to be no end to his
interrogation, she suggested that he meet with the
directress, and he did so promptly. Once again,
lightning struck: after being genuinely fascinated by
the place, now Bernard was about to have his life
profoundly shaken by his meeting with the directress.

* * *

Bernard is sitting very straight in a hardwood chair,
in the very sober office of Soeur Thérèse-de-Jésus,
founder and superior of the Hôpital Saint-Jean-de-
Dieu. Soeur Thérèse is tiny. She has the big sad eyes

of poor children, while her face is perfectly round (unless it is her habit, or the thin strip of white linen that takes the place of a cornet, or, again, the band covering her brow, which gives that impression). Her eyes are so huge they seem to take up half her face.

It is hard to have a sustained conversation with her, for she has hardly started a sentence when she is interrupted by another nun coming to say that a patient has died. Soeur Thérèse instructs her to write to the family of the deceased, if he has one, to tell the vicar so he can say a Mass, and, above all, not to forget the government form: the hospital is entitled to an allowance of three dollars in such circumstances. The other woman nods agreement and withdraws discreetly, then a second nun immediately enters, seeking permission to renew the supply of tincture of iodine, to pay the fees of the veterinarian who came to inspect the horses, and (this in an undertone) to grant a dispensation to the nuns who wish to allow doctors to use the asylum's keys. "Out of the question!" snaps the directress. "Unless they denounce the Ross Law, they aren't getting any keys!"

It's true, then, what the newspapers are saying? That the nuns are striking to protest the government's aim to take over the asylums? To avoid seeming too interested in their conversation, Bernard pretends his mind is on something else. He looks at the images of the Virgin, at the plaster statues on the wooden filing cabinets, and in particular at the magnificent ferns that another nun, who is even tinier than Soeur Thérèse, is carefully watering.

Suddenly aware that the expression on his face may betray his curiosity, he then gazes at the nun's feet: what physical phenomenon enables her to walk so silently, in such heavy shoes, across the hardwood floor? And how is it that the floors are always spotless, never scuffed?

Not only must Soeur Thérèse submit to the comings and goings of the nuns, she must also keep getting up to answer the many calls that are transmitted to her by means of an acoustic horn which is fastened to the wall beside the door. (An excellent invention, she told Bernard at the first call, a brand-new, modern system that cost the hospital a great deal, but that permits her to communicate instantaneously with every nook and cranny of the huge building. After she had taken calls from the procurator's office, the dispensary, the kitchen, and one of the twenty-seven wards, she qualified her opinion: an excellent invention, but it would take time to learn how to use it efficiently.)

How can she follow these two-stage conversations with such ease, and then collect her wits so quickly? Bernard, who has always thought that the thread uniting the two sides of a conversation is even more tenuous and loose than the one that holds together the pieces of happiness in the life of an honest man, has unqualified admiration for the prodigious cerebral capacities of this little bit of a woman.

Bernard is very intimidated by Soeur Thérèse. To thwart this feeling, a rather unusual one for a doctor, he gives her a surreptitious clinical look. If one were to take away her brass crucifix, the rosary of Our Lady of the Seven Sorrows which she wears around her waist, the leather belt that helps her repress evil inclinations, and the twenty pounds of garments that weigh her down, what would be left? Under the heavy black robe which is a reminder of the blemish of original sin which marks us from birth, under the immaculate cornet intended to call down on her the many graces needed to transcend her nature and bring her closer to the Virgin's purity, Bernard imagines a rough homespun headdress, the thickness of eight folds of skirts, and long white stockings, for the skin of nuns must never come into direct contact with black. . . . (Which is heavier: twenty pounds of clothes, or twenty pounds of symbols?) Despite all these attempts at concealment, there would still be a woman's body under all the garments, skin smooth and parchment-like, not white as one might expect but pink, the tender pink of fresh scars.

"Dr. Dansereau, I can only give you a few minutes so let's get right to the point. I confess I don't understand you. You live in a comfortable house, you enjoy an excellent reputation, a stable practice. Why give all that up to come and work in a lunatic asylum? If you were just beginning your career, perhaps I could understand — there's no lack of young idealists — but at your age? What has got into you?"

Emerging abruptly from his reverie, Bernard is briefly disconcerted. His decision is so recent, his reasons are so disreputable, that he can find nothing better to do than stammer something nebulous about the road to Damascus and Our Lord saying, Blessed are the poor in spirit.

"Dr. Dansereau, you wouldn't think it to look at me, but I began my administrative career thirty-six years ago when I oversaw the reception given to the Irish. After that I ran a charitable institution in Burlington, I was present at the debacle in Oregon City, when every single soul left town for the gold-rush, I founded and was in charge of another charitable institution at Valparaiso, in Chile, and then I returned to our beloved Canada to set up this asylum. May God forgive me for my pride, but I believe I know a great deal about men. I have no time to waste, Doctor. So leave religion to the specialists, and let's be serious for a moment, shall we? Are you in trouble with the law?"

"No! Whatever makes you think such a thing, Sister?"

"How much does your medical practice bring you, Dr. Dansereau? A thousand dollars a year? More? If you want to sell that practice and come here to end your days, you must have something to hide. Are your relations with the College of Physicians in order? Have you performed abortions?"

"Of course not, Sister, I swear, I quite simply wish to make myself useful, to help these unfortunate people. . . ."

"Have you ever seen an epileptic fit, Dr. Dansereau? Have you seen men so ravaged by alcohol they can't remember their names? Do you know that we sometimes have to put them in straitjackets to keep them from bashing their heads against the walls all day long? Have you ever seen the devil in the flesh, Dr. Dansereau?"

"No, Sister, I don't believe I've ever met him. And I must add that I'm quite unfamiliar with madness, and I expect that I'd be caring for bodies far more than for souls."

Bernard's reply seems to have reassured Soeur Thérèse, who now looks at him less suspiciously. She goes out briefly to argue *sotto voce* with a nun and to answer some calls on the acoustic horn, then she returns to the attack.

"What do you think of government control of asylums, Dr. Dansereau?"

A few more questions of that nature and Bernard's mind is made up, though he was beginning to think that perhaps Mrs. Robinson's boiled chicken, his Sunday rounds, and Florence's arms were not, after all, the worst future he could envisage. What does she mean to suggest this time? The simplest thing is to tell the truth.

"I've read some articles on the subject in the newspapers: if I've understood rightly, the Protestants want the state to pay for their asylum, but Catholics would be excluded from it. The prime minister quite rightly refused, and now they're building their own hospital in Verdun. According to the newspapers, the discussion appears to be over."

"You're quite mistaken, Dr. Dansereau. Asylums still belong to the religious communities, but medical control has fallen into the hands of the government. They've already appointed a superintendent, an English one into the bargain! Can you imagine! Soon the government will be hiring its own doctors, then they'll pass another law to take over the kitchens, the laundry, and in a few years the whole hospital will belong to it. Have you read Dr. Tuke's report? Drivel. He describes the asylum as a human menagerie. And do you know who this Tuke is? An Englishman from England, and a Protestant! I know those government fellows, I know how they proceed: a campaign of slander in the newspapers, then they pass a law, appoint some of their friends, and the deed is done. The government is an octopus, Doctor, a poisonous octopus. Once it gets its tentacles on the hospitals, it will take on the factories, the banks, even the schools! Look at what has happened in France, which was once the eldest daughter of the Church: it is being governed by Protestants, atheists, Freemasons, even by Jews! Poor France! Are you Catholic, Doctor?"

"Of course, Sister."

"Then you're opposed to the Ross Law?"

"Sister, I'm a physician; I have nothing to do with politics. Whether asylums are run by nuns or by the government is no concern of mine. All I want to do is work with the insane. When you hire electricians to put in lightbulbs or carpenters to build your churches, do you ask them their opinions about the government takeover of asylums? I want to look after patients, Sister, I want to look after patients' bodies. Whether I'm hired by the government or whether it's your congregation that engages me will have no effect on my work."

"Fine. You may be right. But let me warn you: supposing you persist in your decision, officially you will report to Dr. Howard. Always bear in mind, however, that I am the one who's in charge, and no one else! Is that clear? You will work from seven a.m.

until seven p.m., for a salary of four hundred dollars a year. And you may eat in the doctors' refectory free of charge. I'll give you a week to think it all over."

"Will I have to work on Sunday as well?"

"Of course. Do you think patients wait until Monday to fall sick? But don't worry, we'll give you time to attend services here. You can also take off one afternoon per month, if you insist."

Bernard is shaken when he emerges from the office of Soeur Thérèse-de-Jésus. He makes his way down the long corridors — not noticing the nuns, who drop their gaze as he passes — utterly indifferent now to the impeccably waxed floors. Like an automaton he leaves the building, unhitches his horse, gets into the buggy, and sets out down the dirt road that takes him to the iron gate. Still dazed, he casts a brief, final glance at a group of patients who seem to be busily pretending to weed the vegetable garden. As he comes closer to them, the patients start working even harder. He stops his buggy a few feet from the garden. One man turns his head towards Bernard and looks at him. Bernard tells his horse to hurry up. When he is a good distance from the group he will stop the buggy and look behind him: their pace will have slowed down again; some will be pretending to fill their buckets, while others will have stopped working altogether.

Slowly, very slowly, two patients will open the iron gate for him, and the creaking of the metal will penetrate every cell of his memory.

In the fields beside the river, some poor simpletons wearing straw hats are harvesting. Their forks rise rhythmically, the hay piles up in a cart which soon overflows. A carter whips his horse, who finally decides to start up, slowly, very slowly, then another empty cart comes and takes its place, the forks rise rhythmically again, the cart is filled. . . . A nun, only one, appears to be keeping an eye on all these people. (Why is she wearing a black robe in this heat? And all those garments soaked with sweat! . . .) The patients do not talk among themselves, the carters don't heap insults on their horses. Farther away, some women are washing clothes in the river. A weighty silence, only faintly disturbed by cawing crows, surrounds the scene.

Giddyup, old horse, hurry and take me away from this endless stone fence, away from this inferno. Inferno? What is this, Bernard, did you seriously expect to find paradise in the asylum? Get a grip on yourself, old man, this is a time for cool analysis. You wanted to be welcomed as a saviour, but you don't even know what it is you want to save. And what if Soeur Thérèse was right . . . what if you're nothing but an old idealist, what if your decision to come and work at the asylum is simply an old fool's whim, the craze of a rich man who finds repentance difficult? What's this idea of seeking happiness where it's least likely to exist?

* * *

That night he shut himself away in his library and, while drinking several brandies, resumed his self-examination: how could he have fallen under the spell of a site and some buildings? How could he have mistaken some poor lunatics for angels? Wouldn't it make more sense to see them as prisoners?

Be reasonable, Bernard. The mad are prisoners of their madness far more than of the asylum's walls. How could they possibly not be interned? Would they be any happier if they were allowed to roam the streets? How can you think such a thing! This is a civilized country. And aren't the very walls of the asylum, which isolate patients from the rest of the world, a remedy for madness? True, the lunatics are forced to work in the fields, but isn't that healthier than locking them in cells, which was still the practice not so long ago? And is it not a miracle that nuns, those little bits of women apparently without much energy, should have constructed this magnificent modern building where they care for a thousand patients, feeding them, housing them, clothing them, and asking nothing in return? Why do you have a grudge against nuns, Bernard? Do their prayers interfere with your life, don't their activities, when all is said and done, do humanity more good than harm? True, it would make sense for the government to run the asylums, but that's simply not possible now.

A thousand patients. For each of them, he thinks, remembering every one of Soeur Thérèse's words, the government pays the nuns the ridiculous sum of one hundred dollars a year. And with a budget of one hundred thousand dollars, they've managed to build their asylum, cowsheds, stables; to set up shops for making candles, bedsprings, mattresses, brushes, brooms, utensils, and clothing; and to grow their own fruit and vegetables and tobacco. In less than twenty years, they have created a self-sufficient municipality that even exports its surpluses and maintains diplomatic relations with other asylums in Europe and the United States. Think what it would cost the government to take over that hospital. The total budget of the health department would be inadequate. And the nuns still control the Institute for Deaf-Mutes, the Quebec Lunatic Asylum, the Hôtel-Dieu, the convents, the schools. . . . Even if there were no religion, the nuns would still be there, because society needs them. And then?

Now there is nothing in Bernard's mind but the image of a magnificent building, and the vision of a thousand patients. A thousand madmen, a thousand madmen's brains. What an extraordinary laboratory. Would he find in them traces of ideas, emotions, feelings? Does the mind produce ideas in the way those machines produce energy? Isn't it more likely to be chemical in nature, and ideas rather like volatile gases? Or might it be a physical element, so that ideas could be associated with the electrical current produced by the rubbing of atoms? And Florence lives close by. He'd just have to sell the house. . . .

And so it was decided. After a long latency period, Bernard would take up his research where he had abandoned it thirty years before. By offering himself the finest collection of brains imaginable, he would resume his rank in the great army of science triumphant.

3

On this first Sunday in September, Florence rose with the sun so she could attend early Mass. The moment she came home she threw herself into house-cleaning, dusting the same end-table four times, sweeping her gallery whenever a leaf fell on it, and burning cinnamon sticks so the kitchen would be filled with their aroma. At noon she picked at some leftover beef stew, then went out to rock on her gallery. Having nothing else to do, she mused as she waited for Bernard on the singular nature of their association: they could not yet be called a couple and no doubt never would. . . .

Florence has no illusions: they have never exchanged a word of love, not even one of those intimate secrets that people unthinkingly indulge in during those frenzied moments when everything is allowed, only to be forgotten once the revelling has ended. She knows perfectly well that Bernard took a fancy to her because he was lonely and didn't want to remarry, and she realizes that men are so constituted that they must perform that peculiar exercise every Sunday so as to maintain their self-esteem. She knows all that, but doesn't hold it against him. How could she, when she herself has become attached to him for the identical reasons — or very nearly?

* * *

Florence, who was born on a farm at Pointe-aux-Trembles, had been married at sixteen to René Martineau, a farmer from Longue-Pointe. Her parents had, of course, asked her permission before publishing the banns, but she was well aware that, in their eyes, her wishes counted for far less than the acres of good black earth along the river that were in her fiancé's possession. She consented with more resignation than enthusiasm, but she never had any reason to regret it: while René Martineau was not very astute, he was a good man, sturdy, hard-working, and sober. Even though he was the sole owner of the farm, he always asked Florence for her opinion before he embarked on anything, so that after a few years of married life she considered herself her husband's partner, not his servant. During the thirty years of their union, Florence's feelings had not changed: she wasn't madly in love with René, but she had developed a high regard for him, combined perhaps, at certain moments, with a hint of condescension.

After ten years of marriage, still childless, she had gone to Dr. Dansereau to ask his advice. It was the first time she had consulted Bernard, who was highly regarded in the village. She had known at first sight that she could trust this man, who was obviously wise, very learned, and in good health.

With the greatest tact, he asked her some questions about their manner of proceeding and then, satisfied with her answers, prescribed a yellow powder that she must stir into a glass of water and drink at night, just before going to bed. A few months later the treatment had still had no effect, and he replaced the powder with another, a foul-tasting green one this time, which had to be diluted in water as well. As this last treatment was no more successful than the previous one, she resigned herself to submit to a complete examination, which was duly performed, in her husband's presence. When the examination was over, Bernard carefully washed his hands at the basin, then delivered his verdict: "Madame, your Fallopian tubes are obstructed, which makes any nesting impossible. Unfortunately there is nothing to be done. I sympathize with your grief." Faced with a diagnosis so confidently expressed, she had no choice but to accept it — as several of Dr. Dansereau's other patients had already done that year.

The day after the doctor's visit, Florence, pleading that they would never be able to have children in any case, had a frank talk with her husband: henceforth, it would serve no purpose for them to continue to fulfil that conjugal duty which he had hitherto been eager to perform. To Florence's great surprise, René had agreed, offering no argument.

The decision had a beneficial effect on René. In an attempt to divert his energies elsewhere, he threw himself into his work. In addition to growing wheat and oats, he also started raising pigs and sheep, which he sold to the nuns at Saint-Jean-de-Dieu, maintaining and clearing snow from a large section of the Chemin du Roy, and practising the difficult profession of iceman: in the winter he went out before dawn, taking his saw to cut huge blocks from the ice that covered the river, then storing them in the barn under a thick layer of sawdust; when summer came he travelled up and down the streets of Montreal selling these blocks to housewives for their iceboxes. As if all these activities were not enough, he also took on the repair of the church roof, and agreed to serve as a warden in the church.

Florence had no time to be bored. Not only did she assist her husband in all his tasks, she also kept house with great enthusiasm. She was gifted at interior decoration, and spent the long winter days arranging and rearranging all the rooms, occupying any spare time with various sewing projects. Her reputation as a seamstress soon made the rounds of the village, and as a result the curé asked her to be responsible for the upkeep of his priestly vestments. Satisfied with her services, he recommended Florence to his colleagues; some of them travelled great distances, from as far as Terrebonne or Vaucluse, to bring her soutanes, surplices, and chasubles. In the summer she tended the animals and the vegetable garden, as well as maintaining the magnificent flowerbeds around her house, which were planted with geraniums, begonias, and hyacinths. Her flowers were so beautiful that people driving past on the Chemin du Roy would stop to admire them, which overjoyed her.

One day just after Pentecost, a lump no bigger than a kernel of corn appeared on her husband's neck. As the excrescence didn't cause him any pain, René put up with it for one whole year. The lump was almost two inches in diameter when he finally decided to consult Dr. Dansereau. Bernard extracted it in his office and told him not to worry: it was a harmless fibroma, he need only rub a green ointment on the wound to avoid any risk of a recurrence.

Two months later, René began to grow thin. He had always had a hearty appetite, but suddenly meat disgusted him and, what's more, he even stopped smoking his pipe. When he got up in the morning, he complained that he felt as tired as he'd been the night before, despite the tonics Bernard prescribed. By Christmas he could no longer get out of bed. For months on end, Florence watched over him day and night. Dr. Dansereau brought morphine every week, the doses stronger and stronger, until finally, two years later, he died. Because the last two years of her husband's life had been so difficult, Florence did not really experience grief at his passing; rather, it came as a great relief.

Every farmer in the village had come to see her on the day after the funeral, offering to buy her house and her land. She refused curtly, telling them she intended to stay there as long as she lived. During the period when she wore widow's weeds, she tried to look after the farm by herself, succeeding as well as could be expected. At first, some of her neighbours had come to give her a hand with the hardest tasks, but Florence eventually refused all such offers, regarding them as driven by base self-interest.

Her black clothes had hardly been put away when the purchase offers were suddenly transformed into marriage proposals, all of which were rejected. Florence didn't see why she should give away what she had always refused to sell.

One year after her husband's death, facing up to the fact that it would be impossible to continue with all her activities, she reorganized her life accordingly. First, she relinquished the pigs and the sheep; Soeur Thérèse drove a hard bargain and the price she offered left Florence with a ridiculously small profit that bore no relation to the efforts she had expended. After that, she sold off some of the land beside the river, this time to wealthy factory-owners who wanted to put up cottages, and who offered her a much better price than the nuns. The cart that had been used for hauling ice was sold to a grocer looking for work for his son, and the rest of the land was rented out, guaranteeing her an income that, along with her earnings as a seamstress, was enough to assure her a life free from want.

After all the land had been sold off or rented and she found herself alone in the huge empty house, where she spent her days sewing, she began to long for René; suddenly she missed his silent presence, the warmth he left in the bed when he got up before her to cut ice on the river, the smell of his pipe in the evening.

There was no lack of suitors, however; Florence even let some of them keep her company on the gallery of a summer evening. The married ones brought her small presents every week, in the hope that she would grant them what their wives undoubtedly refused. While she gladly accepted these little treats, she was quick to dismiss her suitors as soon as they demanded what seemed to them their due. How dared they even think that a crudely carved softwood statuette, a few strings of beads, or some ribbons from town would open the gates to her secret dominion? These frustrated men soon gave Florence a bad reputation. All over the village, it was said that she gave herself for a few cents, sometimes for nothing, to the first man who asked. Not only did these rumours isolate her from the female community, they also caused her a great many problems: men who didn't understand why she refused them, when allegedly she gave herself to everyone, were liable to turn violent at any moment.

To nip this dangerous situation in the bud, Florence briefly agreed to being courted by André Saint-Cyr, the village butcher. A recent widower, André was the strongest man on the eastern tip of the island, the most feared as well. He had three sons, all of them as strong as he; they were sometimes called on when certain clients threatened mayhem in the local hotels. These strenuous intercessions by the Saint-Cyr family were, however, fairly rare. The hotel-keepers ended up replacing doors, windows, and a fair amount of furniture, and in general they enjoyed peace and quiet for a good ten years.

Keeping company with André Saint-Cyr had been profitable for Florence, at least in the short term. Under his protection, she had nothing to fear from thwarted suitors. Some months later, though, she regretted her actions. André multiplied his proposals, but Florence had never felt the slightest desire to marry him. Uncertain how to extricate herself from this awkward situation, and rightly afraid of provoking André's wrath by too casually declining his repeated demands, she found no better solution than endlessly postponing her decision.

André's patience had been wearing thin when Florence, sitting on her gallery one Sunday afternoon in August, desperately seeking a solution to her problem, saw Bernard go by. She invited him in and, although she was in perfect health, asked him for a general examination, claiming fatigue and vague abdominal pains. Bernard complied, and of course he found nothing abnormal. All the same, he offered her a little flask of tonic, a greenish, malodorous liquid she happily bought from him. On the gallery, she casually asked if he knew of any hideous illness that might be invoked, say to break off an engagement.

Surprised, Bernard reflected for a moment, then quickly listed phthisis, leukemia, and cancer, adding that they were more tragic than terrifying. Then he mentioned syphilis, soft chancre, and blennorrhagia; no young woman afflicted with one of these shameful diseases could aspire to marriage. But maladies that attacked the brain and the soul — epilepsy, a cerebral tumour, all the forms of madness, and hysteria, a more imprecise and a typically feminine affliction — were, in his opinion, even worse.

Florence interrupted: how did one recognize a hysterical woman? It was difficult, Bernard replied: at first glance she appeared perfectly normal. An examination of her genital organs, however, would show a doctor malformations apt to cause a disturbance of the organism, which sooner or later would attack the brain. The behaviour of hysterical women was infantile, and they were generally a sore trial to their family and friends. In his opinion, hysteria was at the root of wickedness, at least in women. Having obtained what she wanted, Florence thanked Bernard, a little more warmly than might have been deemed appropriate in the circumstances.

Shortly after Bernard left, André came back. Florence, who had rubbed her eyes with her fists to make them good and red, told him straightway that her reason for so frequently postponing her decision to marry him was that she feared she was suffering from a strange illness. In fact, Dr. Dansereau had just confirmed her fears: he believed her to be suffering from hysteria. Fortunately, he had prescribed a tonic guaranteed to cure her, she added, showing André the little flask from which Bernard had asked her to inhale when necessary. The smell alone guaranteed the medicine's efficacy; now there was nothing to stand in the way of their marriage.

Sniffing the liquid, André made a face, then declared that perhaps they had better wait until she was fully cured before they went to see the priest; there was no hurry, she should take proper care of herself, and now he had to leave, but he'd certainly come back next week to see her. Immediately after her suitor's departure, Florence rushed to throw the tonic in the stream.

The following Saturday, André had not come back. He delegated one of his sons to notify her that he wanted to step back a little in order to weigh all the implications of the important decision he was about to make, and that his reflections would undoubtedly take several months, perhaps even a year.

So that she would not forget him, he urged her to accept the gift his son had brought: a magnificent sirloin tip from a quarter of beef he had cut up for her as soon as the animal was slaughtered. Florence accepted the offering and asked the son in for a glass of wine; he mumbled some implausible excuse, hopped on his horse, and whipped the poor animal so hard that it whinnied in pain and raced away, horseshoes flying.

When Bernard stopped by a few hours later to enquire about her health, she was sitting on the gallery savouring her immense relief, and welcomed him most enthusiastically. Had he not, quite unwittingly, saved her? She felt wonderfully well, his tonic had cured her completely, would he take a glass of wine? Bernard accepted, they drank a glass and then another, then he suggested that as a precaution she undergo another examination, pointing out that certain exercises also produce an excellent stimulating effect, that indeed they were necessary, for women as much as for men, to maintain the general hygiene of the spirit. . . .

Bernard's suggestion had been the furthest thing from her mind, but she was so astonished by it that she didn't know what to say. In a flash, she interpreted all the messages he had been unconsciously transmitting to her for two weeks now. She felt guilty for having acted without proper judgement, it was her fault and no one else's, she was the one who had roused this man's desire. She had no time to pursue her thoughts any further, for Bernard, having already interpreted her silence as acquiescence, promptly came to her. Florence, who had not let herself be taken by a man for more than a quarter of a century, didn't have the heart to push him away, but opened her arms to him.

After he had left her, she stayed for a long time in her bed. She had not been transported into seventh heaven, far from it, but to her amazement the pain she had experienced hadn't been too severe. Some hours after the doctor's departure, the sheets were still warm and her mind very muddled indeed.

The next day, through the grille of the confessional, she confided to the curé, without however going into detail, that she sometimes had impure thoughts. There was no need for the priest to know everything, and the good Lord was intelligent enough to understand what she was hinting at. Having fervently made her penance, she then felt entirely at peace with her conscience, and ready to begin again. But would Bernard come back?

Yes, he did, the next Sunday at exactly the same time, and he would return every Sunday, with few exceptions, for four years. Never did the subject of marriage come up, nor of her land or her house. He would arrive around two o'clock and drink a glass of wine, then they would go to the bedroom, where, week after week, Florence would submit to a "general examination". Bernard seemed quite satisfied with what he found, and Florence had no complaints.

After his "examination", Bernard would doze for a few moment, then begin to talk. Aside from Monsieur le Curé, who used a lot of words to say nothing and seemed to care little about being understood, Florence had never met a man who talked so much, and about such surprising matters. In the early days of their acquaintance, he had spent hours explaining that the economic system under which they lived was profoundly unjust, and that soon it would be replaced by another, based not on profit but on Justice and Reason; when Science, having attained its maturity, had found ways to fully mechanize the work done in fields and factories, paid labour would no longer be necessary, and all persons, women as well as men, would be able to live in plenty. He patiently described all the obstacles that mankind must surmount before attaining that ideal, assuring her that none of them — of that he was fully convinced — would be insurmountable.

Often, a few days after his visit, Florence would try to remember Bernard's wonderful arguments and repeat them to herself, but she rarely succeeded. It was as if the arguments that had seemed so lucid, so self-evident when they emerged from Bernard's mouth, always rang false in hers. Perhaps it was because he was a doctor that he knew so many unusual words, and could put them together so skilfully.

Over the following weeks, he had explained to her that if medicine continued to progress at the same rate as in the past few years, the diseases that seemed so terrible to us today would soon be as benign as colds, women would be able to have children when they wanted to, and suffering would vanish altogether. Every time, Florence listened to him dreamily, and she continued to dream all week long. From one month to the next, Florence felt as if she were living intimately with an encyclopaedia.

Bernard's way of explaining things gave her the impression, for a moment, that she was prodigiously intelligent; because the impression was fleeting, it intensified all the more the desire to start again.

One day, however, Bernard told her it was perfectly reasonable, from a scientific point of view, to think that God did not exist. That was when she ceased to take his word for everything, although she continued to listen with interest, and sometimes fondly, the way one listens to a little boy describe his imaginary exploits. Lying on the bed beside him, she felt as if she were travelling in time, as if she were sharing his dreams. Were his fine phrases merely idle fancies whose real purpose was to conceal his true thoughts? And then? Were human beings so different from one another that it was worth spending hours isolating what it was that distinguished them from their fellow creatures? Dream on, my little man, you stupendous little man, go on dreaming out loud, Florence told herself, as long as you're talking to me, it doesn't matter what you're saying.

Bernard began to worry her, however, when he decided to sell his office and go to work in a madhouse. Why did he talk with such admiration about that Soeur Thérèse, the same one who had offered her a ludicrous sum for her land? Had Florence done the right thing, letting him move into her place, into her house? Of course.... He would have his own room, upstairs; he would pay her five dollars a month rent — they must keep up appearances — and nothing between them would be changed, he told her again and again. Nothing? Really nothing? He would be there every day, he would come down to her bedroom whenever he wanted, and he expected her to believe that nothing would change!

During the four years she had spent waiting for Bernard, hoping to see him every blessed Sunday, she finally discovered how important was the part that anticipation played in her life. When she thought about René again, she barely dwelt on his conversations, which were, frankly, inconsequential, nor on the warmth he left in the bed, nor on any feature of his face. What she had prized in her life with him was that he had always been a hard worker and, consequently, she had been able to spend long days waiting for him. It was pleasant to rock on the gallery while you waited for someone, although the activity could become tedious if you were really alone. It was the same for preparing meals, and for all those little things that make marriage preferable to the single state. Perhaps the reason she had grown attached to Bernard so quickly was precisely because their liaison was one that enabled her to anticipate him all week.

When he had arrived the day before to take possession of his room, he had hung his clothes in the closet, lined up his shoes under the bed and his books on the dresser, but Florence didn't have the impression that he was moving in for good. He had behaved rather like a traveller preparing to spend a few days in a hotel: if the roof doesn't leak and the bed is comfortable, everything is fine. As soon as his suitcases were unpacked, he wanted to see the barn where René had stored his ice; then he asked her some very odd questions. How long would ice keep under sawdust? Was it possible to install a heating system in one part of the barn so that he could perform experiments on winter nights? Did she have a good supply of glass jars? Listening to a little boy talk about the flying machine he dreamed of building was delightful, Florence thought, but seeing him take hammer and boards from the shed and really set to work was more disturbing. What did he have in mind?

* * *

Suddenly Florence stops rocking; she has just spied Bernard's buggy in the distance, and she doesn't want him to catch her being so blatantly idle. When the horse stops beside the gallery, she pretends to be weeding her begonias. What has he brought this time? He takes some small, rigid cases from his buggy, handling them with infinite care, and carries them directly to the barn, then locks himself inside as soon as the transfer is complete. She hears him hammering, sawing, and swearing.

At six o'clock he is still puttering. Their meal is ready, giving Florence the perfect excuse to take a closer look. She walks into the barn at the very moment Bernard has completed his installations. Proud as a peacock, he shows her his shelves, pretending not to notice that the boards are far from parallel, and his work surface, which slants rather steeply; no sooner has he set a screwdriver down on it than the implement rolls to the ground. . . .

"What do you think?"

"It's fine, but why didn't you use a level and square?"

"No need: I have a good eye."

"I see. If you want supper, it's ready."

Bernard eats with gusto, with great gusto even. Between mouthfuls he lavishes compliments on her: he hasn't eaten so well for ages, it's delicious, absolutely delicious. Vegetable soup, pork roasted with shallots, garden vegetables — it's nothing out of the ordinary, Florence thinks. Bernard seems sincere, and she's delighted. As a handyman he can't hold a candle to René, but what does it matter, since he's so generous with compliments? He has barely finished his dessert when he gets up and tells her he still has work to do in the barn. When she has finished the dishes, she can still hear him hammering, sawing, and swearing. She will go out then and sit on the gallery to finish the sewing that will keep her busy until sunset.

The clock strikes ten and Bernard is still in the barn. Does he intend to spend the night there? She performs her ablutions and gets into bed. Unable to fall asleep, she waits until eleven. At last, she hears the barn door creak. He comes into the house, climbs up to his room, drops first one shoe, then the other, on the floor; the bedsprings creak, the floorboards crack, then silence. Only the ticking of the clock, the dogs baying at the full moon, and the night birds telling each other about their hunting exploits. Florence, half-reassured now, is finally able to sleep.

4

On Monday morning, Bernard arrives at Soeur Thérèse's office on the stroke of seven. In the waiting room, five hefty men sit on straight-backed chairs. Visibly uncomfortable in their Sunday suits, they keep their heads down and pass the time twirling their hats in their hands, or discreetly cleaning their nails, like schoolchildren summoned to the principal's office. Bernard asks a nun who is writing in a huge ledger with a pen:

"May I have a word with Soeur Thérèse?"

"Is it about the heating-oil contract?"

"No, I'm a doctor."

"In that case, I'm afraid Soeur Thérèse can't see you. After she meets with these gentlemen, she has to sign the admission authorizations and the discharges, answer her mail, and greet some visitors from Baltimore."

"What about this afternoon?"

"Out of the question: she intends to spend the rest of the day discussing the new laundry with the architects. And I may as well tell you, you can't talk to her tomorrow either, or the day after, because she's just advised me that she has to go to Quebec. But perhaps I can help you?"

"It's just that I'm supposed to start working

today. . . ."

"Are you Dr. Dansereau? Soeur Thérèse instructed me to tell you to go and see Dr. Howard, the medical superintendent. Turn left, go down the stairs to the basement, and follow the hot-water pipes. It's at the end of the corridor."

"Thank you, Sister."

As he is about to leave the office and venture into the huge building, Bernard sees one of the bidders emerge from Soeur Thérèse's office, a pitiful sight.

"You, sir, ought to be ashamed!" says the directress. "I pray the Lord will watch over your health. I particularly hope that neither you nor any member of your family will ever have to be interned here with us. Next!"

Turn left, go down the stairs. . . . Why did the nun give him that half-smile as she recited the directions? Follow the hot-water pipes. But how is he to distinguish them from the cold-water pipes? The ceiling is so low that Bernard has only to touch them with his fingertips; he follows the pipes for a long time before he reaches the end of the corridor. A low door, a small hand-written sign: *Dr. Howard, Medical Superintendent.* If this is the superintendent's office, Bernard muses, where do they keep the patients! He knocks and a weary voice bids him enter.

Dr. Howard's hair is going thin, but, as if to compensate, his beard is so long and abundant that it completely fills the opening of his double-breasted jacket; a bushy moustache, bright eyes, a round belly, a firm handshake — this is a man, Bernard thinks immediately, who deserves respect. But why is he hidden away in this windowless closet that couldn't even do duty as a cell?

"You'll excuse me, Dr. Dansereau, if I'm unable to offer you a chair. I had to wait two months to be assigned this office; as for the rest of the furniture, I've been told I'll have it within a year. If I stay here for a century, perhaps they will grant me the right to see a patient. I can guess what your questions are: yes, I am indeed the medical superintendent, the head man, at least in theory. My error was to be appointed by the government. The nuns have been ordered not to say one word to me; and they refuse to give me the keys to the dispensary, and they forbid me access to the wards or the lunatics' rooms. As long as their strike goes on, I shall be forced to spend my days in here. If I persist, perhaps they will relent."

"But are the patients being cared for?"

"Of course. The nuns' refusal to speak only applies to government-appointed doctors. The others, the ones hired by Soeur Thérèse, can work in peace, and they're doing a good job, I can't deny that. The hydrotherapy rooms are very well equipped, you'll see. If you want some advice, never speak out about government interference in running asylums, say nothing that might suggest you have liberal ideas, and above all, never say anything against Soeur Thérèse. The woman knows everything that goes on in the hospital before it happens. If she has sent you here, it's to warn you about what your fate will be if you don't behave yourself. That's all I can tell you. If you want to work, go and see Dr. Villeneuve in the doctors' office, he'll tell you what you have to do. Stop by now and then, and let me know what you're doing. One of these days I'll introduce you to Dr. Perreault, the chief physician, and to Dr. Paquette, the second assistant. They were appointed at the same time I was, but they still don't have offices."

Follow the hot-water pipes but in the opposite direction, climb the stairs, turn right after the dispensary, left at the end of the corridor.... Bernard is concerned: one can be wary of having too much pity for patients, but he would never have imagined experiencing such a feeling for the medical superintendent. Florence was right: nuns drive a very hard bargain. But how else could they have managed to construct this huge building? It's quite understandable that, having started from nothing and built everything, they should be concerned about the government's designs. Turn right again after the chapel . . . here we are: *Physicians' Offices.*

Dr. Villeneuve is a chubby, plain-spoken man with a kindly face. The beard along his jawline is carefully trimmed, he wears little metal-rimmed spectacles, and his brain must weigh about eighteen hundred grams. Or perhaps a little less: the man seems rather elderly. Does the brain shrivel with time? Or does it get heavier and crush the spinal column?

"God bless you, Dr. Dansereau! Soeur Thérèse has spoken very highly of you. Thirty years in practice, in the city and in the country: we'll make good use of your experience to tend our poor simpletons. I'll show you around, but first let me introduce you to Soeur Jeanne-de-l'Esprit. Every morning, she will give you a list of the patients who need your help."

Soeur Jeanne? Bernard follows his colleague's gaze to a high wall of forms on a counter. Suddenly a head appears above a pile of paper: "God bless you, Dr. Dansereau! And you too, Dr. Villeneuve!", then immediately disappears. "God bless you, Sister!"

"Let's go," says Dr. Villeneuve. "This is the central pavilion. The administrative offices, the chapel, the procurator's office, the dispensary, the parlours, the doctors' offices, the central kitchen, the morgue, and the hydrotherapy room — which I'm saving for dessert! On your left, the men's wings, on your right, the women's. In each wing, the principle is the same: first are the private rooms, then those for the government patients. Patients suffering from melancholia and persecution are placed in the first ward, epileptics and idiots in the second, the agitated in the third. There is an infirmary in the middle of the wing, and at either end, the Protestants' wards. The dormitories and cells are on the floor above. At the end of each wing there are four boilers, twenty horsepower each, and thirty thousand feet of pipes. Don't worry, you won't be asked to repair them! Now let's go and visit a ward, on the men's side. One will do, they're all alike."

Corridors, corridors, corridors. Whenever Dr. Villeneuve meets someone — a nun, a guard, or a patient running some errand, he calls out, "God bless you!"

"You should adopt that excellent habit too," he advises Bernard *sotto voce*. "You'll be judged for your piety as much as for your medical skills. And you'd be well advised to turn up at chapel now and then as well. I go every morning, myself, but I confess I'm drawn there not so much by prayers or a concern for appearances as by the fact that I can get some rest there. . . . This is the Saint-Etienne ward. At this time of the year, most of our patients are working in the fields. Those who are still in the wards cannot comprehend or do anything at all, and some quite simply refuse to work. Have you visited the Parliament at Quebec when it's in session? It's rather similar."

The only furnishings are a billiard table with its cloth worn thin, a closed piano on which some magnificent ferns are displayed, and shelves that provide a glimpse of chequer sets and decks of cards. None of the patients is playing. Some rock feverishly back and forth, as if they are responsible for driving a huge dynamo, others pace as they recount fantastic stories or repeat a few words, always the same ones, while still others sit and do nothing but stare into space, as if gazing at some terrifying image only they can see.

"Come and let me introduce you to our Romeo!"

Dr. Villeneuve walks up to a patient who is pacing back and forth and repeating softly: "Véronique! Véronique!"

"This is an odd case. The patient's name is Oscar Parent and he used to live on a farm near Joliette. Until the age of twenty he was completely normal. He even learned to read and write — as bad luck would have it. At twenty-one he met Véronique and fell madly in love. Stopped eating and drinking and wrote love-letters all night long. Some weeks later, he began pulling his hair out by the handful and banging his head against the wall, and then he jumped in the river. Fortunately, he was rescued in time. His parents think he's lost his mind."

"How is he being treated?"

"Initially with hot baths to calm his agitation, and now with cold showers. The results have been slow, but encouraging. When he first came here he couldn't walk or talk.... Now then, Romeo, how are you this morning?"

The patient looks vaguely in Dr. Villeneuve's direction and makes no reply. He appears annoyed that his morning promenade has been interrupted, but he just stands there, arms dangling: it doesn't seem to occur to him that he could simply walk around the doctors and continue on his way.

"Here, I've brought you some paper!"

The patient's eyes light up. He becomes as excited as a child about to unwrap a present. He grabs the paper, takes a lead pencil from his pocket, then goes and sits at a table in the covered gallery that is used as an exercise yard.

"He'll spend the rest of the afternoon writing love-letters, to no purpose. The beautiful Véronique has never answered him, and no doubt she never will. If you have writing material at home — any scrap of paper will do — bring it. It's amazing how many patients spend their time writing page after page, usually to complain about some imaginary nasty treatments we submit them to. Here's another interesting one; we call him the accountant. Emile!

Come here, please."

Emile is sitting on a straight-backed chair, utterly motionless. When he hears his name, he seems to emerge from a deep hypnotic state. He comes over, staggering slightly.

"How are you?"

"Poorly, Doctor, very poorly. At breakfast this morning, I'll have you know, certain people whom I won't name didn't clear their plates. They'll drive us to ruin, Doctor, to ruin! Soeur Thérèse would have a fit if she knew about it, and she does so much for us."

"Indeed. But tell me, Emile, since you're so concerned about the hospital's finances, why don't you go out and work in the fields?"

"Because I'm a poor worker and I tire quickly, and the more tired I am, the more I eat, and the more I eat, the more it costs, and the more it costs, the harder it is for Soeur Thérèse. She told me so herself."

"Very well, Emile, you can go and rest now, and God bless you!"

"I don't rest, Doctor, I keep watch. But don't tell anyone. God bless you too, Doctor!"

"You see, Dr. Dansereau, that brave soul was a telegrapher. An alcoholic father, a hysterical aunt, the solitude, the high-pitched sounds that kept bombarding his brain cells — it was inevitable that he'd end up here. Yet his first forty years were altogether normal; he married, had seven children. Last year, his wife died in childbirth. On his way to the hospital, he slipped and struck his head against a wall. All the ingredients for madness, hitherto dormant, rose to the surface: depressive hypermania complicated by erotic urges. Recently, I'm glad to say, his bouts of eroticism have ceased, and now he talks about nothing but money. The nuns consider that progress, but I'm not so sure. Do you have matches? Let's light some pipes; the patients will be grateful."

Bernard has no sooner taken a box of matches from his pocket than he is surrounded by a dozen men. Once their pipes are lit, they go out to the gallery, where they sit on garden chairs and watch the smoke drift through the wire fence.

"As you can see, tobacco provides them with splendid entertainment; that's why the nuns have decided to grow an acre of it. It's excellent. The women don't smoke, but they do take snuff. If you always carry some matches and snuff, you'll be able to soothe the rebels. Now let's go back to the central pavilion, I'll show you the hydrotherapy room."

On their way out, Bernard greets a nun who is watching over the ward: "God bless you, Sister!" — "God bless you, Doctor!" After the door is shut, Bernard worries: a single nun to watch over twenty men?

"Those patients are calm, she's not at any risk. In any case, one nun can often do more than a crew of braggarts. Many a time I've seen a nun, with just a word or a gesture, calm a raving lunatic whom the guards, with all their strength, couldn't restrain. By the way, you should take off your watch chain, one never knows what the sight of such an object may provoke in unhinged individuals. Wearing cufflinks is also inadvisable. And I recommend that you always address them formally. These are small details that one learns eventually. Here we are at the hydrotherapy room. Watch now, you're about to see some of the most modern treatments in the world."

Dr. Villeneuve having ceremoniously opened two large padded doors, Bernard enters a room the size of a gymnasium: along walls and floor run iron pipes with a vast number of taps, valves, controls, and dials; all around the room are twelve bathtubs with nuns bustling about them; and at the back is the shower room. Dr. Villeneuve ushers Bernard to the first tub, where a middle-aged woman is resting.

"This one suffers from a simple mania. When she first came to the asylum, two years ago now, she was often depressed and sometimes hyperactive. She talked so fast her words were unintelligible, in a voice so hoarse that she'd become incapable of producing saliva. Her genital functions were also unsettled, needless to say. At first she was given hot baths every day, sometimes lasting five hours. After six months, the baths were cut back to two hours a day. Now she comes here only once a week. We've been very successful with maniacs. Have you seen the thermometer? It's fitted with a cork float so that it can remain on the surface, with only its reservoir under water. The water temperature is kept at ninety-five degrees Fahrenheit. From time to time, a nun comes and performs ablutions to the patient's nape and forehead, to avoid congestion of the head."

"She's not given any drugs?"

"Five grams of potassium bromide in the morning and two grams of chloral hydrate at bed-time. But it's mainly the baths that have an effect on her mind. One doesn't need lengthy experimenta-

tion to realize the futility of pharmaceutical meas-
ures for treating madness. In fact, drugs provoke far
more madness than they cure. Ah . . . I've just seen
something that should interest you, look over there."

At the back of the room, two nuns are coating
a woman's body with petroleum jelly. She is young,
with dark skin and long black braids that fall to her
hips.

"Her name is Angélique. Angélique Téteki
. . . Tatilké. . . . I'm not sure which. She's an Iroquois.
Soeur Thérèse made quite a fuss when she was
admitted. Since Angélique lives on a reservation,
the directress refused to take her in unless the dominion government paid for her board. Quebec has
no jurisdiction over Indians. In any case, I can tell
you that none of the doctors has ever complained
about having to care for her, and I know some who
would be prepared to pay her board out of their own
pockets. . . . I've drawn this case to your attention
simply to show you that there is no risk of
hypersecretion by the sebaceous glands: once the
skin has been coated with the jelly it is protected."

"What's she suffering from?"

"Circular madness. She was given cold showers at first, but it soon became obvious that warm
baths, preferably with linden blossoms, were preferable. Once a week now, she is given a hot vapour
bath with terebinth, followed by a cold-water im-
mersion and then a spray-shower. It's a pity, but
sometimes we must use restraint. Do you see that
apron tied around her head? It's also attached to the
bathtub, by means of a series of grommets; the
patient cannot escape from it, or splash water out-

side, or put her head under water and drown. As evaporation is limited, the temperature of the water is also easy to control. Very well, let us leave the hydrotherapy room to our distinguished alienists. If you care for the body, you'll seldom have reason to come here. Now I shall take you to see the dispensary. I warn you, you'll be surprised."

"Why is that?"

"You know as well as I do what pharmacists are like: rats in eyeglasses, always shut away inside their grimy shops concocting potions. . . . This is altogether different. Here we are. You can judge for yourself."

This, a dispensary? The room is huge and airy, with light coming in from eight windows. On a large table are the most modern chemical implements — microscopes with three lenses, graduated test-tubes, ultra-sensitive balances — while on the walls there are large glass cupboards with jars arranged in impeccable order and containing everything a doctor could dream of: belladonna, ginseng, and sarsaparilla grown on the premises, castor oil, opium, iodine, ether, chloroform, camphor, arsenic, laudanum, catnip root, hemlock — all within reach! Just say the word to the pink-cheeked nun, Soeur Marie-de-la-Visitation, she'll be happy to assemble the mixture of your choice. Not even the dispensary at McGill University is so well equipped. No more endless arguments with sour-tempered pharmacists who think they know everything and who meddle in your prescriptions, no more of those eternal errors of interpretation, no more complaints from patients about highwaymen's prices! And best of all is what Soeur Marie-de-la-Visitation takes from a big wooden cupboard: a bottle of brandy and three glasses. Who among us doesn't need a little of that excellent cardiac stimulant before undertaking a day's work? God bless you, Soeur-Marie-with-Cheeks-of-Pink!

After they leave the dispensary, both in an excellent humour, doctors Dansereau and Villeneuve go back to the office of Soeur Jeanne-de-l'Esprit, who hands them a list of patients.

"Will you be able to manage, Doctor? If you need anything at all, don't hesitate to ask the nurses; they know everything!"

The nurses! Yes, of course! Remember, Bernard, those first patients you treated at the Hôtel-Dieu when you were still a young doctor? Remember looking at the old lady who was brought in on a stretcher, all curled up? You felt totally helpless. Why do symptoms never look like the ones described in textbooks? You knew hundreds and hundreds of pages by heart, but the lines had blurred, you'd forgotten everything, why had you chosen this insane profession, you'd never be anything but a pitiful country doctor, scarcely more learned than the last of the bonesetters. You'd been pretending to mull things over for ten minutes when an old nurse came to take the patient's pulse.

"What do you think, Doctor? Arthritis, wouldn't you say?"

Arthritis — of course! You nodded and the good nurse went on:

"Do you think a camphor pastille would relieve her?"

"I was just thinking that very thing. In her condition, we could give her two pastilles without risk."

"You're right, Doctor. Do you think we should give her some opium syrup as well, to relieve the pain?"

The lesson had taken hold. For years you perfected a dreamy attitude, stroking your beard until a nurse came and gave her diagnosis and then suggested a treatment, which you always modified slightly, as a matter of form: a few drops more or less, an additional bleeding, a cupping-glass here and there . . . .

As a novice physician once again, he would rediscover during his first day on the job that every one of the nursing sisters at Saint-Jean-de-Dieu was worth her weight in medical manuals, as well as all the doctors in Scotland put together. All he had to do was go to the ward indicated by Soeur Jeanne and find the nurse.

"How are things with my patient, Sister?"

"He has swallowed nothing for two days now, not even his saliva. His breath is very foul and I'm afraid he has gingivitis. His mouth should be rinsed with a boric acid solution, and then checked to see if there are ulcerations. Should that be the case, he'll have to be treated with tincture of iodine. If you wish, I can begin the treatment now, and I can have him taken to the infirmary if his situation deteriorates. What do you think, Doctor?"

"You're absolutely right, Sister."

"While you're here, Doctor, I'd like to ask your opinion about this patient, too. He's always been a heavy smoker, and for a while now the colour of his sputum has been disturbing. I've kept a specimen to show you."

Bernard takes the handkerchief which the nun presents to him, opens it carefully, then folds it up again at once.

"Pulmonary gangrene, isn't it?"

"You're right again, Sister. He must be taken to the infirmary immediately, he doesn't have long."

"Thank you, Doctor, and God bless you."

"God bless you, Sister."

From ward to ward, from patient to patient, from nurse to nurse, Bernard discovers the many advantages of working in an asylum. Never again will he have to compete with charlatans or denounce the old wives' or folk remedies that, too often, are more effective than his own; never again will he have to wonder what fee to ask of his patients, or worry about overdue accounts; never again will he have to wake up in the middle of the night for a difficult delivery at the other end of the village, or plug his nose before performing an operation, for the cleanliness of the patients at Saint-Jean-de-Dieu seems exemplary. Not only those taking hydrotherapy treatments, but also the incurable idiots, who are apparently given a hygienic bath every two weeks. Only the new patients may present a problem. Some, it is said, arrive with lice to their eyelashes, others are afflicted with scabies, still others have so many fleas that, if they aren't mad already, scratching will surely drive them to it. The nuns care for everyone with a spirit of sacrifice that commands admiration. Why, just today Bernard has seen them

give sulphur baths, disinfect clothing, cut hair —
and wash what is left in a xylol solution that leaves
their fingers as white as if they had soaked in Javel
water for an entire day — and they even cut nails
and remove corns. Thank you, God, for giving us
nuns!

When he goes home to Florence's after his
first day at work, Bernard is tired but contented and,
above all, deeply relieved, as one can be on realizing
that, in a difficult situation, one has made the right
choice. As soon as she sees Bernard's buggy on the
road, Florence goes from the gallery to the kitchen.
She stirs the soup a little, adds some salt, sets the
table, goes back outside to rock. The buggy is very
close now; she can see her Bernard, always so elegant in his black hat, talking to his horse. Good
God, has he lost his mind?

He eats with gusto while he recounts his day,
and his words are coherent. Florence is reassured.
Immediately after their meal, he goes out on the
gallery to smoke a cigar, and makes some remarks
that give Florence new cause for concern.

"Tell me, Florence, do you ever take a bath?"

"Now and then, yes. I have a tub in the shed.
Every Saturday, I heat up water and bring the tub
into the kitchen."

"Excellent. I wonder, do you also have a large
rubber sheet, some petroleum jelly, and a few linden
blossoms? I'd like to perform a little experiment."

An hour later, at nightfall, the tub is filled
with hot water and Florence is covering Bernard's
body with a thick coat of petroleum jelly. He will
spend two full hours lying in the tub, almost entirely

covered with a rubber sheet, eyes shut, smiling broadly. What, Florence wonders, can he be thinking about?

5

Sitting on her seat in the train that will take her to Quebec, Soeur Thérèse tirelessly recites her rosary, indifferent to the scenery filing past before her eyes. Thanks to a dispensation in Monseigneur Bourget's own hand, she has the rare privilege of travelling alone. On departing Montreal, she gave a mere hint of a smile to her travelling companions, two rather drab men, one of whom, Henri Massicotte, is a travelling salesman and, it would seem, bored to tears.

No longer able to count the cows since darkness has fallen on the fields, he must be content now with watching his own wavering reflection in the window. He would sell his soul to the devil for a scrap of conversation. But he's out of luck: on the seat beside him the English-speaking member of Parliament, of whom, when they departed Montreal, he tried as best he could to ask a few questions, reads his newspaper. To fill the silence — as well as to take the opportunity to show some samples of the collars and cuffs and neckties he always carries with him, just in case — he tried to strike up a conversation with the politician, but the man immediately launched into a long diatribe against Louis Riel: he had been sentenced and it was a good thing, now all that was left was to hang him and Canada would be rid of the traitor at last. Of all the professions in the world, sales is undoubtedly the one that brings the greatest exposure to compromises of all kinds, but even the greediest merchant has principles. Henri replied that Louis Riel was a hero, and that if he was hanged, the others of his race would have a long memory. At that the politician buried his nose in his newspaper, and hasn't opened his mouth throughout during the journey.

Henri looked out at the cows as he swallowed his anger, but then his irrepressible need to talk came rushing back: to talk about the weather and this and that, to tell some of those ribald tales he had a knack for, to talk to make the time pass, to give himself the feeling he existed. When he observed sitting across from him, alone on her seat, an insignificant little nun who hadn't stopped saying her rosary since the train pulled out of the station, Henri decided, for lack of anything better to do, that he would speak to her. If he asked her some questions, perhaps she would return the favour?

"You'll excuse me, Sister, if I ask what's taking you to Quebec?"

"A meeting with the provincial treasurer."

"The provincial treasurer! You must have heavy responsibilities?"

"I do indeed: I run an asylum."

"A lunatic asylum? I wouldn't get mixed up with a thing like that, Sister, if you paid me a hundred dollars a day."

"Nor would I. I do it free of charge. And now, sir, if it's all the same to you, I'd like to finish my prayers."

Finish them, Sister, finish them, thought the traveller, and say a few decades for me while you're at it. And the little nun continued to tell her beads. How can they keep repeating the same words for hours without going crazy? Henri Massicotte may be skilled at telling juicy stories, and he's certainly excellent at selling collars and cuffs, but where prayers are concerned he's a complete ignoramus.

Just as saying the rosary can be a tedious exercise when performed routinely, so it can become, in the fingers of someone with a wide experience of spiritual exercises, an altogether ineffable experience. The first chaplet takes a great deal of conviction, with eyes carefully shut, the mind concentrating only on the Lord: establishing such a remote communication is no easy task, and it's one that requires tact. But then with the second one feels one's breathing slowing down and sometimes even a slight numbness creeping over one's fingertips. This is a good sign. At the third, unless one is rudely interrupted by some travelling salesman longing for a little conversation, one continues to repeat the Ave's and the Pater's, but now it's as if they are reciting themselves. The fingers move from bead to bead, the words follow one another, but the inner voice is no longer the same; it's as if the Holy Ghost, to thank us for our piety, is whispering the words in our place. The phrases He recites then become a mere pleasant background, the murmur of a spring, a gentle breeze in the branches of a willow, and they act as a filter that holds back all the dust of life, leaving the spirit wide open. One's head, which often seems so cluttered when it is filled with only one's petty everyday concerns, suddenly becomes as vast as the sky, and one's thoughts become luminous. Then we can open ourselves to Him, we know He is there listening to us. Obviously it would be presumptuous to think He will speak to us, though that sometimes happens when we least expect it. Most of the time, He will show Himself in some way other than in words: He will give us courage, cause us to see certain facts in a new light, clarify some difficult decision.

Hail Mary, full of grace.... Twenty-one dollars and sixty-three cents! Can't even read and they accuse me of making an error of twenty-one dollars and sixty-three cents, and that's why I'm taking the train. That treasurer is going to hear about me, Lord. A whim? No, it's a matter of principle. I want to show them that nuns are perfectly capable of administering a hospital, that it's none of the government's business. Besides, I haven't abandoned my patients, Lord, there are two hundred nuns looking after them, not to mention the guards and the doctors. If anything happened, there would still be those three vacuous individuals who twiddle their thumbs all day long; they could make themselves useful, couldn't they?

Our Father, who art in Heaven, hallowed be Thy name, Thy kingdom come.... I know there's not much they can do if they don't have access to the dispensary, and since all the nuns refuse to speak to them . . . . But is it not my duty to protect our Catholic institutions against the designs of the state? I was born Cléophée Têtu, and I'm as stubborn as my name.

Forgive us our trespasses as we forgive those who trespass against us. . . . . If You only knew how tired I am, Lord, if You only knew how I sometimes feel like giving it all up. Do they want my asylum? Let them take it! And let them pay the nuns and start schools for nurses! We shall retire to our convents and we'll pray for them. When I think that I could have become a Carmelite and had peace, blessed Peace! I know, it could be worse: I could have married a travelling salesman or an MP. Forgive me, Lord, I shouldn't complain, I should give thanks to You for having called me, but I'm so tired, I sometimes wonder if I'm worthy to be Your bride.

Glory be unto the Father, and to the Son, and to the Holy Ghost. . . . . Is it a waste of energy for me to get involved in politics, Lord? Look at that Protestant across from me; soon he'll leave his post and another will take his place. If You wanted to give him a push in that direction, Lord, I wouldn't complain. There's no lack of vocations to send people to Parliament, but when it's time for charity, that's another kettle of fish. . . . . I'm so tired, Lord, You can't imagine how tired. Only yesterday I was almost killed again, by a poor simpleton who'd got his hands on a knife. Fortunately You intervened, or it would have been the end of me. Dr. Dansereau stitched me up, but it was You who healed me, I know. Why did You test me that way, Lord? Are You trying to tell me I'm doing too much? Do You think I should just quietly run the asylum and delegate medical control to the government? After all, the minister promised I'd remain responsible for the supervision and the financial management; the community would retain ownership of the building, the leasing contract would be maintained — until the next election, in any case. Then, when the Ross government is defeated, everything will be easier, perhaps, we'll be negotiating among ourselves. . . . But not Dr. Howard, Lord. Promise not to let him take over medical control. Find someone of my own race, a good Catholic, and I'll give up the struggle.

Thy will be done, on Earth as it is in Heaven. . . . Actually, Lord, don't think I'm trying to change the subject, but just between You and me, I'm worried about Dr. Dansereau. When I was making enquiries about him, I learned that he sometimes used to profess pagan ideas. His former parish priest tells me that he's always attended Mass regularly, but that he suspects him of maintaining relations with a certain Florence Martineau, a woman of easy virtue from what people say, and not very charitable either; when I asked her to cede me some land along the river, she refused, and her manner was really quite insolent. . . . And I've also heard that Dr. Dansereau belonged to the library of the Institut Canadien, that he was a Liberal. . . . That's not malicious gossip, Lord, it was a priest who told me. Of course priests can be sinners too, but whom can one trust, Lord, whom can one trust? Dr. Dansereau? Really? *Glory be unto the Father, and to the Son, and to the Holy Ghost.* . . . I leave the matter in Your hands, Lord, You must know what You're doing. But please, Lord, deliver me from Dr. Howard."

Henri Massicotte casts an occasional glance in Soeur Thérèse's direction. He observes that her fingers are moving more slowly now from bead to bead, until they stop altogether. Has she fallen asleep? No, her eyes are wide open, and she now appears quite calm.

The next morning at eight, Soeur Thérèse is at the provincial treasurer's office. The young secretary who receives her, who is busy retouching her nails, doesn't even look up at the nun: the Honourable Minister is not yet in his office, he won't be there before nine, does she have an appointment?

"No, mademoiselle, but the treasurer will see me. May I take a seat?"

"Of course, Sister, but I must warn you: the Honourable Minister is very busy. . . ."

"As am I, mademoiselle. You don't mind if I say my rosary while I'm waiting?"

"No, Sister, but I'm afraid the Honourable Minister won't be able to see you. . . ."

"I'm not deaf, mademoiselle."

Not knowing what to reply, the secretary shrugs and inserts a sheet of paper into her typing machine. You don't call the police to expel a nun, after all. The boss will sort it out. *Dear Sir, In reply to your letter of June 12. . . .* Still, what a life, being a nun: always the same black robe, summer and winter, never any outings or amusements, shut up all day long in a dank cell, praying. . . . Watch those fingers go on her rosary beads! If I could type that fast, I could do a week's work in an hour. . . . Look at that, she wears a wedding ring. I don't imagine she sees her husband very often. All right now, let's concentrate: *In reply to your letter of June 12, I regret to inform you. . . .*

I believe in God, our all-powerful Father, and in Jesus Christ His only Son. . . . How depraved the man must be, dear God, to hire a woman as a secretary! And she's not very fast; I wouldn't give her a job in my asylum. Perhaps she's afraid of damaging her nail-polish. How on earth can she type with such long nails? And would you look at that dress, Lord! There's one who's not afraid of a sunburn! How vulgar!

Give me courage, Lord, as You yourself had on the cross, just a little courage to tackle the treasurer, then I'll go back to my asylum, I promise. . . . What time is it? What on earth is that treasurer up to? Will he even look at his secretary? Has he the faintest idea what she subjects her face to, just to please him? In a few years she'll marry a travelling salesman who'll give her a dozen children. He'll drink up his salary in the tavern and get angry when she wants to buy herself some perfume. Poor girl. Thank you, Lord, for giving me a religious vocation. Is that treasurer ever going to get here? Ah, there he is, finally. He's pretending he doesn't see me, he's whispering to his secretary instead; no, I don't have an appointment, but you're going to see me, *Monsieur le Trésorier,* and don't try any fancy footwork to get rid of me. Têtu was my name, and stubborn I remain."

"Soeur Thérèse, what a surprise! Are you visiting the capital?"

"No, monsieur, I've come especially to see you. May I speak with you in private for a moment?"

"Of course, Sister, of course, but I must warn

you . . ."

" . . . that you're a very busy man. I know. I too am very busy, and I want you to know that I didn't come here to waste your time or mine. Is this your office? May I go in?"

"Of course, of course. What can I do for you, Sister?"

"Last week I received a letter from one of your auditors. He claims that my accounts contained an error of twenty-one dollars and sixty-three cents. I'm quite certain the error is his, *Monsieur le Trésorier*. My accounts are correct."

"A twenty-dollar mistake! Don't tell me you've come all the way from Montreal for such an inconsequential matter!"

"I didn't come from Montreal, I came from Longue-Pointe. And it's not a twenty-dollar mistake, it's twenty-one dollars and sixty-three cents. As provincial treasurer you ought to be more precise. Your auditor has made an error, and I insist that it be corrected, at once, if you would be so kind."

"Look here, Sister, this is ridiculous, my auditors were a little over-zealous, that's all, we aren't going to quarrel over a few dollars. . . ."

"Twenty-one dollars and sixty-three cents."

"Never mind the precise amount, Sister. You administer a budget of more than a hundred thousand dollars, and you do it admirably well, so how important can such a small error be?"

"I regret very much that I must insist, *Monsieur le Trésorier*, but there has been no error. My budget is one hundred and twenty-two thousand dollars and fifty-seven cents, *Monsieur le Trésorier*, and I have never made an error. I've brought you my accounts, you can verify them for yourself."

"See here, Soeur Thérèse, your time is as valuable as mine; here's what I suggest: I'll turn over your account books to my auditors, who will study them thoroughly. If we've made an error, we shall correct it as quickly as possible. And if by any chance the error is yours, I'll make it up out of my own pocket!"

"Out of the question, *Monsieur le Trésorier*. I haven't come from Longue-Pointe to waste my time, and you won't have to reimburse me because there is no error. Fetch your auditors, I'm not leaving here until my accounts have been verified. If your auditors are as speedy as your secretary, I advise you to waste no time. I may as well warn you, I hope to go home on the five o'clock boat. You don't mind if I say my rosary while I wait?"

The treasurer poured out a stream of apologies, explanations and protests, but in vain. There was nothing to be done: Soeur Thérèse had started her first decade.

* * *

Three hours later, five shirtsleeved accountants, visibly exhausted, entered the treasurer's office to submit their report: this is embarrassing, *Monsieur le Trésorier*, but we can't deny we made an error, Soeur Thérèse's accounts are impeccable.

"You were right, Soeur Thérèse. I beg you to accept my apologies, and I assure you that such a situation will never recur. . . ."

"I regret having caused you so much trouble,

Monsieur le Trésorier, but, as you can see, my accounts are properly kept. By the way, will you tell Monsieur Ross that I'm prepared to turn the medical control of my asylum over to the government, and that the three doctors he named will be able to work normally in the future? However, you will agree that perhaps it would be better if our institution's finances were to remain in the nuns' hands a little longer. I look forward to seeing you again, *Monsieur le Trésorier*. I shall pray that your auditors aren't too distracted when they are studying the provincial budget!"

At six o'clock, Soeur Thérèse is sitting on the deck of the boat that will take her back to Longue-Pointe. In another few hours she'll be with her nuns, her patients, and her hospital again, she'll get back in harness with all the energy of which she is capable; but until then, she wants to think about nothing but the wind that is caressing her brow, about the birds that are following the wake of the boat, about the marvellous flying fish she saw off Valparaiso, about the pretty house in Sainte-Hyacinthe where she was born, the wide verandah where she played with her skipping rope as a child. . . . "Thank you, God, for granting me those few moments of vacation."

* * *

While Soeur Thérèse is letting her thoughts drift along with the waves, Bernard has almost completed his second day on the job. A few cases of cowpox, sarsaparilla prescriptions for some lunatics with female complaints, castor oil for others who have trouble evacuating certain materials; he is gradually settling into a routine.

This morning, he began his day by removing from the ears of some patients a variety of substances it is their deplorable habit to bury there, in the vain hope of silencing the voices that plague them. After this delicate operation, he takes a little syringe and injects a warm boric solution. Not only does Bernard need skill and patience, he must also give evidence of psychology: "I guarantee, monsieur, that the voices are silent now; Sister and I have said many prayers for you, and the devil will leave you in peace, I promise." By the twelfth pair of ears, he has perfected the technique, and now he can apply it while thinking of other things. And what if the patients who behave like this are unconsciously trying to touch their sick brains, to extricate the faulty cells?

How many such cells are there in the brain of Emilie Jolicoeur, who died this morning? When Bernard was called to her bedside it was, unfortunately, too late: her pulse had gone, no mist formed on the mirror when he placed it before her nostrils. While the nurse was performing the patient's final toilette, Bernard conscientiously filled out the death certificate.

Emilie Jolicoeur had been a congenital idiot who was brought to the asylum by policemen who found her in an abandoned barn, starved half to death. They had done their best to put some flesh back on her bones, but as she refused all food it was a difficult task; she spent the last three years of her life lying in her little iron bed, staring up at the ceiling.

When he was completing the certificate, Bernard hesitated briefly at the box labelled: "Probable cause of death." The nurse saw him hesitate and suggested that he write *marasmus*. The other boxes had not presented any problems: as she was an orphan there was no one to notify, she had received Extreme Unction, the body would be taken to the morgue, no autopsy would be necessary. . . .

"Tell me, Sister, do we often perform autopsies?"

"Very rarely, only when the family or the police demand it."

"Thank you, Sister, God bless you, and may God bless this poor woman."

"God bless you too, Dr. Dansereau."

All day, Bernard thought about Emilie. Her brain had never had to work, so perhaps it had atrophied like a never-used muscle? Or hardened? Or dried out. . . ? No one would ever come to claim the body, so why not find out?

When his day's work is complete, Bernard hands his report to Soeur Jeanne-de-l'Esprit, goes to the dispensary to drink a few brandies, then comes out carrying a saw. Be brave, Bernard, you have to start somewhere.

* * *

When Bernard comes home, Florence observes that her friend is abnormally pale. He eats in silence, only picking at his food, then goes and shuts himself away in the shed. What has he brought home in his bag, and why does he have that worried expression that lines his brow with such deep wrinkles? If madness is not contagious, as he always maintains, why did he wash his hands for so long before supper?

While Florence is drying the dishes, Bernard places Emilie's brain on his laboratory table. It is a mass of perfectly normal appearance, an almost perfect oval of a fine mother-of-pearl colour, furrowed with convolutions, and weighing one thousand four hundred grams, which is perfectly average, for a woman's brain at least. It seems soft to the touch, its consistency somewhat reminiscent of the belly of a frog or salamander, and the scalpel cuts into it quite easily. The dimensions of the left hemisphere seem smaller than those of the right, yet it weighs virtually the same. . . . Could this be something promising? How many brains must he study before he can formulate valid conclusions? Perhaps the solution will be found in the convolutions? Could all these folds, bulges, patterns, be affected by the patients' humours? Could they be unique, like fingerprints or the lines on the hand? What total area would he obtain if they were unfolded, and would it be marked by ideas? And what if the nature of the convolutions isn't significant at all? What if, instead, it's the depth of the furrows that's important? How can ideas avoid getting lost in this labyrinth? Is it necessary to take a microscope and study every cell of white matter, every cell of grey?

It always seems to us, when we are thinking, that the front part of the brain does all the work: ideas seem to us to be born somewhere between the frontal bone and the brain itself; we never feel ourselves thinking through the nape or the back of the head. Perhaps that suggests a lead? Ideas germinate on the surface of the frontal lobes, instincts in the cerebellum, moral principles in the depths of Rolando's fissure, and the feeling of happiness is a little electrical current that trots along the *pons Varolii*. . . .

Why won't you talk to me, you mass of gelatine, why do you pass on so many crazy ideas and so few flashes of genius, so many superstitions and so little knowledge, so much submissiveness and so little resistance, so much jealousy and so little love? Why so much politics and so little truth? Why does your clock always break down during periods of despair, then run so fast when things are going well? Why make us hear voices when no one is talking, why make amputees feel phantom pains? let us be gnawed at by scruples and remorse? make me like brandy and hate boiled chicken? Why do you want me to raise my eyes to the sky to look at stars I will never reach? How do you arrange it so the newborn baby turns instinctively to its mother's breast, so old people remember only childhood or futile thoughts, when you can't even explain your own workings to me? Old plug of tobacco! Yes, you're just an old plug of tobacco, to be tossed in the garbage when it has no more taste. . . .

But why am I getting all worked up like this? It's only the brain of a poor idiot, after all. Even if I had the brain of the greatest scholar of all time in front of me, it would be just as silent. I mustn't expect it to reveal secrets to me that it's hidden from the greatest surgeons and the most illustrious philosophers. I'll need years and years of patience. Draw up a chart of the convolutions, measure the depth of the furrows, examine the cells one by one, weigh the hemispheres, cut up the lobes, make mistakes and start over, again and again, until a small fragment of truth makes another infinity of questions appear. . . .

Perhaps, one day, someone will invent a little wax roll that can be grafted to the brain at birth to record all conversations, thoughts, and dreams. At the moment of death, the roll will go first to the doctor, who won't have to perform an autopsy, then to the priest, who will then know with certainty whether the soul is in Heaven, Hell, or Purgatory, and finally to the family, who can proceed to tear each other to pieces in full knowledge of the facts. Until that happens, he'll have to make do with a mass of dead cells.

"Bernard? It's eleven o'clock, what on earth are you doing?"

"I'm finishing an experiment, then I'll come in. Don't worry."

How did you make me hear Florence's voice through the door? How can you immediately associate that worried voice with a sweet perfume, a penetrating warmth? So long, old plug, sleep well in your glass jar. Here, let me give you a label: *No. 1. Idiot — 56-year-old female — Cause of death: marasmus — Sept. 7, 1885.* Good-night, old plug! And may God bless Emilie's soul.

6

As he has done every morning for a little more than two years, Bernard arrives at the doctors' office on the stroke of seven.

"What's new this morning, Soeur Jeanne?"

"Plenty of work, Dr. Dansereau; there was a fight on the men's side last night. The infirmary is full."

"What happened?"

"I've no idea. All I can tell you is that there are as many Protestants as Catholics, and you'll need plenty of thread; the Protestants had knives and the Catholics had pitch-forks."

"Are there any dead?"

"No, at least not yet. Soeur Marie is already on the spot with bandages and thread, and so is Dr. Villeneuve; he was wakened as soon as the injured arrived. They're expecting you."

"I'll go right away. God bless you, Soeur Jeanne."

"God bless you too, Dr. Dansereau."

A fight! What can have happened? Usually they fight with their fists, or sometimes with knives stolen from the kitchens, but pitch-forks . . . in January! Bernard races to the infirmary.

"God bless you, Dr. Dansereau! Can you help

me sew up this one? It will take me a while to repair his skull; would you see about his stomach?"

"God bless you too, Dr. Villeneuve. Give me some thread, I'll take care of it. Were the internal organs affected?"

"I don't know, he was unconscious when I got here. The nurses attended to the most urgent matters first by stopping the haemorrhaging, but he'd already lost a lot of blood. One of his brothers is interned here, and I considered performing a transfusion, but the chance of success is so slight, even between brothers. . . . He seems robust, I think he'll pull through. Try to make loose stitches, we'll undoubtedly have to pick them out when he regains his strength."

While Dr. Villeneuve sews up the scalp, Bernard removes one of the three bandages that cover the abdomen. Fortunately, the wound seems superficial. The dark red blood flows in a steady stream: some small veins have been cut, but none of the arteries. While a nurse mops up the wound, Bernard threads his needle and starts making sutures. Soon both doctors' hands are rising and falling at the same rhythm.

"How are the others?"

"Superficial wounds. We've looked after the most urgent. Fortunately, the guards intervened in time, and the nurses did their work, otherwise we'd have lost some. God bless the nurses. But . . . tell me, what's that on your finger?"

"That? A thimble. I got the idea of using one from watching a seamstress; I don't like pricking my fingers. I have several more at home; I could bring you one if you wish."

"That's very kind. Is that the same person who showed you how to make stitches? You do it very well."

"Yes, I took that idea from buttonholes; they look better and they're more solid too. Now tell me, how did the fight begin?"

"It's this man we're sewing up who led off. His name is Clifford Harvey; he's a Protestant, from an old family of Orangemen in the Eastern Townships. He's a rebel, a megalomaniac, a born leader. . . . Would you hold my knot for a moment, while I thread another needle? Thank you. . . . Since Clifford was convinced that he'd been interned because of his religion, that the asylum is actually a papist prison and he himself a prisoner of war, it was easy for him to talk some of his coreligionists into trying to escape. They'd even started assembling provisions and weapons. Nothing terribly dangerous: just some bread, fruit, ropes, knives. . . . One of the Irish Catholics got wind of it and thought they were preparing an insurrection. He warned Romuald Séguin, the former papal Zouave. That was when things began heating up. You know Romuald thinks he's still in Rome, leading the troops of Zouaves who put up such brave resistance to repeated assaults by Garibaldi's troops. He's a loudmouth, and he infuriated the French Canadians when he reminded them that Clifford had applauded the hanging of Louis Riel — which is true, incidentally — and he even managed to sign up some Creoles for his battalion, by telling them that Clifford had joined the ranks of the Confederate army — which is also true — and wanted to kill all the Negroes in the asylum — which is less certain. Around five o'clock this morning, the Protestants had tied up their guard and were preparing to make their getaway. Unfortunately for them, the Zouave army was waiting at the door to the ward. A nun came and woke me at half past five, and I've been sewing ever since. The last time I saw such butchery was during a hockey game at the Victoria Skating Rink: the National against the Shamrock. . . . How's that abdomen coming along?"

"Fine, I've almost finished. How is it that the other doctors haven't come to lend a hand?"

"Well, you see, our distinguished alienists are far too important to look after a few measly cuts! When one has studied in Paris, one doesn't mingle with the small fry. They must be having a meeting somewhere. . . . Would you lend me your scissors? Thank you. When you've finished with your button-holes, will you examine Romuald? He's complaining of abdominal pain. It seems to me that our Zouave is trying to get out of working. In the meantime, I'll take care of Clifford; the poor man's joints are black and blue. Then, if you'll allow me, I shall go to the chapel to meditate. I've been sewing for almost three hours; my fingers need some prayers. Romeo needs to be examined too: his thigh was slashed with a knife."

"Romeo? Don't tell me he was fighting?"

"No, fighting's not in his nature. He simply happened to be there and got caught between the two sides. An innocent victim of the war. . . ."

As Dr. Villeneuve had suspected, Romuald

wasn't really in bad shape. Bernard merely performed a few palpations, mysterious ones, to say the least, then winked at the nurse and prescribed a strong dose of castor oil. While the Zouave was being purged, Bernard went over to Romeo.

"Tell me, Romeo, what happened?"

Romeo looks up at the ceiling as if he's heard nothing. Bernard lifts the sheet, removes the bandage, disinfects the wound, and starts to sew a buttonhole.

"It isn't serious, Romeo, but you should stay on your back for at least a week; I'm afraid the muscle's been cut."

Romeo still doesn't react.

"You could use the time to write. In fact, I've brought you paper and a pencil. Be careful not to press too hard; it's tissue paper. Do you think you can manage not to tear it?"

"Paper? Thank you, Dr. Dansereau, thank you very much. I'll be extremely careful, Dr. Dansereau, I'll write as gently as I can. If you only knew how gently I write; in fact I don't even write, I stroke the paper. God bless you a thousand times, Doctor."

"Watch out, hold still while I close up your wound. As soon as I've finished I'll give you the paper, I promise. . . . Where did you learn to write, Romeo?"

"At school, with the Brothers of the Sacred Heart. I even started classical studies."

"Why did you give it up?"

"My father died, I was the oldest. . . . I had to go back to the farm."

"And how did you meet Véronique?"

"What Véronique?"

"What do you mean, what Véronique, isn't she the one you're always writing to? Isn't it because of her that you're here?"

"Ah, yes, I see what you mean. I loved her very much, it's true, but that's all over now, she's married."

"How about you, what are you doing here?"

"Me? I'm here because I'm unhappy. When I jumped in the river, everyone thought it was because of Véronique. The doctor assumed I'd lost my mind because of a broken heart, and the curé did too, for that matter; so I finally believed it myself. It's easier to accept unhappiness if you have a good reason for being unhappy, isn't that so? Now I know it wasn't her fault — hers or anyone else's. . . . No, the unhappiness is in my head; and it doesn't want to come out. It's like hammer-blows. . . ."

"Where do they strike? In the front, the sides, the back?"

"The back, near the nape of my neck."

"Do you take baths?"

"Only for cleanliness. Dr. Paquette says there's nothing more to be done for me. I enjoyed the hot baths, though."

"When you go back to your room, try to look at the ferns for as long as possible."

"Why?"

"Just to see. Perhaps it will ease the pain. Now then, I have to go. Here's your paper. Don't forget the ferns. Let me know."

"Thank you, Doctor. Before you go, may I ask

you a favour?"

"What's that?"

"Don't call me Romeo, please. My name is Oscar, Oscar Parent."

"Oscar Parent, I solemnly swear that if I ever find a vaccine against unhappiness, I'll try it on you first."

"What did you say?"

"Nothing, nothing, I was thinking out loud."

* * *

At noon the doctors' refectory is deserted. Bernard is disappointed, for, during the two years he has been working at the asylum, he and Dr. Villeneuve have got in the habit of eating lunch and then smoking a huge cigar together, while talking about this and that. In the end, Bernard has learned to appreciate this man with the sanguine temperament, who never asks indiscreet questions and who, when he allows himself to make a declaration or to state a position — a rare occurrence — always has enough tact to balance it with one of those remarks that allows the other party to express his opinion in turn, without provoking an escalation: "In my opinion," "I sometimes think that. . .," "I'm no expert, but it seems to me that. . . ." The only criticism Bernard could make of Dr. Villeneuve is of his inconstancy: sometimes he doesn't come to the staff refectory, leaving him alone with Dr. Paquette. . . .

Unlike Dr. Villeneuve, Dr. Paquette seems unacquainted with doubt. Whether the subject is politics, mental health, or religion, he always offers peremptory declarations tangled with great indisputable principles and specious arguments, until, at some point, his interlocutors are forced to reply. Dr. Paquette is genuinely pleased when he sees them fall into his trap; like a starving spider who feels his web vibrating, he throws himself at his opponent and surrounds him with the sticky thread of his arguments, then paralyses the victims by pinning them with one of his definitive proofs. Bernard is not the kind to brave a rabid dog or a gang of hoodlums: he would rather cross the street; and when he encounters someone who has studied in Paris, he goes to another table.

There is a good chance that this morning's events will lead the conversation onto political ground. Dr. Paquette should be here soon. . . . He'll have something critical to say about the nuns' cooking, something sarcastic about chokecherry wine. . . . Why not bolt his meal, take advantage of the mild weather, and go for a walk in the garden? Thank you, Soeur Berthe, I won't have any more dessert, the sugar pie was delicious but I want to take a walk. God bless you, Soeur Berthe.

* * *

Bernard lingers briefly in the yard, looking at the skating rink. Some lunatics armed with big shovels are removing the last of the snow that has accumulated on the ice, while others struggle with long strips of lamp-wick, with which they will fasten circles of barrel-hoop to their boots to serve as blades. Although the day is mild, not everyone can handle these materials with ease; some are forced to ask the nuns for help.

What an amazing sight it is to see them moving silently across the ice. The most awkward ones have trouble staying on their feet, and their arms trace broad and useless spirals in the air, while the more dextrous glide elegantly despite their makeshift skates and heavy coats. They go in circles, utterly indifferent to the beginners' pirouettes and spectacular falls; they skate rings around their misfortune. Some nuns will come out and join them presently; for a few moments they will be allowed to go back to their childhood. . . . Heavy black robes, pretty red cheeks, scattered laughter, like spatterings of grace, prayers addressed to the winter.

Bernard walks a little longer, turning onto the elm-lined lane to the graveyard. The asylum was built recently, yet the graveyard is already full. But who is that just next to the Calvary? That round, stocky silhouette, slightly hunched, the ridiculous beaver hat, can only belong to Dr. Villeneuve. At whose grave has he come to meditate? It's none of your business, Bernard, turn around discreetly, go back to the asylum, leave him in peace. Bernard would like to go back, but his feet are stuck in the snow, his eyes remain on Dr. Villeneuve's silhouette. The latter, who has felt his colleague's gaze on him like a friendly tap on the shoulder, turns around.

"God bless you, Dr. Dansereau. Do you know someone in the cemetery?"

"No, I was just getting some fresh air, sorry to disturb you."

"Not at all, I was about to leave. I come here once a week to say a prayer over my mother's grave. See the little cross in the second row, on the left of the bad thief? An insignificant little cross; it's all that's left of one of the hospital's first patients. She was first taken in by Soeur Thérèse, at the Saint-Isidore convent.... She was an exceptional woman, a devoted, attentive mother who deserved a Christian husband. Instead, she was made pregnant by a young carter who, once his vile deed was done, fled to the United States and was never heard from again. One day, some relatives told us he had died. His liver had burst."

"You needn't feel obliged to tell me all that, Dr. Villeneuve."

"I know. It's precisely because I don't feel obliged that I want to tell you. It will help you understand many things."

Be quiet, Bernard. Look at the little cross too, and be quiet.

"When I was born, my mother could have abandoned me as so many others have done, but she wanted to keep me. She worked like a slave all her life, in a tobacco factory during the day, cleaning rich people's houses at night. So that she could spend more time with me, she used to take me with her; while I played with old spools of thread she scrubbed her floors. 'Look around you, my boy, take a good look; when you grow up you'll have a house as fine as this one.' I'd put down my spools and look at the polished floors, the enormous rooms, the velvet drapes, the bookcases, the piano, and I'd think, she's crazy, I'll never have that kind of money. She *was* crazy, in fact, but I didn't know that yet. How she managed to put me under the protection of a kind man named Gamelin, I don't know. When he died in 1827, he left my mother enough money to pay for my education. I was five years old at the time. It was Madame Gamelin who administered my inheritance. Not only did she look after the insane, she took care of me as well. A saintly woman, Madame Gamelin. Were you aware that she became known as 'the angel of the political prisoners' during the 1837 troubles?"

"No, I didn't know that. But what makes you say your mother was crazy? From what you've told me, she sounds perfectly sane."

"She suffered from mental degeneration, however, a disease that takes some time before it appears. Until I finished medical school, she was incoherent at times but I thought it was due to fatigue, to overwork. That was what she said as well, though she knew perfectly well that she was suffering from an incurable disease. Once my future was assured, the dam burst: in the space of a few months, she'd become unrecognizable. She had always been absolutely reserved, and now she started to use crude language, to forget my name and then her own, she stopped washing. . . . It was Madame Gamelin who took her in. And that's the story. Now you know why I've never married, why I've spent my life caring for the insane, even though I'm convinced that no treatment for madness will ever be found."

"Why didn't you marry?"

"My father was alcoholic, my mother was insane. If I had fathered children, they would have been insane too. Heredity, Dr. Dansereau, heredity is the only cause of madness. Read the patients' histories: alcoholism and poverty are transmitted from father to son as surely as hysteria is transmitted from mother to daughter. There are some rare exceptions, I grant you, but when both parents have problems, madness is no longer in the realm of the probable, it is inevitable. An alcoholic father and an uneducated mother will invariably engender idiots; if the father is the uneducated one and the mother the alcoholic, the children will be imbeciles; when the father is a bastard and the mother a hysteric, the children will most assuredly be maniacs. There is no solution for madness. One can relieve the symptoms, but there is no cure for hereditary flaws. The only solution is for people like me, who know they are afflicted, to refrain from procreating."

"But your own example refutes your arguments, Dr. Villeneuve: despite your antecedents, you yourself are perfectly sane."

"With mental health even more than general health, there is no difference in kind between health and disease, it's only a matter of degree. Who is to say that I too won't suffer from degeneration? And you know as well as I do, inherited characteristics sometimes skip a generation. No, I mustn't take any risks. It's a pity . . . because I was successful with women, I knew how to make them laugh."

"So you've never . . . I mean, you. . . ."

"Set your mind at ease, Doctor, I take care of my hygiene. I have one free afternoon a month and I know where to go; I take precautions. What else do you want me to do with my money? I live in the asylum, I eat all my meals there. . . . Now then, time to get back to work. I thank you for listening to me."

"Not at all, it was most interesting."

"You're not obliged to believe me, Doctor. If you only knew how much I'd prefer not to know those things about myself. . . . By the way, while I think of it, did you know that Berthe died this morning? Remember her, she was in the Sainte-Cunégonde ward, the poor idiot who was always smiling. If ever there existed a happy lunatic, it was Berthe. You were very interested in her case, I believe?"

"Indeed. Is her body already in the morgue?"

"Very likely. The poor woman had no family, so I'd be surprised if anyone came to claim it. That will make one more white cross in the cemetery. . . . Have you talked with Soeur Thérèse recently?"

"No, why?"

"She's given me a message for you: she wishes to see you in her office first thing tomorrow morning. She said she's very interested in your research."

"My research? Is that all she said?"

"No. It's none of my business, Dr. Dansereau, but I didn't know you were doing research."

"Sometimes, yes, in my spare time, but I didn't know Soeur Thérèse was aware of it."

"Soeur Thérèse knows everything. And, in addition, she arranges things so that other people know. Why do you think she charged me with giving you that message? But don't worry about me, Dr. Dansereau. Should you feel like it, keep me informed, and if not, I won't hold it against you. In either case, I'll say nothing to our distinguished colleagues."

"Thank you, Dr. Villeneuve. I shall keep you

informed, I promise, if I continue to work for the asylum. . . ."

"You have nothing to fear from Soeur Thérèse. If she'd wanted to dismiss you, she'd have done it long ago. Now, back to work."

* * *

Dear little thirteen-hundred-gram brain, you may be the last in my collection, so try to cooperate, will you? Give up some of your secrets, tell me about Berthe. . . . How did she manage to keep her smile though she was an idiot? To be insensitive to sarcasm despite her ugliness? To be incapable of the slightest meanness? For once, brain, be something besides an old limp plug. Help me, I beg you, make me find the fern-cells at the base of the nape, and the others close to the optic nerve, and those that hide in the hollow of the inner ear. Be kind, little brain. If you let me extract a few cells, I'll preserve them in a huge block of ice, and then one day, perhaps, I shall be able to inject them into Oscar, poor Oscar, who is doomed to unhappiness. . . .

How could I be so naive, how could I think I'd be able to remove so many brains from their cases without anyone noticing? Twice, three times a week, taking a metal-saw down to the morgue; it couldn't last. Soeur Marie-de-la-Visitation must have had suspicions and talked about them with Soeur Thérèse, or perhaps someone saw me going out with my little bag. . . .

Two hundred and sixty-four times I went down to the morgue, with saw in hand and a few brandies in my gullet. I sliced across the skull from temple to temple, inside the hairline, being very careful not to damage the skin on the forehead; I opened the head very gently, like a fiancée lifting the lid of a jewel box; I cut through the frontal bone, severed the optic nerves and spinal cord, then I delicately removed the brain and closed the lid again, replaced the skin on the forehead and the hair, and went home with no one the wiser. My technique is flawless, no one could suspect that the heads I leave are empty, that the bodies families sometimes come to claim are lighter by two or three pounds.

Hours and hours closed up inside the barn talking to my old horse; measuring the depth of the furrows with an instrument of my own devising, reproducing the convolutions on tissue paper so I could hold them against the light to compare them — a total waste of time, as it turns out. If I'd got the idea of studying animals earlier, I wouldn't have wasted six months of my life drawing. Sheep, horses, and cattle have very complicated, very deep convolutions, while the brains of rats and birds are perfectly smooth. Now, if horses are more intelligent than hens, sheep are much stupider than rats; it's perfectly obvious. And even if we admit that convolutions are a factor in intelligence, we're no further ahead: aside from idiots, the insane are just as intelligent as normal people; but their intelligence is warped, which is a different matter.

Hours spent weighing old plugs, hemisphere after hemisphere, lobe after lobe, almost cell after cell. I should have known from my very first experiments that it was quite useless. Jar number sixteen:

Clara Pontbriand. A poor servant girl, interned for religious monomania. She thought she was Salome. When she died, the guards were very relieved; she had a way of looking at their necks that gave them gooseflesh. Poor Clara couldn't read or write, she could barely count to three, and she was convinced that if bathwater got inside her through her navel, she would give birth to a frog. Yet her brain weighs one thousand three hundred grams, much more than Cromwell's. No, the size of the brain has no influence either on mental health or on intelligence. One brain will be huge and full of nonsense, another will be minuscule and brilliant. But still I went on weighing them: it was convenient for classification.

Two hundred and sixty-four times I almost gave up, but I continued. And to think that I was on the point of making a discovery. Let me explain, old horse. When sensations reach the brain they spend a brief time in the frontal lobes, where a few cells sort them very rapidly. Colours, temperatures, shapes, weights, ideas, everything is measured, weighed, hefted, labelled at lightning speed. Next comes the question of storage. When one has a logical mind, everything is filed in the appropriate compartment, and the oldest information can be found as easily as a book in a library. The cells for logic are the librarians of the mind. How many logic cells are there? Where are they located? I don't know. Perhaps it's not so important.

Now, let us combine two ideas: I observe brains and Florence grows flowers. What do a brain and a flower have in common? Nothing. And yet, when you think about it, it's perfectly obvious: the nerves are like roots that sink into the body and, through the sensory organs, into the entire universe. That nourishment is transported to the spinal column, which rises, like a long stem, to the brain, and it, in turn, is an efflorescence of the spinal column. The nerves are roots, the spinal column a stem, the brain a flower. Are you still following me? All impressions, with no exception, pass through the roots, rise up the stem, and finally arrive at the brain. Depending on the treatment they undergo, those data, which at the outset were neutral, will become the components of joy or sorrow, of happiness or unhappiness. Where does the transformation occur? At the junction of stem and flower, of the spinal column and the brain. Necessarily. So it's there that we must look and nowhere else. That's where the key to happiness will be found. And that's why I'm removing some of Berthe's brain cells before I put the rest in a jar.

What will I find if I observe these cells under a microscope? Nerve cells just like all others of the same kind. They have different shapes and are connected by a granular substance in which they are suspended. Each one has a very specific role to play: this one, perhaps, stores very old memories, that one, which resembles an apple, makes us love women. And what will I find if I continue looking? Giant cells like those found deep in the convolutions, pyramidal cells linked by odd little branches that bear a strange resemblance to ferns. All the brains of idiots present cells of that kind. Those who suffer from hallucinations all have the same kind of cells, which are joined together in the same place, like grapes in a bunch; those individuals are unhappy. Idiots, in contrast, are very often blissful, placid, always ready to be of service, gentle and engaging as children. . . . Look, in fact, here's a magnificent fern-cell, and here's another, and another. . . . If Oscar observes ferns carefully, will his brain cells bunch together differently, to mimic them?

What am I going to do tomorrow? Deny vigorously, feign indignation to gain time, or quite simply admit everything? If I do confess, I'll be back in private practice—and stripped of everything: my office, my patients; my name stricken from the lists of every hospital in the province; my only recourse will be to exile myself to the United States or Ontario. Can you picture yourself in Ontario, Bernard? Starting your career all over, at your age? Have you any idea what you'd be eating in Ontario? Boiled chicken. Boiled chicken until the end of your days. Twenty-one fern-cells, twenty-two, twenty-three, a real nursery! Thank you, dear Berthe. . . .

Had Soeur Thérèse gone and investigated? It would be just like her. Did she open a skull? How much does she know? Everything, she must know everything. She's going to dismiss me, that's certain. How could a nun tolerate the profanation of cadavers in her establishment? It's over. Quickly now, let's remove the cells from this little brain: twenty-five, twenty-six, twenty-seven fern-cells. . . . I'll put them on ice. . . . Not a hint of a bunch of grapes yet! And to think, I may have been very close to the goal. . . .

7

"Good morning, Dr. Dansereau, I've been expecting you. You don't appear to be in top form this morning. Are you ill?"

"No, Soeur Thérèse, just a little tired."

"Good, Dr. Dansereau, I'm glad to hear it, we need a doctor who's in good health. I've asked you to come at such an early hour so that you and I can have time for a little talk. You've been working here for more than two years now, but we've hardly had a ten-minute conversation. That's not enough. I like to know what my staff are thinking and I like them to be happy. How do you find life in the asylum, Dr. Dansereau?"

"Everything's going well, I think I've adapted fairly readily, and I don't regret my choice."

"As you can see, Doctor, I'm very pleased. Do you enjoy the refectory food?"

"Yes, I find it quite satisfactory."

"Of course it's not refined cuisine, but one must do one's best with what one has. Do you know what I sometimes think, Dr. Dansereau? I think that our poor simpletons are quite fortunate. Have you ever wondered what their lives would be like if they hadn't been taken in here? They would be working in dusty factories, for starvation wages that wouldn't even buy food for their families. At the smallest crisis, they would be forced to join the multitudes of the unemployed. They'd starve to death or exile themselves to the United States, where they'd work in the mills and soon lose their language and their souls. Or else they'd go up to Temiscaming to clear a bit of land; they'd spend a few years felling trees they wouldn't even have the right to sell and, in the end, they'd be reduced to cultivating rocks and snow. As for the women, well, the less said, the better. If they don't want to see themselves forced to carry children for nine months of every year, and to give birth in pain — just to see the youngsters die a little later because they weren't able to pay the doctor — the only solution for them is to teach a hundred children for a salary of sixty dollars a year, or to become the bride of Our Lord and take care of those who are even more unfortunate than themselves. . . . Dr. Dansereau, our patients have privileges: they are housed, clothed, fed, they enjoy free medical care, they can play billiards and cards, they're even entitled to hot baths and showers. Just think, in the old country the bourgeois spend a fortune for spas! Here they have no money, no obligations, not even the obligation to work, although they are strongly urged to do so — for their own good. . . . If I'm not mistaken, Dr. Dansereau, you used to be a habitué of the Institut Canadien. Indeed, I've heard that when Monseigneur Bourget condemned the Institut, despite the threat of excommunication that hung over you, you were a fierce supporter of maintaining the association. Which makes you what is called a free-thinker."

"That's ancient history, Soeur Thérèse, I was very young at the time."

"No matter how old you were; our ideas don't change all that often in the course of a lifetime. So you're a free-thinker, a partisan of the separation of Church and state, you have read books on the Index, perhaps you even share the ideas of those European utopians who think they can refashion the world. Now, tell me: do you know a single utopian who has created a society more perfect than ours? Absolute security, free medication, recreation, voluntary work. . . . The ideal society is *here*, Dr. Dansereau, don't you agree?"

"I find that a surprising idea. It merits reflection."

"Don't try to wriggle out of this: all the conditions for an ideal society are brought together *here*, in this asylum. Is there a single one missing?"

"Liberty," replied Bernard.

"Why do they need liberty when they have everything they could desire? And how can you explain the fact that, despite that, most of them are only waiting to be cured so they can leave here, to become unemployed, cultivate rocks, or bring forth children in pain? It's a strange paradox, don't you think?"

"Undoubtedly, Soeur Thérèse, but what are you getting at?"

"This: I have no need of an ideal society that neither you nor I will see in our lifetimes. The only thing that matters dearly to me here on earth is my asylum. We have arrived at an acceptable compromise with the new government. The Protestants will soon have their new asylum; perhaps the criticisms will stop. *To all appearances,* everything is going well. It is only a respite, however, Dr. Dansereau, a brief respite; the enemy is already preparing for battle, he is within our very walls. You know Dr. Paquette as well as I do, and you know that he is a fierce proponent of government control of our asylum. He doesn't even have the decency to conceal it — as you do so well."

"How can you pretend to know what I think, Soeur Thérèse?"

"When you've spent your life with the insane, Doctor, you know what men think. But don't worry: I need you, Dr. Dansereau, I need you just as you are, with your ideas and your . . . your experiments."

What until now has been only bland drawing-room chat has suddenly taken another turn. Like travellers stretching their legs after a long stage, Soeur Thérèse, who spoke the last few words *sotto voce,* almost confidentially, rises from her chair, looks out the window, glances at the acoustic horn, which has been strangely silent since their conversation began, and finally comes back and resumes her seat. Bernard, who hasn't taken his eyes off her, does the same and tries, quite unsuccessfully, as it happens, to find a less uncomfortable position on his wooden chair; but even if he were seated in the deepest upholstered armchair, sampling the finest brandy in the world, he would be equally ill at ease. During this brief pause Bernard, who has always had trouble sifting his ideas, even has time to think about the theatre and to reconcile himself with stage directors.... He has never been able to tolerate those stage directors who keep their actors in constant motion as if they're possessed by the devil, and who can't abide having two characters sit face to face and carry on a conversation. Why must one actor always remain seated while the other hovers around him flailing his arms like a jumping-jack? When Soeur Thérèse takes her seat again, he has had time to chase away this mad idea. He decides to make the first move. Let the chips fall where they may, he cannot bear to go on playing the part of a mouse held captive by a particularly sadistic cat.

"Soeur Thérèse, you have a very roundabout way of getting to the point. If you want to talk about my experiments, just say so. I'm prepared to explain without hiding anything."

"Dr. Dansereau, it's important that we understand one another. A great deal happens in an asylum, so much that I couldn't possibly know every detail, despite what some people say. Among the facts of which I am unaware are some, I'm certain, that may run counter to Christian morality; that is why it is my duty to inform myself, even to make enquiries, so that any such reprehensible actions will cease. In spite of all my zeal, it is possible that some of these acts have been perpetrated for years without my ever having the slightest suspicion. And so no one can reproach me for not doing my duty, can they? Now, let's stop beating about the bush. I've known for some time now that you've asked the nuns to advise you when one of our patients dies. Why? Do you simply want to offer a few prayers for the salvation of his soul, which would be entirely to your credit? If that is the case, I congratulate you. I also know that you have the fine habit of consulting the books in our library, especially those that deal with the latest discoveries on the workings of the brain. Such healthy curiosity is equally commendable, and we could cite you as an example to certain young doctors who, on the grounds that they have studied in Paris, claim to know everything. I have also learned — and this is where matters become complicated — that you have been seen on several occasions going to the morgue with a saw, and coming out shortly after with a small bag containing, among other things, chunks of ice — at least, that is what has been deduced. Such behaviour is, to say the least, odd, and some people are concerned about it."

"I'm prepared to tell you everything, Soeur Thérèse."

"Let me finish, Doctor, if you please! I've spent a long time working on this brain-teaser — if you'll forgive me the expression — but now I believe I have solved it. Of what earthly use is a saw to a man, unless he's engaged in some kind of tinkering? I know that when our doctors have free time, they seek out solitude; the morgue, along with the chapel, is certainly the quietest place in the asylum. As for your bag, I believe it's quite normal for you to bring along a snack. So you see how simple it is? I'm not mistaken, am I? Tell me I'm not mistaken."

"No, Sister."

"I'm very glad to hear you say so, and I thank the Lord. Now that we understand one another better, Dr. Dansereau, I'm sure you can tell me about

your tinkering. I have very little time for woodwork-
ing, so I'm most interested to hear about it."

"Shall I tell you right now?"

"We still have some time, I've left orders not
to be disturbed under any circumstances, the acoustic horn has been turned off. . . . So go ahead, I'm
listening."

"You see, I am indeed very interested in
wood, and particularly in . . . in planks that come
from, well, from diseased trees."

"Is that so? And what have you learned
about those trees?"

"Very little, in fact. I've wondered, for example, if the veins — which strongly resemble the
convolutions of the brain — might be able to teach
me something about the causes of those diseases.
Unfortunately, I've not yet found anything conclusive in that respect."

"What a pity. It's easy to imagine the extraordinary repercussions such a discovery could have
on the work of nurserymen and . . . gardeners."

"Quite right, Soeur Thérèse. Then I attempted
to learn whether the weight of the planks extracted
from diseased trees possessed any special character-
istic. Were they more compact, denser, did they
have harder knots? Alas, my research has not yet
yielded any significant results. Very recently, however, I have managed to elaborate what I believe to
be a promising theory. Trees, you see, can be divided
into two broad categories: those that are healthy —
which I would call, figuratively speaking, *happy*
trees — and diseased trees, which, to use the same
figure, would be *unhappy*. After observing some of

the cells from these trees, I found that the unhappy trees had a large concentration of cells that closely resembled bunches of grapes, whereas those in the happy trees seemed to be largely made up of cells that looked more like ferns. I am convinced that if there were a way to inject some of those fern-cells into the unhappy trees, we could cure them."

"Have you performed any experiments along those lines?"

"No. I've preserved some fern-cells on ice, but I haven't dared inject them into ... into any of the asylum's magnificent trees. The risk is far too great."

"Indeed. What you have to say is very interesting, Dr. Dansereau, very interesting indeed, but I must tell you frankly what I think: you'll never succeed. If Providence wanted certain trees to be unhappy and others happy, surely there were reasons. What are fifty years of suffering on earth when Paradise awaits for eternity? For there must be trees in Paradise, I have no doubt of that; surely the saints have earned the privilege of a little shade. Which does not erase our duty to strive to relieve suffering, of course, but let us not be so proud as to want to take the place of God. Having said that, I wish you to publish your research."

"I beg your pardon?"

"I wish you to publish your research, to give speeches. I want everyone to be aware of the important experiments you are performing. You could very well publish your results without making reference to the means that you used to obtain them, could you not? You see, Doctor, having recently met the provincial treasurer myself, I have good reason to believe that the asylum's finances will remain in the hands of the nuns for a long time yet. Medically, it's another matter. The government has only to pay the salaries of two or three doctors to obtain — for far too low a price, in my opinion — the management of the asylum. What do those doctors do, aside from being present when the nuns bathe the patients, and receiving money for their trips to Paris? They spy, they criticize, they try to undermine our work from within. Rather than help us care for our poor patients, they try to interfere, with the sole aim of one day being able to pose as saviours. After they've had their fill of disparaging us, they will alert the newspapers, cry scandal, and even — they're quite capable of this — publish our patients' ravings to support their theories. And what will the government do then? It will take the opportunity to seize control of the asylums, hospitals, and schools; and who will they put at the head of those establishments? Those who would emulate Dr. Paquette. But there are some very nasty surprises in store for the government: once Dr. Paquette is in charge of the asylum, do you think he'll be content with prayers and fresh water? Of course not. He'll want higher salaries, budgets, credits, and soon the government will be caught in a trap and have no choice but to increase taxes, even to levy a tax on incomes!"

"Don't you think you're exaggerating, Soeur Thérèse? The population would never accept such a thing."

"I hope that sad situation doesn't come about during your lifetime, Doctor, but I'm convinced it is inevitable. Unless, of course, we succeed in proving that nuns are not only capable of administering hospital finances far better than the province could ever do, but that they can also provide the medical care, even be at the forefront of research. And that is why I need you, Dr. Dansereau. You will publish your articles, you will give papers in Paris, London, and New York, and we shall defeat Dr. Paquette on his own ground!"

"But how do you expect me to publish when I have no convincing results?"

"According to my calculations, you have studied at least two hundred planks. Didn't you tell me you'd found that neither the convolutions nor the weight has any influence on the health of the trees? I know people who would have published less than that! And what you've told me about those 'fern-cells' and 'grape-cells' certainly merits a series of papers. Have you been to Europe, Dr. Dansereau?"

"Never."

"At your age, it's time to think about it. What good is research if you can't take advantage of it to travel?"

"It's a tempting proposal, Soeur Thérèse, but I repeat, I haven't yet found anything conclusive. If I start publishing articles and delivering papers in Europe, when will I get the time to continue my research? And what if I find no legitimate conclusions? If I set off a controversy that I'm not even in a position to sustain, there's a risk that your strategy will turn against you."

"How much time do you need to complete your work?"

"I've no idea. A year, two years. . . . And

perhaps I'll never finish. . . ."

"That's a long time."

"Give me two years, Soeur Thérèse, two years with no obligation to publish any articles or deliver any papers, and I swear I'll do my utmost to reach some conclusion."

"I shall grant you that time, Doctor, and I shall pray every day for the Holy Ghost to light your way. I shall also leave instructions to give you easier access to the dispensary, in case you should need anything. . . . I was intending to give you a small laboratory, too, so that you could work on the premises, but that would be too dangerous."

"Thank you, Soeur Thérèse."

"Don't thank me yet, Doctor, I still have a few small things to ask you."

"What's that?"

"First, I believe that with your two hundred and some-odd planks you ought to have enough raw material. If you need more, I suggest that you don't use the hospital budget. Wood is expensive, you understand, so I think you ought to use it parsimoniously. . . ."

"I understand."

"After that, I would ask you to use the greatest caution when the time comes to attempt . . . grafts: perform them only if you are absolutely certain of the results, or at least if you can first ensure that the pa . . . that the trees will not suffer. When you do those . . . grafts, I would be grateful, too, if you said nothing to me about them."

"Agreed, Soeur Thérèse."

"And . . . something would relieve my conscience of a heavy burden. . . . You see, Doctor, I can accept your status as a free-thinker; I can also, if necessary, close my eyes to certain activities of which I disapprove, because I have decided to trust you; I think you deserve that much. However, certain rumours are circulating about you . . . rumours that are so many thorns driven into my heart. . . . Dr. Dansereau, I would like you to put an end to your cohabitation, that is, I would like you to marry Madame Martineau. That really would be a great relief to me, Doctor."

"Who told you such a thing?"

"Don't deny facts, Doctor, and don't lie to me; for a doctor, you're very bad at it."

"Very well. What you are asking me to do is, to say the least, surprising. And I cannot give you such an undertaking without discussing it with her. What if she refuses?"

"Come on, Doctor, you know very well that's impossible; what woman in our province would refuse to marry a doctor? If you won't do it for yourself, do it for me, Dr. Dansereau, I beg you."

"I'll talk to her about it, Soeur Thérèse."

"Thank you. And now I think it's time to get to work. I'm very pleased to have had this conversation with you, Doctor, and I shall pray for you."

* * *

That evening, after a day when he'd had trouble concentrating on his work, Bernard did not go to the morgue. After donning coat and boots, he went instead to the henhouse, a small wooden building located on a distant road that skirted the stables

119

before disappearing into the deserted fields. The henhouse was so low that, with the first snowfall, it disappeared completely behind the white mounds. Access to it was along a small path hardly wider than a shovel. During the winter, everyone forgot about the henhouse, the hens, the roosters — and Wilfrid, the attendant in charge of the hens.

The path was so quiet, the air so still, and the snow so white that Bernard hesitated before knocking. When he finally made up his mind to do so, the silence was broken at once by the hens' cackling. He opened the door slowly and Wilfrid appeared, in his undershirt, amid a swirl of feathers. In a flash, Bernard saw again the pillow fights that had been a tradition at boarding school, just before the summer holiday.

"Come in, Doctor, and shut the door. You ought to take off your coat; snow's a good insulator, you know, and the hens give off a lot of warmth. You, hens, be quiet! Behave yourselves, we have company! You too, Gertrude!"

To Bernard's amazement, the hens fell silent at once. He felt rather daunted: all those hens looking at him, their heads to one side . . . and Wilfrid, usually so timid — he was only another patient like all those in the Saint-Etienne ward — suddenly seemed a foot taller. With head high and chest thrown out, he looked like a king on vacation.

"This is a surprise, Doctor, I don't often get a chance to see visitors. . . . What can I do for you?"

"I just want to ask a few questions about your hens. Since you're an expert in the field. . . . How many hens do you have, Wilfrid?"

"One thousand two hundred laying hens, twenty roosters, and more than four thousand chickens. The asylum consumes a thousand dozen eggs per month, and *a lot* of chickens. Next Sunday, I'll kill five hundred just for supper."

"And ... you know them all by name?"

"Hardly. Just my layers."

"Still, it's a lot. . . . Now, I want to ask a question that may surprise you, but it's of great scientific interest to me: in your opinion, are hens happy?"

"Hens? Happy? Of course."

"And what makes them happy?"

"Certainly not the roosters, I have to say. If you could see the way they treat them! When you have such a large number to choose from, there's no need to be polite. But still ... they could be more careful. No, roosters are brutes. The hens can get along without them very nicely, too. . . . In fact, it really doesn't take much to make them happy: good food, a bit of gravel, some sun, and, most of all, a good pile of manure."

"Why?"

"Hens love to scratch around in manure; not for worms, just for the pleasure of scratching."

"I see. And how long do you fatten your hens before you kill them?"

"Twelve weeks."

"Perfect. Could you do me a favour, Wilfrid? It's for a very important experiment. . . . The next time some chickens hatch, I'd like you to divide them into two identical batches, then give the first batch all the conditions you've just mentioned —

good food, gravel, manure; but give the other batch neither manure, sun, nor gravel. Before you kill them, let me know; I'd like to study their brains."

"I see. But tell me, Doctor, no offence but . . . does Soeur Thérèse know about this? Because, you see, unhappy hens don't make good eating, and if the patients complain, Soeur Thérèse may give my job to someone else. I wouldn't want to be separated from my hens, you understand."

"I understand very well, and you have nothing to fear. I'll tell Soeur Thérèse. She'll be very pleased with you when she finds out you've helped me."

"In that case, I'll do what you ask and I'll give the guards the tough chickens. But . . . how will you get their brains out?"

"With a little metal saw. I should be able to do it without too much damage."

"Can I give you some advice, Doctor? When you're going to take out their brains, don't look them in the eye."

"Why not?"

"Because . . . because most hens are very nice, but you can't say the same about the roosters, and . . . and I'll be giving you roosters' heads."

"And so?"

"You must never look a rooster in the eye, Doctor, ever. It's the devil looking at you through his eyes."

"I see. I'll be careful, you were right to warn me. When will I be able to come for my heads?"

"Let's see. . . . It's January now. Let's say the beginning of April. I'll let you know."

As he was leaving Wilfrid's, Bernard pulled up his coat collar and quickly walked to the stable. Had a cold wind just risen, or was it the fact that he hadn't noticed before he went into the henhouse the tiny scrap of spring that was lost in the snow?

8

The wind, blowing directly from the north, plays at imitating the owl's cry as it sweeps into the chimney; the snow rounds off the angles of the windowpanes, and Florence is curled up under her comforter. What day is it? Sunday. Why this perishing cold, Lord, how do You expect us to even think of paying tribute unto You in weather like this?

It seems to me there were cats sleeping in my bed. How many? Twenty, thirty, fifty, at least fifty white cats keeping me warm. It felt good. Or it did until they started purring. What a racket! And then that suffocating smell of incense. . . . Why was my bed in a church?

On Sunday morning, it always takes Florence a long time to wake up. She enjoys the cloudy zone of sleep where dreams unravel and reason, still asleep, tries its best to knit them up again. She opens a lazy eye, then closes it at once; yes, she is in her bed, the sweet smell of tea rises from the kitchen, Bernard must be up already . . . has he left for work? No, Soeur Thérèse has given him a day off, the first in two and a half years. Why isn't he in bed? What's he up to now? With her eyes still shut, she slips her hand under the quilt, on the other side: the sheets are barely warm; he must have got up with the sun.

The nave was empty, the choir deserted, there was nothing but the bed, in the very heart of the church, with thousands of vigil lights all around it. Though it was his own wedding, Bernard wasn't present. Lost in thought as usual, rooting around in imaginary cells, looking for chunks of happiness. . . . His own wedding? Was I dreaming, or did he really ask for my hand? What on earth is it all about? There's something fishy about this sudden decision. Linden blossoms, there was the smell of linden blossoms in the church.... But where was the priest? In the choir-loft, a Little Sister of Providence had started to play the harmonium. As soon as the ceremony was over, she and Bernard had gone away hand in hand. The nun was very tiny, and her shoulders shook as if she were laughing. Soeur Thérèse. It was Soeur Thérèse who suggested that he marry me. What business is it of hers? I may as well admit it, the last drops of sleep have evaporated. The dream has vanished. For ever. . . . Now I must pull myself out of bed, get up, get ready for Mass.

A thin crust of ice has formed on the water jug, which Bernard has a bad habit of leaving too close to the window. Florence dips one corner of her washcloth in the icy water, vigorously rubs her eyes and temples, then starts to brush and comb her heavy hair. While the brush is slowly gliding, pulling her head towards the right, then towards the left, she doesn't take her eyes off the mirror: why should I get married? And for whom? For myself, for Bernard, or for Soeur Thérèse?

She ties the sash of her housecoat on her way downstairs, then looks at the hook by the front door:

Bernard's coat isn't there, nor are his boots or hat. When he goes to the stable he doesn't bother with a hat; that means he's gone to the river to cut ice. He's out of his mind, in weather like this. And why didn't he light a fire before he left, for heaven's sake?

Florence lifts one of the stove-lids, looks inside: Bernard has indeed made a fire of little branches, enough to boil water for his tea, but he laid a huge maple log over the branches, which obviously stifled it. Imagine, at his age he can't even light a fire properly! Men!

Yes, but what would you do without him? What would your life be like if he weren't in it? Who would you talk to about your joys and sorrows, about the weather, about the spring that will soon be here, about your hyacinth bulbs that may not have made it through the winter? He doesn't listen much, it's true, but at least he sometimes pretends to. Whenever you criticize him for his lack of interest, he protests on principle, then finally admits that his mind was elsewhere. Embarrassed, repentant, he promises to try, and for a few days he does his best to take an interest in your sewing or the village gossip. Sometimes it will last a whole week. Then you'll tell about the problems you have when you work with silk, and you'll see his gaze become distant. He'll be thinking about his cells, imagining himself mending them with invisible thread. . . . Men aren't made to listen, and priests are no exception: they hide behind their grilles, and after they've listened impatiently to your confession, they impose their penitence — always the same one: three Our Fathers, three Hail Mary's, three Glorias.

There it goes, the fire's burning again; you can put back the lid, your water will soon be boiling, you'll drink your cup of tea as you wonder if you're allowed to sweeten it, as Bernard does so often. The sugar is completely dissolved in the water, he says, so it can't really be considered a solid, and it's permissible to consume it before taking communion. But sugar is still sugar; aren't we supposed to begin fasting at midnight? When you mix science and religion, it's hard to understand anything.

After she has put the kettle on to boil, Florence goes to the window, scratching gently with her fingernails at the frost that overnight has traced a pretty forest of filmy fir trees. In the distance, on the river, she catches sight first of the old horse, breathing so hard that two huge gusts of vapour stream from his nostrils — when will he reconcile himself to getting rid of that old horse? — then of Bernard, busy sawing blocks of ice. Is he even thinking about me?

* * *

You see, old horse, I *think* the presence of fern-cells is a necessary condition for happiness, but I'm not absolutely certain. Perhaps every cell has a precise role, even several indissociable roles to play. How can I find out? If the cells for happiness also contain the germs of idiocy, I'll be at a dead end. What sensible man would give up a few inches of his intelligence in exchange for acres of happiness?

Let's suppose I find the right cells and inject them into a diseased brain, how could I predict the reaction, how would I know exactly what dose was needed for each one? What if I injected nightmares, hallucinations, tortures? And who knows, perhaps a small proportion of grape-cells in the mixture is necessary? Don't painters add a touch of black to give depth to their blues? Two years, old horse, two years to work out some problems the greatest minds have never solved. Can you hold on for another two years? In a few weeks I'll have hundreds of hens' brains. If I can make a hen happy, just one single poor little hen.... Assuming that I succeed, will the hen be more idiotic than she was? How do you measure the intelligence of a hen? Do you know, old horse? All right, I know, you're cold, you want to go home. I'm cold too, and Florence must be waiting for me to go to church.

Know what, old horse? I didn't need so many blocks of ice, I could have waited. I could have stayed in my bed and left you in your stable. But I couldn't sleep. I was staring at the ceiling, tormenting myself.... Might as well tell you, it's because of Florence. I asked her for her hand. I thought it would be a mere formality but no, she made quite a scene. It's been more than two years we've been living as man and wife, and she seems to have no complaints. So why is she reluctant to make it official? A signature at the bottom of a notary's paper, a bit of fuss at the church, what difference would it make? I shouldn't have mentioned Soeur Thérèse, that's for sure.

"Would you mind telling me, Bernard, who on earth put such an idea in your head?"

"To be perfectly honest, Soeur Thérèse mentioned it and. . . ."

You should have seen the look in her eyes! She was furious, absolutely furious. Have you ever seen Florence when she's angry? That's something I wouldn't wish on anyone, not even Dr. Paquette. What difference does it make if it was Soeur Thérèse's idea? Women are so complicated, old horse, it would take a combination of the brains of Benjamin Franklin, Auguste Comte, and Lavoisier to understand them. The advantage of science is, there's always time to repeat experiments that fail. In life, you don't have the time. One word too many, just one word. . . .

I'd be quite happy to get married. It would be tidy, and our brains need tidiness—to be sure they get some rest and to allow them to see to nobler tasks.

Have you ever asked yourself what would happen if someone came up with a universal love potion, a long-lasting aphrodisiac, the recipe for Cupid's dart? What a godsend for the young man about to marry! Rather than listen to his heart, he would heed only his reason. The girl next door is sturdy and healthy, a good cook, capable of rearing children, she'd make an ideal wife but . . . he doesn't feel the slightest desire for her. Never mind: when the couple are exchanging the rings, they'll swallow a couple of pills, and that will be that. The sturdy, simple young woman will become Juliet, the timid young man to whom Providence forgot to issue any charm will be transformed into Romeo. No more balls, no more lengthy period of getting acquainted, broken engagements, family dramas, no more endless quests for kindred spirits — such an appalling waste of time. No more failed marriages or regrets that are dragged through a long and unsuccessful married life like a ball and chain. No more rancour, sarcasm, the daily gall of the unloved wife, the infidelities of the unsatisfied husband. No more children brought up in an atmosphere of civil war, who go on to become bad parents in turn. The family as nucleus of society? Yes, old horse, I'll go along with that, but a scientific family.

Now imagine the young girl who wants neither husband nor children, who simply wants a quiet life, free from want. Or perhaps she dreams of travel and responsibilities — which society grants to women only on condition that they don a nun's habit. A little pill and *voilà!* The young girl is in love with the Lord for ever, she can utter her vows with complete peace of mind. If a merchant puts such a product up for sale, I'll be his first customer. I'm a man of science, I've never understood about love. It's like horses: there are race horses and draught horses. Why are you stopping again, horse? Just one more little push, we're almost there, then you can rest. Are you tired of listening to me? All right, I'll be quiet. You know, old fellow, you're beginning to frighten me.

* * *

The tea, drunk in little sips, warms her insides; the stove is crackling as she looks at the enamelled bathtub, the rubber sheet that still covers it, the floating thermometer they've forgotten on the table .... No, Bernard really isn't a bad sort. Oh, he drinks a little too much, of course, but wine makes him sad, never violent, and what man doesn't drink in this country of ice and misery? The poor chap looks after madmen all day, surely he's entitled to some escape.

Bernard Dansereau, doctor to the insane. A doctor, Florence, imagine! A doctor wants to marry you, you who have practically no education, and you're playing hard to get! Why didn't you simply say yes right away? After all, he's not asking you for much. Just to grant him a few minutes a week, Saturday night after your bath. . . .

You can't imagine him going away, but you can't imagine yourself with a ring on your finger either, you can't bear the thought of being called Madame Bernard Dansereau. The look on their faces, the parish gossips, when they find out that you're Madame Bernard Dansereau, the doctor's wife. . . . But there it is, after first belonging to your father, you'd belong to a husband again; you'd be a minor once more, you'd lose your name, your house, your land, you'd be forced to ask a man who doesn't know a thing about it for permission to sell or lease your property, you'd even lose the right to vote against the mayor who wants to raise taxes again. . . .

I'm well aware that I offend You, Lord, but why do You insist that people marry when they can no longer have children? What wrong do I commit by simply living with him? Bernard thinks of nothing but his cells, he doesn't care about my land. So why does he want us to get married? And does he really want it? It's certainly not to please You, Lord, I know him too well. . . . Do I really know him? It's very easy to seem uninterested in the things of this world when you have nothing, but give the holiest of men a piece of land and right away he'll start making plans. A little road here, a little house there, we'll cut the trees, raise some sheep, put up fences. . . . Men cannot leave things as they are, it goes against their nature.

"Morning, Florence. Did you sleep well?"

"Very well. You?"

"Yes, I did. I got up early because I needed some ice for my experiments. . . ."

"Honestly, you could have waited. We have to hurry or we'll be late for Mass."

"I don't know if we'll be able to go; my horse is very weak and I'd rather he rested."

"We'll take mine, then. Go hitch him up, I'll be there in a minute."

As she dons her coat, Florence can't help thinking that Bernard is lying: that man tossed and turned in bed all right, there are bags under his eyes down to his chin, and he dares to say that he slept well.

While Bernard is hitching Florence's horse to his buggy, he muses that if she says she slept well, it means she's made her decision. How long will she wait before she tells him?

* * *

Bernard, driving the buggy, made tremendous efforts to look straight ahead of him. He wanted to say something to lighten the silence, but as he could think of nothing but his marriage proposal, he kept quiet. As for Florence, she too looked straight ahead, silent. It was a very long trip.

The Mass had just started when they arrived at the church; they were lucky to find two empty seats at the back. The windows were shut and the air was heavy with a mixture of the smells of incense, wet coats, burning wax — and old sins. Bernard looked up at the ceiling: surely the architects hadn't anticipated that the air would be so heavy. Then he watched the curé: how much does a priest's brain weigh? Now and then he gazed out of the corner of his eye at his companion, who seemed to be far more pious than usual: is she asking the Holy Ghost for enlightenment? Should I pray to Him too?

Florence had shut her eyes to help her think, but she was constantly being distracted by some minor detail: why doesn't Bernard sit at the front of the church, as his rank requires? Is he ashamed to be seen in my company? Why doesn't the priest ask me to mend his soutanes? Would he have more respect for me if I were the doctor's wife? It was time for the *ite missa est* and she still hadn't made her decision.

On the way home, Bernard was on pins and needles. He had to wait until the exit to the village before Florence finally consented to speak.

"Bernard, I want to talk about something. I've been wanting to tell you for a long time, but I was afraid of hurting you."

"Go ahead, tell me, I'm not afraid."

"It's about your horse. He's very old and I think you should get rid of him; you ought to be thinking about buying another. For the time being I can lend you mine."

"Yes, he's old, I agree; however, I think he's still quite capable of pulling the buggy to the asylum."

"To the asylum, perhaps, but you ask him to

pull blocks of ice; that's much too heavy for him.
And there's something else. . . ."

"What's that?"

"Well, you're a doctor. Aren't you embarrassed to be seen with an old nag?"

"I don't think it has much influence on my
patients, in their condition. . . ."

"I'm not talking about your lunatics, I'm
talking about the people in the village. The humblest
roadman is proud of his horse. And you, a doctor,
you go around with an animal that should be six feet
underground. It's bad enough that people say all
sorts of things about us, if they start laughing at your
horse too. . . ."

"You surprise me, Florence; since when do
you let yourself be impressed by village gossips? Let
me remind you that he's my horse, not yours. When
I want to get rid of him, I'll tell you."

"He may be *your* horse, but *I'm* the one they
see in *your* buggy. And now that we're engaged. . . ."

"You accept?"

"I didn't say that! I said that we were engaged, that's all."

"I see. . . . And in your opinion, how long will
the engagement last?"

"Indefinitely. Tell me, have you made a will?"

"No. I had one when I was married, but I
revoked it when I moved in with you."

"And since then?"

"I've often thought about drawing up another, but I've never had the opportunity."

"Excellent. I don't either. As soon as we're
back at the house, we'll take care of it. You see,

Bernard, I've thought it over carefully and I still don't know what made you propose to me. You don't need my land, and I don't see you as a farmer. Is it respect for conventions? Religion? That's not your style. Is it love? No, you don't really love me. Don't argue, you're a bad liar. If it isn't my land or religion or love, then what is it? The truth is, you'd never have thought of proposing if Soeur Thérèse hadn't insisted."

"I assure you, that has nothing to do with it."

"You don't know me very well, Bernard. In any case, the prospect of drawing up a will doesn't displease me. At our age, we have to think about the future. I'm still capable of earning my living. So are you, but for how much longer? A will is the best form of protection. I'll leave you everything I own, you do the same, and we won't have to worry about our old age. Do you think it's possible to get married through a will?"

"What do you mean?"

"Exactly what I said. While we're both alive we'll be engaged, but if one of us should die we'd automatically be married. Do you think that's possible?"

"Perhaps, I don't know. . . . But what would be the advantage?"

"And what would be the advantage to this marriage? You're the one who wants to sign a piece of paper, so why not a will?"

"I've never heard of such a thing before. I'll think about it."

* * *

That night, Bernard planned to pretend to work in

the stable. If he talked to his old horse about it, perhaps he'd have a better understanding of this business about marriage and wills. It didn't turn out that way. When he was taking Florence's horse back to the stable after Mass, he noticed his own horse lying on his side. When Bernard asked what was wrong, the animal barely managed to raise his big head, to lift his heavy eyelids.

9

"Whoa there, horsey, calm down! Did Florence teach you to run like that? Glad to be getting some air, eh? Well, so am I, but if you go too fast, you'll be no farther ahead: you'll have to spend the whole day in the stable at the asylum. Good, that's better, easy does it now. . . . He's young and full of pep, but he can't think past the tip of his nose. You can't imagine how I'm not looking forward to the asylum this morning! Have to give dear Dr. Paquette a hand. You don't know him? Tallish fellow, with a fine black beard and a thick head of hair that makes him look like a rooster, which he is if you ask me, in more ways than one. And what does he need me for? To help him try out a new treatment for hysteria. That's right, hysteria. You don't know what that is? Never mind, I don't feel like explaining everything. Anyway, you wouldn't be interested. All you want to do is walk and run. Walk away, you dumb animal, you'll still end up like your stable-mate. I'll give him an injection tonight, and tomorrow he'll be in horses' paradise. It'll happen to you too. You'd rather run and not think about it? Well, you may be right.

Walk, you dumb animal, you. . . . Who am I going to talk to? To Soeur Thérèse, who pretends she doesn't understand, to Florence, who sighs whenever I say the word 'cell', to Dr. Villeneuve, who swears by heredity, to Dr. Paquette, who listens to no one but himself, to a horse who thinks about nothing but running? . . . If I keep it all inside my head, my cells will become congested and I won't understand anything. Who can I talk to? To the madmen, the snow, the sun, to Viviane? The chaplain? Perhaps that isn't such a bad idea. He's bound by the secrecy of the confessional, so he'll have to keep it to himself. The problem with Abbé Leclerc is, he's a chatterbox. He'll want to speak his piece, give me advice, maybe even tell me the story of his life. No, there's nothing like an old horse. Two long ears and a big blank brain, that's all I ask for. If all the confessors were replaced by horses or rabbits, there'd be no complaints.

Laudanum, remember to get some laudanum from the dispensary. A horse-sized dose, for my confessor. Thank you, Soeur Marie-of-the-Rosy-Cheeks. A brandy? I won't say no, Sister; one drink to forget about Dr. Paquette, another to forget the syringe of laudanum, another to forget the end of winter. . . . God bless you, Soeur Marie-of-the-Blessed-Lightheadedness, who always has a remedy for days that are too long, who can set off whirlwinds in the brain-cells, who stirs up sand and dust, who takes leaden ideas and gives them wings.

* * *

"Morning, Dr. Dansereau. How are you today?"

"Not all that well, actually. Why did you ask me to assist you, Dr. Paquette?"

"Because, unfortunately, I only have two

hands."

"Couldn't you have asked a nun?"

"It's hard to imagine a nun applying the treatment I have in mind. Why so grumpy, Dr. Dansereau? Aren't you interested in science? Don't you aspire to improve your mind?"

"You're in charge. Now, about this hysterical woman?"

"A splendid case, as you'll see, a splendid case indeed. Her name is Idola Valiquette, you must have noticed her. She was in the Sainte-Cécile ward. Her husband owns a laundry, she's blonde with blue eyes...."

"Yes, I know who she is. A very pretty woman."

"I didn't force you to say that. If she hadn't been so pretty I'm sure her husband wouldn't have hesitated to put her away after her first attacks. When he finally decided to entrust her to us, it was too late for hydrotherapy. For a while now her attacks have been longer and more regular. At precisely eight o'clock every morning, her limbs are shaken by such strong muscular tremors, you'd swear she was having an epileptic fit. After that she becomes unconscious, then wakes up about ten minutes later. That's when it starts to get interesting. Follow me, we'll go to see her. I've asked Soeur Marthe-du-Très-Saint-Nom-de-Jésus to watch her, she'll give us her report. She may have a name that's as long as the month of November, but she's still an excellent nurse. You have to hand that to the nuns. . . .

"Has it started, Soeur Marthe?"

"Yes, Dr. Paquette: she vomited up her breakfast, complained about ovarian pain, and then the attack began. She's sleeping now. We bound her feet and wrists as you requested."

"Excellent. How long ago did she lose consciousness?"

"About ten minutes."

"Did she describe her dreams?"

"Yes: blood, fire, red monks, and other things I'd rather not talk about."

"We'll go there directly. In the normal course of events, she should have an attack of 'clownism', which is very interesting, Dr. Dansereau, you'll see. Are you coming too, Soeur Marthe?"

"With your permission, Dr. Paquette, I prefer not to. Other patients will undoubtedly be needing my services."

"I'm afraid I may need you, Sister. Come."

Soeur Marthe shoots a desperate look at Dr. Dansereau, who responds with a shrug: Dr. Paquette is the medical superintendent, so it's best to go along with him. As they enter the room, Idola is being shaken by what look like excruciating spasms; then her feet begin to pull at the solid leather straps, as if they are trying to push into her body. Her contortions force her into the shape of a perfect circle: only her head and feet touch the bed, while the rest of her body is thrust upwards as if pulled by an irresistible magnet. Under her nightgown, all her muscles are painfully tense. She remains frozen in this uncomfortable posture for two long minutes, then her body finally relaxes.

"Magnificent crisis, Dr. Dansereau, don't you think?"

"The poor woman must be exhausted. What treatment were you considering?"

"We must wait until she has calmed down completely. Clownism is generally followed by an erotic phase. That's where we come in. Look, it's starting! Her pelvis is moving and soon she'll begin crying out. I don't know if she learned her vocabulary from her launderer husband, but she has a most varied repertoire. I've never heard anything like it, not even in Paris. Very well, let us begin. We're going to massage her ovaries. In her present state, she won't complain. Dr. Charcot himself taught me this treatment. It's a question of gently massaging the ovarian zone, clockwise, like this, do you see? Go ahead, each man to his ovary. Yes, that's fine, don't be afraid to press firmly. Look at her eyes: the lips are drooping, the pupils are slowly rolling back, they're half-hidden by the lids. . . . Have you seen this attitude before?"

"How long must we massage her?"

"A good ten minutes. Don't tell me you find it embarrassing?"

"Not at all."

"Do you know that it's possible to provoke this kind of attack with a turpentine injection? The patient immediately goes into convulsions like those in an epileptic fit. It's very interesting."

"Have you tried that?"

"Of course. Science is not conceived without experiments. . . . Ovarian massage, Dr. Dansereau: there's nothing like it to end hysteria. There is a method that's more natural and more effective, but it's difficult to apply in an asylum. If all women would agree to perform preventive exercises, and if all husbands fulfilled their duty conscientiously, hysteria would disappear from the list of diseases. What do you think, Soeur Marthe?"

"I think that if you don't need me any more, I'll return to the ward."

"Go ahead, Sister, go right ahead.... Tell me, Dr. Dansereau, are you married?"

"I'm a widower."

"But you do enjoy yourself now and then, don't you? By the way you perform that massage, you seem rather good with your hands."

"You ask a great many questions, Dr. Paquette. Allow me to ask one as well: why do you enjoy embarrassing the nuns? Why force poor Soeur Marthe to be present during this treatment?"

"In war, any tactics are good. For the moment the nuns are stronger, but we'll wear them down, I guarantee it. As long as nuns have control over the asylums, no progress will be possible. It's faith against science, obscurantism against enlightenment, stagnation against progress. And you, a former member of the library of the Institut Canadien, surely won't contradict me."

"How do you know I was at the Institut?"

"Everything is found out in the end. Soeur Thérèse isn't the only one with information, you know. By the way, how do you manage to stay in her good graces?"

"What do you mean?"

"Don't play dumb. When I took over from Dr. Howard, Soeur Thérèse summoned me to her office to give her orders: no blasphemy, no atheistic propaganda, no keeping Dr. Dansereau from his work. What have you done to her, for heaven's sake? Administered a treatment for hysteria?"

"I think she's quite simply grateful: during my first day's work at the asylum, she was attacked by a madman with a knife. I took care of her . . ."

" . . . and you expect me to think that a simple little bandage has earned you her protection? You must really think I'm an idiot: the stupidest nurse could have bandaged her. She insisted that you be allowed to work in peace. Exactly what mysterious work are you doing?"

"I have no secret activity. I care for bodies while others care for souls."

"And is it to help you care for those bodies that you have direct access to the dispensary and the morgue? Has it been a long time since you completed your medical studies?"

"Yes, a very long time."

"And do you think being a village doctor was enough to keep you abreast of the latest scientific developments? Do you seriously believe that the confinements of fat farmers' wives and prescriptions for camphor pastilles can replace long years of study in Paris? You seem to think that any simple country doctor can claim superiority to alienists who have studied in Europe."

"I've never claimed anything of the sort. As I told you, I merely care for bodies."

"You insist on playing the innocent. Very well, as you wish. But let me warn you, Dr. Dansereau: I have an even tougher hide than Soeur Thérèse. In a few years there won't be a single nun left in the asylums, and those who delayed the march of progress will have some accounts to settle."

"I don't doubt it, Dr. Paquette. It's just that I don't imagine that day will come during my lifetime."

"And what about Galileo?"

"What does Galileo have to do with it?"

"It's obvious: the Church condemned Galileo, you defend the Church, therefore you condemn Galileo. On one side, progress, on the other, reaction. Enlightenment or obscurantism, science or superstition: there is no middle ground. I like to know who my enemies are; now that I know which camp you're in, I'm satisfied. There will be no quarter, doctor. You've been warned."

"I appreciate your concern. Do you suppose the treatment is finished now?"

"What treatment?"

"The ovaries. . . . We've been massaging them for ten minutes, haven't we? The patient seems quite calm to me. How much longer must we go on?"

"I'd forgotten all about her. . . . You're right, I believe she is calm now. Thank you, Dr. Dansereau, that will be all for today."

"Not at all. Shall I ask Soeur Marthe to remove the straps?"

"Do that: *you* know how to talk to the nuns."

That's it, horse, we're going home. A wasted day. What a nuisance, that Paquette. "I don't know that I can talk to them, but I can tell you I've learned a lot from being with them. How to stand up to sarcasm, among other things." No, that's too long, not direct enough. Besides, he'd think I was really in their camp. What's all this about camps and wars of attrition? Will we never see the end of it? "Thank you for letting me have the opportunity to assist you, Dr. Paquette: you give a first-rate ovarian massage!" That's better. Still a little long, a touch too servile, but it's much smoother. Ovaries, work in something about ovaries. . . . "I may know how to talk to nuns, Dr. Paquette, but when it comes to massaging ovaries, you're the champion!" Oh, why bother? I've never been good at repartee, I may as well resign myself to it. It has to do with the speed of the brain-cells, I imagine, and mine are desperately slow. But they're determined, and where memory's concerned, well now. . . . It may take me five years to come up with an answer, Dr. Paquette, but I shall find one, you can count on that.

When a fellow's young like you, horsey, he's an idealist, wants to change the world. In the end, though, you inevitably get mixed up with politics. You sign a membership card without giving it too much thought, read a sentence or two, subscribe to a newspaper, then you spend the rest of your life regretting it. There'll always be someone to dig up our youthful errors. You aren't listening, are you? You think I'm just an old fool? Fine, keep walking, I'll talk to myself. Not too fast, do you hear? There's a syringe filled with laudanum in my kit; I don't want it to break. I'm in no hurry to use it, so slow down, will you? Look at the river, try to think about something else. About the spring that's just around the corner, about the sun that's getting warmer, the

snowstorms still waiting for us, spring break-up. . . .
Spring. . . . Hens, hens' brains. . . . What size is a hen's
brain, anyway? Will I need a magnifying glass and
tweezers? I'd have been better off working with
pigs, they're closest to humans: same skin, same
weight, and pigs are happier than other. . . . Happy
as a pig. A pig's brain, think about getting a pig's
brain. . . . If happiness really does transform the
brains of pigs, it shouldn't be too hard to see. The
brains of alcoholics become swollen, so much so that
the convolutions disappear. But is it the alcohol that
swells the brain, or unhappiness? Will the brain of a
happy hen be as different from that of an unhappy
hen as an alcoholic's brain is from a normal one?

Now, let's suppose that happiness transforms
the brain. What are we to conclude? That we must
reform society at once and devote the maximum of
our resources to education? Take children from their
mothers in the first year, give them so many fern-
cells they'll be prepared to face the worst misfortunes. . . . Who knows? Perhaps we'll learn that
unhappiness is related to the kind of education we
receive? That generation after generation of parents
have been motivated only by the prospect of wreak-
ing vengeance for their own unhappiness by shutting children away in prisons. . . . That would make
teachers particularly vindictive then, recruited from
among the most belligerent human beings: women
no one wanted, powerless men thirsting for revenge
. . . . No, no, Bernard; teachers may be frustrated
people, but they do disseminate knowledge, they're
creatures of enlightenment and reason. You wouldn't
want a society without reason, after all. . . . If you

showed some logic, you'd have to admit your own reasoning doesn't hold water: if unhappiness springs from education, it should follow that, before the invention of schools, mankind was happy. And why would happy men suddenly get the incongruous idea of making their offspring unhappy? Whatever its origins, unhappiness is well and truly implanted in the brain, whence it must be extirpated, and that is your mission, that and nothing else. Now you've arrived. You've managed to forget your old horse for a good fifteen minutes.... That's not so bad: who said that philosophical speculations served no purpose?

* * *

Bernard unhitches Florence's horse and ties him to the stable door: he's still young, better spare him the sight. He opens his bag, takes out a huge syringe, squeezes it until a few millilitres of the precious fluid spurt out. There are still sixty millilitres left, enough to kill an elephant. He won't suffer. Everything's ready, I just have to open the heavy door, go inside, pat my old companion one last time.... Dear God, if only he could have died during the day....

But the old horse isn't dead. Still lying on his side, he barely lifts his head at the sound of his master's footsteps. He looks at the syringe that's pointed at him, then at Bernard's eyes, and he heaves a long sigh before laying his head on the straw. He knows.

"Don't worry, old friend, it won't hurt any more than a bee-sting. Then it will be over. Now, where can I give the injection? Your hide is so tough,

I'm liable to break my needle. . . . Inside the ear, I have no choice: the skin is thin, you can see the veins. That lovely ear, I've bent it so often. There, it's done. The laudanum is already flowing in your bloodstream, heading directly for your heart, which will send little drops to your legs, your stomach, your brain. . . . Your eyes close one last time, you fall into a deep sleep filled with dreams. You're walking on a fine soft road with no pebbles or flies, across meadows, fields of oats, you try to open your eyelids but it's over, you've stopped resisting, you follow your dreams, those fragments of dream that blend together in a mosaic of colours, of smells of the past. . . .

You're still breathing, softly, very softly; but your nostrils barely open. Your brain no longer has the strength to command your lungs, which are expelling their last breath of air. Your heart is still beating, the old pump offers a little resistance through force of habit, but it sends your brain only bad black blood, with no oxygen. The brain-cells will die one by one, starting with those that control memory. Have I told you what happens when drowning victims are revived? If they've spent too long under water, their recent memory is obliterated, but their memories of childhood are intact. In the asylum we have a few adults like that, who have lapsed into childhood. When we're able to cure them, they often reproach us for it. It will be the same for you: your memories will be obliterated one by one, starting with the most recent, those that haven't yet had time to be classified by your logic cells. Your memory will be destroyed in reverse, unfurling like a measuring tape. You're already forgotten the injection, the stable, the winter that's drawing to an end, you know nothing about Florence's stable or the road that goes to the asylum. We're in Hochelaga, the night bell has just rung, the two of us are going to deliver a poor woman in the neighbourhood around the Viau cookie factory on rue Notre-Dame. Do you remember the smell of baking? You're very young now, the farmer assures me that you're gentle and strong, that you used to belong to an old lady who only took you out to go to Mass, that you'd make an excellent doctor's horse. You were a fine-looking creature, as fine as the farmer was a liar: you weren't docile at all, it took me a long time to get you to pull my buggy with calm and dignity, but you did become an excellent doctor's horse in the end. When I wanted to calm you I always had to speak softly, very softly, never raising my voice. The things I told you about patients and treatments!

Now you're a colt again, you don't belong to me yet, spring has returned, you're still sucking at your mother's teat, you've just been born, and now it's dark and warm.... There, you have no memory, you're new, absolutely new. Your memory is coiled up, now you don't even know that you used to be a horse, that you were alive, you don't know what it is to die; you can't be afraid. At the moment of death you know nothing about what you're losing and you may even be perfectly happy, like those drowning victims who reproach us for saving them.

Can you still hear me? Have you realized that your heart has stopped beating? After your memory has gone, you'll lose the cells for pleasure and pain one by one, the ones that govern dreams, reflexes, anxieties. . . . Perhaps there will still be a few pale glimmers, shadows of sensations, will-o'-the-wisps. . . .

Five minutes. It's over now, all the cells in your brain are dead, and if your legs are still jerking in spasms, it's just the nerves relaxing one last time. You know nothing about it. After the brain, the other major organs will die one by one, cell by cell. First the liver and kidneys, they can't survive without their ration of clean blood, then the muscles, and after that, long after, comes the turn of the adipose cells, of the bones, the teeth. . . . Your skin will continue to live for a few more hours, your hair will keep growing for two or three days, but already you will be gone, you'll have left your carcass behind. . . .

It's over now, well and truly over. So long, old horse. There will be another, I can't help it, but he'll never take your place. So long, old horse, and thanks for everything, for carrying me and for listening to me.

10

Saint-Jean-de-Dieu, April 2, 1889

Dear Dr. Dansereau I know you're too busy to listen to me and also perhaps I'm not there when you come to see me that's why I decided to write because I think what I have to tell you is important and if I write it will be better because you'll have time to read me without being interrupted.

Last Thursday before supper I was following your advice as usual I stood up on the piano bench to look at the fern but Soeur Pudentienne-du-Précieux-Sang the one that's old and short she said it was dangerous that I could fall down and hurt myself and she asked me why I was doing it so I told her I wanted to look at the fern because you told me it was good for me so then she said as a matter of fact she was going to tend the fern because it was sick and that maybe I could help her if I wanted. I said yes and she held the bench while I lifted the fern off the piano it's very heavy because of the earth that was in the flowerpot and she also told me to take away the plate that was under it for the water when there's too much of it and then the lace cloth that had to be washed and be careful not to scratch the piano and then we went out on the gallery to tend the plant.

It's true the plant was sick but Soeur Pudentienne knew what to do she told me it was sick because it got too much water and its roots were rotten and then I saw it was true there were insects in the earth like little white spiders that had started eating the roots and if it doesn't have roots it can't live we'd have to spray it to get rid of the spiders so I sprayed it I was very careful not to break them because roots are very fragile and Soeur Pudentienne went to get fresh clean earth and I stayed alone with the plant to keep an eye on it.

I got rid of the spiders by spraying them and I was thinking it was the same inside my head but that I'm sicker than the plant that's why insects are black instead of being white and they're bigger too and there's not just spiders there's also snakes and mice and toads and blind birds that frighten me because they have red eyes and sharp beaks and they're always squawk-ing but I explained that to you before. I was afraid of insects so I looked at the leaves of the fern the ones that weren't sick and it helped me as usual and I was able to go on removing the insects.

When there were no more insects Soeur Pudentienne still wasn't back so I did as she said and I took off the dry leaves that were dead and I crushed every one of those leaves with my fingers to make a powder because I thought we could put the powder in the new earth that it might be better for the plant to be with its dead leaves and Soeur Pudentienne came back and she told me it was a good idea. She washed the flowerpot carefully because insects lay eggs that are too small for us to see with our eyes she put stones in the bottom so water wouldn't stay in the pot too long and on top of the stones she put a little earth and then the plant and then some more earth on the roots and she told me the earth mustn't be packed down too hard so the roots could find their way and that the plant was healed now and that it was because of me that I'd saved its life.

So then I tried to tell Soeur Pudentienne that I was afraid of insects because I had the same kind in my head and I told her about the snakes and the blind birds with red eyes but she told me you shouldn't talk about such things, you should pray to the Blessed Virgin because the Blessed Virgin can crush serpents with her feet and that if I prayed she'd come and crush them but she didn't know about the birds and maybe I'd be better off with the Holy Ghost. I told her I'd try to pray but that when I looked at the leaves I felt better and that if she wanted me to help her save the lives of other sick ferns I wanted to help her. She said she'd talk to Soeur Thérèse about it and that if she got permission why not.

Afterwards she talked to Soeur Thérèse about it and since then I've been helping her she's glad because she's old and the pots are too heavy and she says I'm good at saving plants but she'd prefer it if I don't talk about the blind birds so I don't. Soeur Pudentienne doesn't want me to talk to her but she's always talking not to me but to the plants when she thinks I'm not there she whispers all sorts of things and I asked her why she did it and she told me it was good for the plants but I think it's good for her too because maybe she has blind birds in her head and she'd rather talk to the plants about them and it's a good thing to do because if you make a hole in the bottom of flowerpots for when there's too much water it runs out so maybe it's good for us human beings too.

So then I started talking to the plants and I told them that when I was a child in Joliette one day I saw a magician he had this kind of metal milk can except it was smaller and he went around the hall talking very fast and he stopped at every child and took money out of our ears and nose it was very funny because it made a noise when it landed in the milk can but he didn't get to me because I was sitting at the back and that's why I'm sick but maybe I'll get better on account of the ferns and Dr. Dansereau because he's a good doctor and some day maybe he'll make a hole in my head to drain all the sickness away.

I also have to tell you that the other day Dr. Paquette came to see me I was wondering what he wanted because it was the first time he'd talked to me since he decided I'll never get better he asked me why you often come and give me paper and if you'd told me anything about the experiments you were doing but I told him I

didn't know you did experiments and it's true I
don't know but if you do and it's to get rid of
unhappiness I want to tell you that you can do
whatever you want in my head even make holes
and if I die it won't be serious. I have to go now
because I'm out of paper if you have any more
thank you in advance.

Oscar Parent

Oscar folds his sheets of tissue paper in four, tucks
his pencil behind his ear, looks behind him in case
anyone should see him heading for the piano, then
discreetly lifts the panel to hide his precious letters.
He slips his hand in above the tuning pegs, and soon
the paper will join the rest of his writing, thousands
of sheets of paper of every size, both sides covered
with very fine writing that no one except Oscar can
decipher. As he drops in his letter, he remembers
that he wanted Dr. Dansereau to read it; in fact that's
why he's taken such pains with his handwriting. It's
unwise, then, to consign it to oblivion. But where can
he hide it? Soeur Pudentienne will be coming for
him soon to tend the plants, but she doesn't like to
see him write. . . . If he shoved his letter between two
strings, perhaps he would be able to retrieve it? No,
that's not a good idea; the nuns often play the piano
in the evening, in fact they're always saying it has a
particularly rich tone. . . . Too late: Soeur Pudentienne
has already come into the room and now she's
approaching him. Caught in the act, Oscar can think
of nothing better than to pretend that he's scratching
his leg and, while doing so, to hide the folded pages
in his sock.

"I've brought you a little present, Oscar. Look, it's a picture of the Virgin trampling a serpent. You see, I told you she knew what to do. You should pray to the Blessed Virgin, Oscar, it's much better than ruining your eyes writing nonsense. What have you hidden in your sock?"

"Nothing, Sister."

"Oscar, you know you mustn't lie, especially to a nun. What have you hidden in your sock?"

"A letter."

"A letter? And to whom have you written?"

"Dr. Dansereau. I told him he could make a hole in my head to get rid of the unhappiness."

"A hole in your head? Whatever made you think of such a thing?"

"It was Dr. Dansereau that told me. He's going to make a hole in my head and all the unhappiness will run out. It's like the water in the plant pots, it's the same thing."

"Don't be silly, Oscar. You know very well it's Our Lord who gave you life and it's He who will take it away when He chooses. If He wanted to put unhappiness in your head, it's His business! I'd pray to the Blessed Virgin if I were you, she's often kinder than Our Lord."

"Yes, Sister."

"Very well. Now you're going to tend the ferns. Start by yourself, I must go and see about Soeur Thérèse's plants, but I'll be right back. Don't tell anyone what we've been talking about, do you understand?"

"Yes, Sister."

A hole in the head, Sweet Jesus! What will

Soeur Thérèse say?

* * *

The first time Soeur Thérèse saw Soeur Pudentienne-du-Précieux-Sang, about ten years before, a single glance was all she needed to assess the new recruit: she was old and her constitution seemed frail, so it would be futile even to consider making a nurse of her. As she didn't know how to read or write, she could not become a secretary either; her mental health was little better than her physical condition, so it would have been too risky to assign her the supervision of the dormitories: neither her heart nor her soul was sturdy enough to bear the screams, the nightmares, the epileptic fits. And so Soeur Thérèse had assigned her to the kitchens, where she remained for only two weeks. Incapable of understanding the simplest instructions, Soeur Pudentienne was useless there, and the rest of the staff were irritated by her endless chatter. After that she was transferred successively to the laundry, the broom-factory, the procurator's office, and the stables, but with no more success. Despite her obedient attitude and good will, her ability was so limited and her mind so impervious to any form of learning that no one ever asked her to do anything.

Having despaired of finding any tasks at which she might prove useful to the community, Soeur Thérèse finally gave her a variety of assignments: replacing the oil in the sanctuary lamp, dusting the statues in the chapel, cleaning the pianos, handing out the internal mail, and watering the ferns.

In strictly budgetary terms, Soeur Pudentienne was a millstone around the community's neck, but Soeur Thérèse told herself that perhaps Soeur Pudentienne's admirable devotion to the Virgin Mary would bring her invisible dividends one day. Indeed, only a few months after her appointment, the ferns had started to grow in almost miraculous fashion; never before could the nuns remember seeing plants more lush, or greener foliage.

It hadn't taken Soeur Thérèse long to interpret this sign from Heaven correctly: she placed ferns in all the wards of the asylum, as well as in the procurator's office, the dispensary, the private rooms, the doctors' offices, and finally her own office. No one objected. Most saw it as merely a nun's whim, which none the less indicated a commendable concern for decoration. Others, more perceptively, were sure the plants would have a calming effect on agitated patients. But no one ever suspected that they were actually an essential component of the formidable information network set up by Soeur Thérèse. Nor did visitors, patients, or staff ever have an inkling that Soeur Pudentienne, the silly old woman who was being kept on at the asylum out of charity, was, because of her very silliness and the fact that she was an incorrigible chatterbox, the most formidable informer imaginable.

Utterly incapable of selfishness, it would never have crossed her mind to seek any personal advantage from her unofficial role of tattletale, which in all probability she had no idea she was filling. She repeated phrases gleaned here and there, but like a parrot, understanding nothing. She described things as she had seen them, never attempting to interpret the raw truth or to lie in order to make her account more interesting. She seemed to share with young children an innate faculty for ferreting out what others are attempting to conceal, to discover unknown hiding places as if by chance.

Soeur Thérèse never had reason to regret her decision; indeed, she often congratulated herself for making it. Once again she was verifying the great Christian principle which maintains that any ordeal, no matter how painful, conceals within itself a portion of revelation.

* * *

Soon the ritual had become unalterable. At half past nine every morning, Soeur Thérèse was at her desk, busy with her correspondence; she had hardly dipped her pen in the inkwell when Soeur Pudentienne knocked discreetly and came into the office pushing the little cart, which looked rather like a tea-wagon, on which she transported her tools: a watering can, fertilizer she concocted herself, an atomizer, and nail scissors for removing the dead tips of fern fronds. Soeur Thérèse always pretended to be concentrating on her work and put on a show of listening with only half an ear to Soeur Pudentienne's endless chatter; it would be best if her informer was never aware of the job she was doing in spite of herself. Actually, as Soeur Thérèse's letters were usually only a tedious string of set phrases and expressions, there was no reason for her not to give Soeur Pudentienne's declarations all the attention they deserved.

"God bless you, Your Reverence! How are the ferns this morning?"

"I haven't had time to look at them, Soeur Pudentienne, I've too much work to do."

"I'll take care of them, Soeur Thérèse, you go on working, I won't make any noise. . . . Soeur Thérèse, do you think the Blessed Virgin knew how to write?"

"Of course she did! Why do you ask such a question?"

"Just to know. It's funny, but I've always thought she wouldn't need to be able to write to give birth to the baby Jesus. What about Saint Joseph?"

"Saint Joseph?"

"Did Saint Joseph know how to write? You don't need to write to be a carpenter. Perhaps he didn't know how to write."

"It's possible. Though I don't see what difference it can make, I'll speak to the chaplain about it. Now, please, tend to your plants and let me work."

"Very well, Your Reverence, I won't bother you any more. The reason I asked, see, is because I'm always telling Oscar he should stop writing, it's no good for his eyes or his head. I never write, and I'm none the worse for it. This morning Oscar told me he'd written a letter to Dr. Dansereau asking him to make a hole in his head. . . ."

"What on earth are you talking about, Soeur Pudentienne? A hole in Oscar's head?"

Soeur Pudentienne, while continuing her gardener's tasks, was watching Soeur Thérèse: at Dr. Dansereau's name the other nun had promptly stopped writing. Soeur Pudentienne was well aware that the directress would be interested in what she had to say.

"Yes, a hole in his head. He said it's to get rid of the unhappiness and that Dr. Dansereau would do it. What I find odd is, it's been a long time since Dr. Dansereau came to see him. Now it's Dr. Paquette who's interested in Oscar. He's always asking why Dr. Dansereau gives him paper and if he knows anything about the 'experiments'. . . ."

"And what does Oscar say?"

"Nothing. He talks about his spiders and snakes. I told him he should pray to the Blessed Virgin, because she knows how to crush serpents. Do you think I did the right thing?"

"You did very well. Did you talk to Dr. Dansereau about it?"

"Of course not, Your Reverence:;you forbade us to talk to the doctors."

"That was a long time ago, Soeur Pudentienne. And besides, I didn't forbid it, I *suggested* it, that's different."

"I've always followed your suggestions, Soeur Thérèse."

"And so you should. Don't mention this hole to anyone else, especially not Dr. Paquette, do you understand? Everything you know you've heard from Oscar, and Oscar is crazy. So . . . you must never give any credibility to what simpletons say, Soeur Pudentienne, none at all, do you understand?"

"Yes, Your Reverence. But if Dr. Dansereau makes a hole in his head, am I supposed to tell you?"

"There won't be any hole, Soeur Pudentienne!

I know Dr. Dansereau very well and he'd never do such a thing."

"If you say so, that puts my mind at rest. I wanted to talk to you about it because I was worried, and you told us to let you know everything the doctors do. . . ."

"Very well. Now if you've finished with the plants, would you leave me alone, please."

"I've just finished, Your Reverence. God bless you, Your Reverence."

"God bless you too, Soeur Pudentienne. . . ."

Should I believe her? Should I pay any attention to the words of a madman repeated by a silly fool? The problem is, Dr. Dansereau would be quite capable of. . . . Are You sure I can still trust him, Lord? It's true that he doesn't go to the morgue any more, and he is engaged to be married; it means he's trying to mend his ways. But now that I think of it, why did he look so uncomfortable when I asked about his wedding date? Do You know? Of course You do. Forgive me, Lord. Should I warn him that Dr. Paquette's on his trail?

Soeur Thérèse jumps to her feet and heads for the acoustic horn.

"Soeur Jeanne? This is Soeur Thérèse. Do you know where I can get in touch with Dr. Dansereau this morning?"

"This is his day off, Your Reverence."

"In the middle of the week?"

"Yes, Your Reverence. He said he had your permission to go to Montreal."

"You're right, I'd forgotten. I'm sorry to bother you."

"Not at all. Do you want me to give him a message?"

"No, that won't be necessary. Or, actually, yes. . . . Tell him it's too soon to tap the maples yet, the forests aren't safe just now."

"I beg your pardon, Your Reverence?"

"Don't pretend you didn't understand, Soeur Jeanne. Simply repeat what I told you."

Why on earth did he go to Montreal? To desecrate graveyards? Amuse himself with loose women, go to hotels? Perhaps he simply had to buy some instruments for his study of hens' brains. . . . What will he find out? Why does he never tell me anything, Lord?

* * *

Bernard wasn't thinking about hens or the asylum, let alone about maple trees; he was peacefully driving down rue Notre-Dame, savouring his day off. He felt as if he hadn't seen Montreal for ages. Numerous factories had sprung up along the river, everywhere houses were being built for the workers, and the streets were crisscrossed by streetcar tracks. Quiet walks on country roads may be excellent for the lungs, but there's nothing like a visit to the city to restore the brain: prosperity and progress excite the scientific cells.

At the corner of Craig, he stopped off at his favourite merchant's to buy a new pair of Italian shoes. The fragrance of the soft leather, the salesman's respectful attentiveness, the feeling that he was walking on a new planet. . . . Five dollars was a little dear, but there's nothing like buying a new pair of shoes to make one feel like a new man. After that he replenished his wardrobe: two shirts of the finest quality at a dollar each, some collars and cuffs, a pure wool suit for four dollars. He spent his whole salary, but he didn't care ... he would dip into his savings. It's not every day that a man becomes engaged to be married.

After that, he dined alone in a restaurant on Place d'Armes, where he sampled the best puff pastry in town. After eating his fill, he absent-mindedly read the newspaper, then went to the jewellery shop. On the way home, he held the reins with one hand while the other hand was in his pocket, firmly clutching the box that held the ring he'd just bought — the most beautiful engagement ring he had ever seen. Altogether worthy of a doctor's wife. As soon as he was inside the house, he offered the ring to Florence. Filled with emotion, she slipped it onto her finger, then pulled it off immediately to take a closer look. Dreamily, she rotated it in her fingers for a moment, then put it back in its case, which she proceeded to stow in the fireproof metal box where she kept important papers. Bernard dared not ask why she didn't want to wear it. Directly after supper, he shut himself away in the barn.

* * *

Removing hens' brains from their bony shells is a delicate operation that demands much dexterity, unusual self-control, and unwavering patience. After hours of strenuous labour, the novice bench scientist has managed to split open only half of his supply of skulls, to no purpose. Either the metal-saw crushes the bones, rendering the brain useless, or it goes right through, which yields the same result. If the researcher persists, he will eventually discover a method which has the advantage of being infallible but the drawback of taking an inordinate amount of time: it consists of first removing all the skin and then, as if he were cutting glass, using the scalpel to make a shallow circular groove that will mark the bone without cutting all the way through it. After that, he will take the top of the skull between the thumb and forefinger of his left hand, and the base between those of the right. Sometimes, if the groove has been properly cut, a simple movement of both hands, twisting the halves in opposite directions, will cause the skull to snap open. The researcher will then have the good fortune to obtain a perfect brain to add to his collection. Nine times out of ten, though, he will have to bring out the scalpel again and resign himself to tapping the skull on a corner of the workbench, as if he were tapping an egg against a bowl. Because precision is essential if the operation is to succeed, the scientist has to be perfectly sober, otherwise he will waste his precious brains, thereby adding to his exasperation.

It is only persistent, almost excessive determination that will enable him, after hours of unflagging effort, to obtain fifty properly decorticated brains. Fifty pinkish little masses with no convolutions, fifty little lumps not much bigger than a pea, fifty little balls of dead cells. Not even enough to make a soup.

His troubles far from over, he must now weigh them, separate the hemispheres, and finally examine under a microscope all the cells in proximity to the point where the brain joins the spinal cord. His patience then will be at the breaking-point, but curiously it is his pride that will suffer most. He will discover, in fact, that the brain cells of hens are similar in every respect to those of humans: the same kind of white cells, the same grey cells surrounding the central channel of the cerebrospinal axis, the same granular substance in which everything is suspended. Of course, there are certain significant differences — the frontal lobes are less well developed, the organization of the cells seems more primitive — but is it not humiliating to note that there is no natural difference, overall, between the brain of a chicken and that of Louis Pasteur? The study of hens' brains is beyond any doubt the most depressing activity imaginable.

Bernard doesn't let this get him down. Of the fifty brains in his collection, twenty-three belonged to happy fowl. What's special about them? Very little, in fact. Their brains are generally marginally heavier than those of their unfortunate neighbours, but the difference compared with the average was so small, it would be rash to infer from it a general law. The slight swelling of the posterior section of the left parietal lobe has led Bernard to formulate the hypothesis that, all things being equal, the right hemispheres of happy hens should be a little less heavy, and it has been very easy to verify that.

Microscopic study of the cells extracted from the spinal cord region has revealed, moreover, the total absence of giant or pyramidal cells from both the happy and the unhappy brains. In the latter, however, more extensive study has turned up in his microscope a hint of a cellular organization that might, just possibly, suggest bunches of grapes, a structure never found in happy brains. Bernard has thus been able to confirm the hunch of Gall, father of phrenology, that the brain is undeniably influenced by behaviour. Just as the immoderate use of alcohol influences the development of the liver, then, the practice of happiness changes the configuration of the brain. . . . This discovery, paramount though it is, leaves Bernard highly perplexed. What other researchers would hail as a phenomenal victory for modern science, what he himself, if he were not so tired, would normally see as an important stage in his research, has actually left an aftertaste of failure: the secret of happiness is to be found in happiness itself. Could there be a worse tautology?

What does the researcher do when the eye-piece of his microscope fills him with nothing but disgust? when he discovers that he has completely wasted his time, and when the results of his research appear to him in their worst light? He gathers up the remaining brains and puts them on ice, shuts the stable door without even bidding his horse goodnight, goes back to the house, and heads straight for the pantry, where a long-neglected friend awaits: a good bottle of brandy.

11

Bernard shuts his eyes, heaves a long sigh, and at once feels himself glide slowly down a smooth, warm slope. With utter confidence in the restorative virtues of sleep, he allows himself to fall to the very bottom of the abyss, where the light never enters, where even the blackest dreams dare not venture. An eternity later, he can feel Florence shaking his shoulder. In the distance a voice is calling him. The tone is firm, but he can barely hear it. "It's six o'clock, Bernard, you have to go to work. Bernard? Can you hear me, Bernard? It's six o'clock. . . ."

Bravely he tries to cling to the walls of the abyss, but the slope is too steep, the surface too slippery. . . . He gives up. "It's ten after six, Bernard. Bernard?" The voice comes from the kitchen now and it blends with the clatter of cutlery, the poker, the stove lid. Ten minutes after six. Some of his brain cells become more alert and try to remind the others that, in certain civilized countries, human beings have had the peculiar idea of carving the days into twenty-four divisions, and those in turn into sixty parts, associating them with tasks each more unpleasant than the others: waking up, washing, dressing, hitching an inconsequential horse to a buggy, going to work, tending madmen. . . . A few cells resist this tyranny, but no sooner have they started to get organized than Florence's voice drifts up for the third time, nipping any resistance in the bud: "Bernard! It's twenty after six! You'll be late!"

Struggling hard to push aside the dream fragments that are trying to hold him back, shutting out the siren song that endlessly invites him to drop again to the bottom, the very bottom of the abyss, he sets out on the slow climb up the slippery wall. It takes a heroic effort but he finally opens his eyes, and a sunbeam enters the bedroom, striking him full in the eye and causing a sharp pain.

Bernard is still not fully awake when he somehow manages to make his way to the kitchen. The first sip of tea scalds his throat. (What is this perfumed water? If I poured in the few drops of brandy left in my bottle, it would go down more easily....) Then a second sip.... At the pit of his stomach, an interminable concert of gurgling and rumbling.... Twenty-seven minutes after six. Please, God, make this an easy day with no complications or operations — give me a hundred pairs of ears to unplug, I'll do it, a hundred splinters to remove, I shall discharge my duties conscientiously, but no operations, dear God, no operations....

"A strange time to be praying!"

"Morning, Florence. How do you know I'm praying?"

"By reading your lips. I can even finish your prayer if you want: please, God, deliver me from my headache, shrink my tongue, give me the strength to open my eyes.... If you want my opinion, He won't listen. Don't you think it would be better if you didn't go to work?"

"No, I have to. Is there any bread left?"

"Poor Bernard, it's right in front of you."

In front of me? As a matter of fact it is. No operations, God. . . . A few mouthfuls of bread to quiet the stomach and we're off. Stand up, dress in overcoat and boots, open the door, suffer an onslaught of sunbeams, take a deep breath of fresh air, walk to the barn, open the heavy cedar door, curse the rusty hinges, hitch up that dunce of a horse: relax, young fellow, you'll be old some day too. Watch Florence wave from the window — after all, it's just one bad day to get through — and be on your way.

When Bernard's buggy disappears on the horizon, Florence puts away the dishes, then she takes her knitting and sits in the rocking chair. Why do all the men in this miserable country have to drink? Don't they have problems enough with the cold and hard work? As if liquor could dissolve the big knot of hardship in their stomachs. Will they never understand that they're born with hardship and they'll die with it too? Florence's fingers slow down, her needles click more quietly, then finally stop altogether. The hands settle onto the knees, the head is lost among the clouds that slowly travel across the squares of sky that are perfectly set off by the windowframe. Bernard has gone, he will come back, a whole day to wait for him. . . . Sighing, she picks up her knitting again.

* * *

"God bless you, Soeur Jeanne. What's new this

morning?"

"Nothing special, Dr. Dansereau. First you must go and look in on Pierre-Henri Champagne in the Saint-Luc ward: he was found paralysed in his bed. I asked for hemlock to be brought, the nurse knows. While you're there you must certify the death of Tancrède Laporte. I took care of the forms; the family is well off, we'll ask them to provide the coffin. After that, you go to the women's wing. They say Jeanne Sénécal — you know, the woman from Chambly who drowned? — has regained her memory. The trouble is, she's not getting better, she was screaming all night, she'll need a sedative syrup. . . ."

Sedatives, sprains, strains, only routine, thank God. . . .

"At eleven o'clock you're to go to Soeur Thérèse's office, she isn't feeling well."

"Soeur Thérèse? What's wrong?"

"I don't know."

"Perhaps I should go right away?"

"Out of the question! She's negotiating with the electricians. She insisted that you go at eleven o'clock, and you'd be well advised not to cross her."

* * *

Pierre-Henri Champagne is an interesting case: when he was a reporter at *La Presse* he was reputed to be able to write on any subject, very quickly. If a Montreal merchant withdrew an advertisement at the last minute, Champagne would be called on to turn out a few pieces. Politics, sports, recipes, minor accidents, practical advice, or gardening, in ten minutes the article was ready to be printed. Then, at the height of his career, he began to slip. Too much work, too much drinking — so prevalent in those circles — lack of sleep. . . . One day he didn't show up at the paper. They looked for him everywhere, but in vain. Two weeks later, a colleague ran into him. He was sitting at the end of the Sutherland wharf, looking terribly haggard as he watched the boats go by. Melancholic depression.

Bernard pays scant attention to the comments of Nurse Girard, one of the asylum's few lay nurses. He has trouble concentrating: the brandy vapours that linger in his brain, Soeur Thérèse's illness, Nurse Girard's lovely voice, her magnificent black hair gathered into a knot under her immaculate nurse's cap, the dose of hemlock to administer, the unfortunate journalist, everything is confused. . . . Twice he botches the injection. Receding vein, he pleads, somewhat shamefaced: the vein is so prominent it could be diagnosed as varicose.

"Do you think he'll pull through, Doctor?"

"I don't know. It was a fairly large dose, but the patient is more than six feet tall, so he should react well. It all depends on the origin of the paralysis. . . . I'll be back late this afternoon."

"And in the meantime?"

"No special treatment. Or rather, yes: come to see him every hour, bend over him, and smile. That will do him more good than anything."

* * *

At ten to eleven, Bernard leaves the Sainte-Cécile ward and heads for Soeur Thérèse's office. He stops briefly in the bathroom, long enough to rinse his mouth and make an awkward attempt to slick down the cowlick at the top of his head. Every time he overindulges in brandy, the same phenomenon occurs: it's as if his hair is rebelling against the alcohol. In vain he runs his hand back and forth over his head, wetting the hair: the tuft still stands. Finally, he must resort to soap.

He arrives at Soeur Thérèse's office on the stroke of eleven, just as the chief electrician is leaving, a look of vexation on his face.

"Good morning, Soeur Thérèse, how are you?"

"Not very well, Doctor. Do you know how much that man is asking for a measly seven hundred electric lights? Even if I calculate the savings in wax and gas, it will take me two years to pay him. I asked for more time and do you know what he had the gall to tell me? That he'd charge interest! Interest, have you ever heard of such a thing! If that's the way it is, I told him, he can take down his lamps and roll up his wire at once. I'll have nothing to do with his electricity."

"How can you say such a thing, Soeur Thérèse? Electricity is progress, and besides, have you thought about the risk of fire? Oil lamps are extremely dangerous."

"Dr. Dansereau, you fill me with despair. You're undoubtedly an excellent physician, but I would never make you responsible for running the asylum. The day the doctors take over the hospitals, all the province's money will go to them. But I didn't ask you here to talk about electricity. I haven't been feeling well for a few days now. I'm always tired, I often sneeze, my throat smarts. . . . Probably a bad cold. Do you have some medicine that would get me back on my feet?"

"First, Soeur Thérèse, I have to know what's wrong with you."

"That's not necessary. It's a bad cold, I tell you. All I need is a tonic to perk me up."

"Forgive me for insisting, Soeur Thérèse, but I think it would be better if I give you an examination."

"What kind of examination?"

"First I must look in your eyes and down your throat, then I have to listen to your chest. It will just take a moment."

"No, no, I don't need an examination."

"Soeur Thérèse. . . ."

Bernard knows instinctively the tone of voice that is appropriate: firm and reassuring, the same voice one uses to let children know that one is serious.

"Very well, but you will listen to my chest *from the back*, only on the back."

"But Soeur Thérèse. . . ."

"Don't be stubborn, Doctor. You will listen *from my back* or not at all. It's that or nothing."

"Very well, as you wish."

Just as Bernard is positioning himself behind Soeur Thérèse, her office door opens. First a foot appears, holding the door open, then a nun enters, pushing a cart.

"What are you doing here, Soeur Pudentienne?"

"I came to water my plants, Sister. I couldn't get here before. . . ."

"Come back later. Now get out, do you hear? Why do you persist in coming in without knocking?"

"But Soeur Thérèse, it's what I do every day. . . ."

"Out!"

"Very well, Your Reverence."

"And you, Doctor, hurry up. Do you see what kind of situation you've placed me in with your examination? God forgive me."

"You must unfasten your robe, Sister."

"Out of the question!"

"That's an order, Sister."

"What right do you have to give me orders?"

"The right of a doctor who is concerned about his patient's health. I regret this as much as you do, Soeur Thérèse, but it's necessary."

"Very well. In that case, you will put out the lights."

"The lights are already out, Soeur Thérèse. That light comes from the sun; I'm afraid I can't do anything about it. What are you so afraid of?"

"Afraid? Me? I'm not afraid. Go on, listen to my chest. Will this do?"

"I'm afraid not. How many layers of clothing do you have?"

Soeur Thérèse finally extricates a shoulder, slender and milky white, that still bears the scar left by the knife wielded by a patient some years earlier. Bernard has been careful to warm the stethoscope in his hand so that Soeur Thérèse won't be startled when he slips it onto the narrow surface of skin she has uncovered.

God, how fast the heart is beating! True, she's very small, and heartbeats are inversely proportional to size — a man's pulse is slower than a cat's, which is slower than a mouse's.... But all the same, all the same, one hundred and forty isn't normal!

"Very well, what's wrong with me?"

"I've barely started. And if you keep talking I can't hear anything.... Try to relax, Soeur Thérèse, breathe deeply."

"Relax! How do you expect me to relax when anyone could walk in at any moment and see me here half-naked!"

"You're not half-naked, Soeur Thérèse, and anyway no one can criticize you for looking after your health; the asylum needs you. Think of your patients . . . and breathe deeply."

One hundred and twenty.... One hundred and ten.... Good, that's better. We'll put it down to nervousness. Now the lungs: breathe in . . . out . . . in . . . take a deep breath . . . now let it out. Good, now again.... No. Nothing in the lungs or the bronchial tubes.

"Very well, that's enough. What's wrong with me?"

"For the moment, a simple cold, but complications can always set in. Do you have any muscle pain? Stiffness?"

"Yes, when I get up in the morning."

"Do you always wear camphor around your neck?"

"How do you know?"

"I smelled it. Do you always wear it?"

"Yes. And a scapular medal as well, if you want to know everything."

"That's fine. Don't forget to change the camphor once a week. Try to keep warm, and get plenty of rest. Avoid contact with the patients. It will probably pass."

"Tell me the truth, Dr. Dansereau, what are you afraid of?"

"For the moment, I see nothing serious. You never know what to expect with influenza. . . . Sometimes it will be just a cold, but epidemics may be fatal. . . ."

"Is that all? Dear Lord, if that's all it is, I'll get over it! Thank you, Doctor. Now sit down and close your eyes, please, while I get dressed again. I need to talk to you."

"If you want me to tell you about the state of my research," says Bernard as he resumes his seat, "I may as well say right away that I've found nothing."

"I know, I could see it in your eyes."

"What do you see in my eyes?"

"You look half-asleep, as you always are when you drink too much. And when you drink, it's because your research is at a standstill. . . . By the way, have I ever told you what happened to me when I went to Oregon?"

"No, I don't think so, but why. . . ."

"It was in 1852. I'd left Burlington, in Vermont, to go to Oregon City, at the other end of the continent, to found a charitable institution. When I got off the stagecoach all that was left of the city was a few boards and a huge cloud of dust: they'd discovered gold in California and everyone had left town. I was all alone in a deserted city. I was desperate. A month-long journey for nothing. . . . I prayed to the Lord, who advised me to go back home. When I was on board the boat that would take me to Los Angeles, where I could get a train going east, a tremendous storm blew up just as we were pulling in to San Francisco. The sails ripped, the rudder broke. . . . We drifted aimlessly for a month, then finally came ashore at Valparaiso, in Chile! On the wharf a priest greeted me, a French Canadian like you and me: 'Soeur Thérèse,' he told me later, 'it was Providence that sent you. We needed someone to run our hospice.' I ended up staying for five years! I ran that hospice, founded a hospital, then I came home to Montreal to look after the asylum. . . . And that's it."

"It's a wonderful story, but why do you tell me it today?"

"Because I'm going to Europe next week. First I'll be visiting asylums in Scotland and Belgium, then I'll go to Paris, where I shall attend the International Conference on Mental Medicine. I'd have liked you to accompany me, to communicate the results of your research, but . . . another time, I suppose. Dr. Bourque will be coming with me, as will Dr. Paquette — unfortunately — and Dr. Vallée from Quebec City. We'll be back in three months, God willing. During that time, you'll have no one to be responsible to. For three months I'll know nothing about what is going on at the asylum. I confess that I'm concerned. So much can happen in three months. An epidemic, a fire, an earthquake. . . .

Someone could even get the bright idea of cutting down all the trees at the asylum and I'd know nothing about it. What could I do, three thousand miles away?"

"Are you really afraid that something could happen to the *trees*, Soeur Thérèse?"

"No. What could happen, however, is that a patient or a member of the staff could be struck with compassion for the sick trees and try new methods to heal them. . . . The Lord may not want us to take His place, but He can sometimes shut His eyes for a just cause. You understand, of course, the trees would have to be on the point of death. . . . You never know what can happen with experiments. You think you're on your way home and you end up in Chile, on the other side of the continent. Nothing ever happens the way we want it, Dr. Dansereau, but we always land somewhere. When I came back from Chile in 1863, there was nothing here but a fallow field. One hundred and sixty-six *arpents*, purchased for three thousand dollars. On that land there now stands an asylum — one that is the envy of the entire world. Do you think that would have been possible if we'd given up? No, Doctor, and the madmen would still be sleeping in quarters no better than dungeons. Every time we despaired, the Lord came to our aid. I shall pray for you, Dr. Dansereau."

"Thank you, Sister, but I'm afraid you'll have to pray very hard."

"We can never pray hard enough. While you're here, let me give you a letter that was erroneously addressed to me. It's signed Oscar Parent. . . . He's counting on you a great deal, I believe. . . . I read it by mistake and I apologize. . . . You know Soeur Pudentienne: she's so absent-minded. . . ."

"Dear Dr. Dansereau. . . ." Bernard has stopped listening; from the first lines he understands that he must succeed. Soeur Thérèse protests her innocence for another few moments, then falls silent; the mere sight of Bernard's eyes speeding across Oscar's prose tells her she has won.

* * *

Bernard arrives at the refectory at noon. Dr. Villeneuve has just left his seat; Dr. Paquette is about to start eating. Bernard won't be able to escape him. He spends a long time washing his hands, wondering what demeanour to adopt, and then, after a long look at himself in the mirror — the cowlick is pointing heavenwards again; when did it spring up? Did Soeur Thérèse notice? — he takes a seat, still faintly sheepish, at Dr. Paquette's table.

"Hello, Dr. Dansereau! We're in luck today, there's chicken on the menu. A change from porridge and cornmeal mush, isn't it?"

"I'm quite fond of porridge."

"It's obvious you've never been to Paris, dear Doctor! When I think that in just a few weeks I shall be eating in the finest restaurants. . . . It really is a pity you can't come; the Paris congress will bring together the most brilliant alienists in the world! Of course, much of the proceedings would mean little to a general practitioner. . . . This chicken is disgusting."

"Really? Mine's delicious."

"No, it's disgusting. The only thing they can

make here is coffee. Actually, I wonder how they manage even that. Ah, Paris! . . . You're leaving already, Doctor?"

"Yes, I'm going out for a breath of air. Good day, Dr. Paquette."

Leaving the asylum, Bernard heads straight for the henhouse. A few steps along the muddy road, some deep breaths, the warmth of the sun. . . .

"Wilfrid, my friend, I need your help again. Would you be able to recognize a happy hen?"

"Of course, nothing simpler."

"How do you do it?"

"When you look into her eyes, you see something that looks like blonde hair: it's the Archangel Gabriel. And if you keep watching, you'll see his wing-tip and his shiny sword. Do you want to look? Take this one, she's so happy the Angel Gabriel has a halo. Can you see it?"

"No, I can't see anything."

"It's a question of practice. It will come."

"If I were to make her unhappy, would the angel disappear?"

"Obviously. When hens are unhappy, the devil appears. I thought I told you that before."

"And if we made an unhappy hen happy, what would happen?"

"The devil would leave and the angel would come back. Didn't they teach you anything at the university?"

"The happiness of hens wasn't a compulsory subject. Wilfrid, I need you. Do you know what we're going to do? We're going to take some unhappy hens and we're going to mix all sorts of substances into their food. Perhaps we'll find a drug for unhappiness. Tomorrow I'll go to the dispensary and bring you some substances: laudanum, hemlock, zinc. . . ."

"I'd be glad to help, but if you ask me, you won't get anywhere unless you add a few seeds of Indian hemp."

"Have you tried it?"

"Of course. I've also tried ginseng, spruce gum, ants, mustard blossoms, dandelion roots. . . . No, take my word, hemp seed is the only thing that works."

"How does it affect them?"

"They're excited at first, then they calm down a little. They start walking slower, their movements aren't so jerky, they peck quietly: they look so happy, they almost seem to be smiling! The little black balls in their eyes get bigger, and when you look at them you don't see the devil, only his hoof-prints. They're happy, there's no doubt about it."

"And have you . . . have you ever thought of trying those seeds?"

"I've tried them, yes."

"And?"

"I got sick. I don't have a hen's stomach."

"But did you feel less unhappy?"

"Oh no! Anyway, I've never been unhappy."

"Then why are you here?"

"Because I'm crazy. Haven't you noticed? But even though I'm crazy, I'm not unhappy. If you're looking for the recipe for happiness, forget about Indian hemp."

"Why is that?"

"Because the effect doesn't last. After an hour or two, the devil comes back. I use hemp when I'm about to kill them, to drive the devil away. It's my way of giving them the last rites. If I were you, though, I'd try magnets."

"Magnets?"

"You know what magnets are, don't you? Just place two little magnets on either side of a hen's head and the devil is gone in an instant. But of course they have to be blessed, otherwise nothing changes. Don't tell anyone, but I'm the one who steals the holy water from the chapel. I pour a few drops into a quart of water, mix it up so all of it will be blessed, sprinkle a little on the magnets, then attach them to the hens' temples, and that's it."

"That's splendid."

"If you say so. But I should warn you: if you try to use it for another purpose, it won't work."

"Why not?"

"Because it doesn't make the slightest difference in how the chickens taste: they die happy, but they're still tough. It's not genuine happiness, do you understand? And before you ask, I can tell you that, yes, I've tried sleeping with magnets on my temples, but it doesn't change anything: when I wake up I'm just as crazy as before. The only difference is, I'm in a good mood."

"That's not a bad start. How long does it take to achieve that result?"

"Depends. . . . For a hen a few hours is enough, but for humans it takes longer. I started to see results at the beginning of the second year, but I admit I'm pig-headed."

"Have you talked to the doctors about it?"

"How do you expect me to talk to the doctors, they only come here to complain about my chickens! They're right, too. If one of the crazy people doesn't like a doctor or a guard, he'll come to see me and we'll fix it so they only get tough chicken, or eggs that aren't too fresh. . . . If you want to spot who treats the patients kindly, watch them eat their chicken."

"That's not very nice, but I understand."

"That's nothing, Dr. Dansereau, I should tell you what's in their coffee!"

* * *

Magnets. . . . Let's suppose we find some particles of iron in the grape-cells, and the iron, attracted by the magnet, breaks up the bunches of grapes along its way; or let's suppose magnetic currents pass through the brain and are responsible for the make-up of the ferns, a fluid that. . . . A compass, the brain contains a kind of compass that simply needs to be correctly oriented — in fact, when we talk about crazy people, don't we say they've lost their bearings? Let's suppose. . . . To hell with suppositions, what I need is some magnets. But where do you find magnets in a madhouse? The dispensary, let's try there.

"God bless you, Dr. Dansereau. A brandy?"

"No thank you, Soeur Marie. But do you have any magnets?"

"No. If I were you I'd go and see Dr. Villeneuve. Last week I saw him performing magic tricks for the patients: he put a key on a piece of cardboard, then he pretended to be commanding the key to move. ... It was very amusing. Actually, you could ask him right away, here he is now."

"Hello, Dr. Villeneuve. Soeur Marie tells me you know where to get magnets?"

"Magnets? Certainly, in fact I have quite a few. Why do you ask? Trying to find a needle in a haystack?"

"Precisely. A very small needle in a very large stack of hay. No, it's to use in some experiments."

"Like Mesmer?"

"Like who?"

"Mesmer. Have you never heard of him? An Austrian physician who thought he could cure diseases by placing magnets in his patients' hands. It was in the late eighteenth century. He was interested in hypnosis, too; he had some famous patients, crowned heads, even the Mozart family. His experiments created such a stir that a committee was set up to study them, with Benjamin Franklin and Lavoisier among the members."

"What happened?"

"They concluded that animal magnetism was a fraud. You see, Mesmer was an odd bird. Some of the young girls he hypnotized had a big surprise when they woke up. The same thing happened with Lord Durham, do you remember?"

"Yes, I remember. I even attended a hypnosis session at university; it was very impressive. ... But what about magnets? Did Lavoisier and Franklin forbid the use of magnets?"

"I don't think so."

"Did you eat chicken at noon today?"

"Yes."

"How was it?"

"Delicious. I don't understand Dr. Paquette's complaints: whenever there's chicken or an omelette on the menu. . . ."

"Dr. Villeneuve, I must talk to you. . . . Can you come to my house tonight?"

12

Soeur Thérèse, who had done a lot of travelling in her life, knew how to appreciate the breakfasts, the long solitary strolls, the small purchases and conversations with coachmen, all those little things that one does at home without giving them too much thought, but that one really savours when one is abroad. Unlike a great many travellers, however, she never used the excuse of being away from home to neglect her spiritual duties, even less to commit acts that the moral code would have condemned.

When she was travelling, there was nothing she enjoyed as much as performing her religious duties, even adding an extra measure of zeal. As soon as she was awake, she would kneel at the foot of her bed and pray for the health of her one thousand patients, of her two hundred nuns, naming them one by one so the Lord wouldn't overlook any of them, and for her doctors and the lay staff, sometimes adding an amendment to her insurance policy, addressed directly to the Holy Ghost, asking that He might shed His light on Dr. Dansereau's research. She liked to think that her prayers, coming from another place, would arrive in Heaven more quickly, and that the Lord would pay more attention to them.

Before she went to sleep at night, she would

kneel again and ask the Lord to watch over her buildings. For that she had composed a long obsecration intended to protect each of the asylum's wings and annexes against all forms of disaster: flood, fire, earthquake, tidal wave, lightning, earth slide, hailstorm, invasion of termites, tornadoes and typhoons — the list was endless. Obviously, she could have got off more lightly by simply requesting permanent, total protection against cataclysm in any form, but she was convinced that, when it came to prayer, the Lord did not admire economy. Slapdash effort is peculiar to mortals; eternal beings are concerned about detail. She told herself, as well, that competition was strong at bedtime: from everywhere on earth at that hour there arose thousands of prayers! Those that weren't sincere wouldn't fly very high, but still there must be several hundred pressing against the gates of Heaven. To cross that final threshold, it was important to stand out, and Soeur Thérèse applied herself unreservedly to doing that. To judge by the reassuring letters she received from the asylum almost daily, her prayers were effective.

Whether she was in Scotland, England, Belgium, Italy, or France — the final stage of her journey — she never failed to attend daily Mass. She took communion as often as possible, too, and the slight subtle differences in taste that distinguished the bread in each of these countries only heightened her appreciation of the Lord's presence.

Of all the sacraments, however, none brought her so much grace as the sacrament of penitence. The asylum chaplains were excellent confessors, no doubt, with absolute respect for the secrecy of the confessional, but it was hard to search the depths of one's soul in the presence of someone you rubbed shoulders with every day. At Saint-Jean-de-Dieu, she generally limited her confession to small, inconsequential sins. When she thought her faults were more serious, she would talk vaguely about "wicked thoughts", without ever specifying their content. But now, three thousand miles from home, across from a confessor with an imperfect understanding of French whom she was unlikely ever to see again, her confessions were truly satisfying.

She had observed that the priests in different countries sometimes had divergent views. A mortal sin was still a mortal sin, needless to say, but the interpretation of the Church's precepts differed in some aspects which, while minor, were still important. A fault that had brought her only a tiny little penitence in Belgium had a far worse reception in Italy, while another sin that had been considered almost mortal in Scotland became a trifle, at most, in France. In theological terms there was obviously something disturbing about these different perceptions, but they were convenient, too, if you knew how to use them.

Finding herself with a few free moments before the start of the final day's meetings of the International Conference on Mental Medicine in Paris, she had decided to make use of them by going to confession one last time. She had opened the heavy door of the confessional, knelt down, and slowly recited a few preliminary prayers; in that way her eyes could grow accustomed to the dark.

Even though the priest was merely God's representative on earth, she still wanted to know whom she was dealing with. Through the wire grille with ornamental crosses that covered the opening, she could see nothing but his greying hair — which was reassuring — and his white hand resting on his chin. The man had a fine strong bass voice, so she decided she would trust him. After confessing a few minor sins and reciting the usual formulas, she remained in the confessional and cleared her throat to let the priest know that it would be advisable for him to help her along. The old priest, who had seen worse, grasped the message.

"Is there anything else, Sister?"

"No, Father.... That is.... May I ask you a question?"

"Of course, Sister, go ahead."

"Tell me, Father, does it ever happen that you have conversations with Our Lord?"

"Of course. Whenever we pray, we are in communication with Him, that's quite obvious...."

"Have you ever heard His voice, Father?"

"Sometimes, in the secrecy of my heart, I have the innermost conviction that I hear Him, yes."

"What does His voice sound like, Father?"

"What do you mean?"

"Does He speak quickly or slowly? In a deep voice or a high one? In French or Latin? How can we be sure that He is speaking to us?"

"I see what you mean.... That's a delicate question, and I fear there is no infallible method for recognizing Him. Indeed, I think it is improper to speak of a *voice* in His case.... But if you were to tell me instead what is worrying you, Sister?"

" . . . What I want to know is whether it's possible for the devil to imitate the voice of Our Lord."

"Indeed it is, Sister, indeed it is. There is no deceit of which he is not capable. We must always be wary of voices, especially the ones we hear at night. Is that the kind of voice you hear, Sister?"

"Let's suppose that the Lord is speaking to you, Father, or rather, let's suppose that you are convinced He is speaking to you. Let's suppose that He speaks in His usual voice and tells you to trust a person you're acquainted with, a lay woman, for example, for whom you may feel admiration or even affection. . . . Do you believe that would be the devil's work?"

"If you want me to help you, I beg you to answer my questions: do you have wicked thoughts at night, Sister, the kind that come from the base instincts?"

"No, Father, of course not! I was only wondering if you knew a way to recognize the voice of God when He speaks to you. . . ."

"I don't know, Sister. The only thing I can suggest is that you pray, and pray, and pray some more. Now I shall ask you to recite your act of contrition."

"Very well, Father."

As she recited her prayer, Soeur Thérèse told herself that the priest had not done his work properly and that he had sinned through lack of curiosity. Therefore she would ignore his advice.

So far, she had consulted seven priests. Only

one, at the beginning of her journey, had told her she had indeed heard the devil's voice; but he was an Irishman, and she had decided you couldn't altogether trust the Irish. Although they called themselves Catholics, they didn't speak a Christian language; moreover, it had seemed to her when she looked through the grille that his nose was rather large. Why should she trust an Irishman who was, perhaps, also a Jew? The priests she consulted in Belgium, two chubby, red-faced fellows, had been unwilling to offer an opinion. Confessors in Italy and France, clearly more conscientious, had pressed her with questions, finally concluding that there was nothing terribly serious, that when the devil wanted his victim to succumb to wicked thoughts, he had more terrifying means at his disposal — they knew something about them! — and so she had nothing to worry about for the moment. Since four priests had absolved her of her sins, she could go about her business with her soul at peace. Still, to set her mind at rest, she had offered up all the penances they imposed on her.

* * *

Now that she had duly met her religious obligations, she had the rest of the day to herself. At every stage of her journey, she had taken advantage of the numerous opportunities she was given to improve herself.

In England and Scotland she had visited a good many asylums, but found none that had more modern equipment than Saint-Jean-de-Dieu, which filled her with an altogether legitimate feeling of pride. She had also observed that the Anglo-Saxons were not great believers in the powers of hydrotherapy, advocating fresh air instead. While their asylums were disappointing, the gardens surrounding them were sheer wonders. Soeur Thérèse walked for hours along winding paths, admiring willows that wept beside old streams, lawns that were as carefully clipped as Dr. Dansereau's beard, and fruit trees that appeared to be highly productive. While the doctors discussed the respective merits of hydrotherapy and fresh air, she made sketches of garden designs, noted the names of certain particularly interesting plants, and inquired of the gardeners how to care for them: where could she obtain seeds, did they have medicinal properties, would they resist the harsh Canadian climate? She had been very surprised to meet at every turn doctors, nuns, and even gardeners who spoke impeccable French. What an odd race the English were! As gifted as they were at learning foreign languages *when they were at home*, how that gift evaporated when they came to live in Canada. . . .

In Belgium she visited more asylums, and she had a high regard for their architecture. Instead of the large structures of the English and the Americans, the Belgians seemed to prefer a system of small separate pavilions linked by tree-lined lanes. If there were some way, she thought, to bring together in a single place Belgian architects and English gardeners, asylums would truly be little pieces of Heaven on earth. For several days she toyed with the idea of separate pavilions, then reluctantly had to abandon it. In America, she noted in her report, the style was unfortunately impracticable: "Merely heating such an expanse would be prohibitively expensive. Our snowstorms would render communications impossible; we would require a separate kitchen for each pavilion; we would have to double all our services."

In France she visited the asylum at Cîteaux, near Lyons, and the one at Mettray, founded by the illustrious Dr. Demetz. She had expected a great deal from these visits, but left them cruelly disappointed. As far as their architecture was concerned, there was nothing particularly interesting about the French asylums. Of course, they had a certain elegance, but they weren't nearly as spacious as the North American asylums and, most important, they were poorly heated. The care they offered had nothing at all to distinguish it from what was available elsewhere in the world, while the hygienic conditions struck her as downright deplorable. And yet her hosts told her, again and again, that she had wasted her time visiting asylums in Belgium and England, because it was quite obvious that true mental health existed only in France. When she told them that she had seen very modern hospitals in America and that Saint-Jean-de-Dieu had no reason to envy any other asylum, they seemed to turn suddenly deaf. Weary from so much insincerity, she finally told them that, in fact, there were no genuine hospitals in Canada, that the sick were simply dropped into holes dug in the snow, and that only those who were at the point of death were entitled to a small tent made of wolf-skins. She made quite an impression on her hosts. . . .

* * *

She had attended sessions from August 6 through 10. Five long days of sitting on straight-backed chairs, listening to boring speeches; five interminable days she could have put to far better use with her own people. As for doctors Bourque, Paquette, and Vallée, they seemed to derive a great deal of pleasure from all the chatter. . . . If it had been up to her, she would have forbidden the holding of such shamefully wasteful international conferences; if these gentlemen needed to exchange observations so badly, could they not do so in writing?

None the less, she had to admit that there had been a few interesting presentations, such as the one by the old German who had discoursed wittily about the first experiments with hydrotherapy: in his asylum, baths sometimes lasted for as long as eighteen months. If the madmen weren't cured, at least they emerged with a fine set of gills. In the gardens of that asylum, they had even built a bridge across a pond; a lunatic would be attracted there by some clever ruse, then a mechanism would be activated that caused a trapdoor in the middle of the bridge to open and the madman would fall into the water. They believed firmly in the therapeutic value of surprise. . . . Because it couldn't be repeated, the practice obviously had not been pursued. The old German was a splendid raconteur and his heavy accent only added to his charm, so that he enjoyed a huge success. At scholarly conferences, these pages out of history permit one to measure the progress achieved, while providing those in attendance with a tremendous sense of self-satisfaction. The scholar concluded his presentation by assuring his audience that, in fifty years at most, madness would have ceased to exist; he received an ovation. Soeur Thérèse applauded politely. An end to madness? Surely not! If God had placed madness in human heads, it would take much more than a few baths to remove it.

She had also very much enjoyed the presentation by a French alienist who had recalled the principal stages in the doctrine of cerebral locations. Nineteen years before, in 1870, two Germans, messrs Fritsch and Hitzig, who had already observed that if an electric current crossed the head from left to right it would cause certain muscles in the eyes to move, had discovered, while exploring the various points on the brain's surface (which had been laid bare by trepanation), that all motor centres were located in the parietal lobe and the posterior half of the frontal lobe. The speaker had presented all this information very rapidly, *sotto voce*, as if he were discussing shameful diseases. Then he had sipped some water, cleared his throat, and solemnly added that it was a Frenchman who had made the most interesting discovery: the illustrious Dr. Charcot had found that sensitivity was located in the posterior part of the parietal lobe, and his latest research seemed to indicate that the faculty of speech was found in the second and, even more, the third frontal convolutions of the left anterior lobe. Soeur Thérèse jotted all this in a notebook for Dr. Dansereau. Unfortunately, the French alienist's presentation had been interrupted by a German scholar who replied that there was no doubt that the doctrine of cerebral locations was German, and that the French were a decade behind Germany, fatherland of Science. Then an American had intervened and the discussion had almost turned into a brawl. Abandoning her notes, Soeur Thérèse simply wrote: "I thank God for allowing me to be born in a country that is not a great power and probably never will be."

The same day, Dr. Bourque was asked to make a speech. That excellent man spoke with a great deal of modesty and warmth about the progress being made in mental medicine in Canada: the province of Quebec, with its one million, six hundred thousand souls, possessed four very modern asylums, for which thanks were due to the nuns, who had built them all from nothing. Then he spoke out in favour of leasing — the best way to administer an asylum in a new country such as Canada, and the best system that existed for both patients and governments. Soeur Thérèse had barely had time to savour these reasonable, sensible remarks when Dr. Paquette, who had been waiting for just such an opportunity, spoke up to denounce his colleague: it was the state, he declared, that must take care of its lunatics. He went on to denounce the nuns, who checked any progress, and the system of leasing, which must be brought to an end once and for all. She listened calmly and with a look that was almost benevolent to Dr. Paquette's remarks; only her fingers, which ran a little faster along the beads of her rosary, betrayed a certain nervousness.

Dr. Paquette's intervention sparked a great debate: some supported him, others vigorously defended the work of the nuns, while others, more pragmatic, wondered if they could do without this gratuitous contribution. Throughout the debate, which was very spirited, Soeur Thérèse remained unmoved. After a while she put away her rosary, and finally took from her purse the long letter that had been waiting for her upon her arrival in Paris. She had turned the thick envelope over and over in her fingers, then put it away in her purse, but not before she had fingered it at length. Picking up her rosary again while the argument was raging, she addressed Our Lord to tell Him not to worry: Dr. Paquette could hold forth as long as he wanted, Soeur Thérèse would get even with him.

* * *

After the closing banquet on August 10, the Canadian participants approached Soeur Thérèse to ask if she wanted to hold a final meeting on the eve of their departure, to take stock of their journey. From Dr. Bourque's tone she sensed that the request was dictated only by politeness, and so she amused herself by pretending to mull it over for a good long time before she replied.

"To tell you the truth, Dr. Bourque, I don't think that will be necessary. We'll have all the time we need during our crossing. And we've worked well, so it would be only fitting, I think, to give ourselves some rest. Why not amuse yourselves a little? We're in Paris, after all, there should be plenty for you to do."

"What about you, Soeur Thérèse?"

"Me? I shall rest in my room, I'm feeling a little tired. Go ahead, Dr. Bourque, have some fun.

You too, Dr. Paquette."

* * *

One hour later, doctors Bourque, Paquette, and Vallée were attending a performance that Soeur Thérèse would undoubtedly not have approved of: it was hard to carry on a conversation in such a noisy place, and the atmosphere was not conducive to profound reflections. Yet Dr. Paquette's brow was as furrowed as a bust of Beethoven.

"Just between us, Dr. Bourque, don't you find Soeur Thérèse's behaviour peculiar?"

"What do you mean?"

"I mean she hasn't replied to my speech. . . . And do you find it normal for her to incite us to debauchery?"

"Debauchery! That's going rather far, Dr. Paquette. I find this show very interesting, the dancing girls are very talented, and I'm most impressed by the choreography. . . ."

"It's still peculiar. She's got something up her sleeve, I'm sure of it."

"Soeur Thérèse isn't as terrible as she seems, Dr. Paquette. She improves on acquaintance. If you weren't so inflexible. . . ."

"Inflexible, me? She's the inflexible one."

"Don't you think we should resume this conversation somewhere else, Dr. Paquette? Relax, for heaven's sake, relax and enjoy these final moments!"

"I still say she has something up her sleeve. . . ."

* * *

In the meantime, Soeur Thérèse was sitting at her desk, transcribing her notes of these last days. Then she knelt to say her prayers, which that night, she had to confess, she rushed a little. Finally, she got into bed and, for the tenth time, reread the long letter from Dr. Villeneuve.

13

Longue-Pointe, July 10, 1889

Dear Soeur Thérèse,

When, on the eve of your departure, you summoned me to your office to ask in so many words that I keep an eye on Dr. Dansereau during your absence, I confess that I was deeply shocked. What? You would have me spy on one of my colleagues, denounce his actions, play double agent? Even though one practises one's profession in an asylum, one has one's honour. You told me then that I had misunderstood, that it was not a question of spying but rather of coming to the assistance of a colleague who had an unfortunate fondness for alcohol, of a doctor whom we at the asylum sorely needed, as well as a scholar who was conducting important research. You stirred my curiosity, I confess, but that was certainly not the main reason for my consent. If I promised to write you as soon as I had witnessed any important event concerning him, please be assured that it was chiefly because of the high esteem in which I have always held you. I am doing something now that I would do for no one else.

I am writing to you today, then, from our beloved asylum, to tell you that Dr. Dansereau is indeed a great scholar, that he has made a discovery which could well be fundamental in the treatment of mental maladies, and that I am infinitely grateful to you for having given me this mission. Had it not been for your request, I should never have had the opportunity to participate in his fascinating investigations. When I have described to you the experiments we performed during your absence, you will see that my enthusiasm, which it is still difficult for me to hide, is not at all false, and you will have no peace, I am certain, until you have returned to our beautiful country.

Let us return, then, if you will, to the time when I was leaving your office. Shortly afterwards, chance — or rather Providence, let there be no doubt about it — brought me together with Dr. Dansereau, who was in conversation with Soeur Jeanne in the doctors' office. No sooner had I entered than he asked if I still had those little magnets with which, as you undoubtedly know, I sometimes perform magic tricks for the amusement of our patients. As my reply was affirmative, he began at once to pour out a torrent of theories regarding the functioning of the brain. If he is to be believed, one need only arrange a few magnets on either side of a patient's skull and his trouble will dissipate immediately. He told me that he had already performed experiments on hens, and that they had proven conclusive; all that remained now was to try the treatment on humans, and for that he needed my assistance.

This was not the first time I had heard him make such statements. You know as well as I do that, while Dr. Dansereau is pleasant company, he has an unfortunate tendency to express such speculations whenever he is under the influence of an intoxicating beverage. On the day in question, although he was feverish, he appeared none the less to be quite sober. If you had not stirred my curiosity just a few moments earlier, it is most likely that I would have declined his invitation and merely agreed to lend him my magnets, nothing more. But I consented to assist him in his research and accompanied him that same evening on a visit to his laboratory.

Permit me to digress for a moment here to tell you that the widow Martineau, in whose house Dr. Dansereau lives, struck me as an excellent Christian as well as a remarkable hostess, two inseparable qualities in French Canadian women. I attempted, as you had requested I do, to have them name the exact date for their marriage, but received only an evasive reply. I can however tell you that they are well and truly betrothed: Madame Martineau showed me her ring, which for reasons unknown to me she keeps hidden in a metal box.

Now let me resume my account. After an abundant meal washed down with plentiful quantities of that red-currant wine for which the Sisters of Providence are renowned, we went to visit what Dr. Dansereau calls his laboratory (although it consists in fact of a rather crude installation in one section of the barn). Imagine my surprise when I saw an impressive collection of human brains, preserved in glass jars bearing labels on which I could read the names of some of our recently deceased patients. When he declared that he had assembled this odd collection with your wholehearted consent, I confess that I was only partly reassured. He invited me then to examine through the microscope some cells extracted from the brains of patients whose lives had been particularly unhappy. He declared that if I observed these cells carefully, I should find something resembling bunches of grapes. While I looked as best I could, I confess that I discerned no trace of any such formation, nor of the fern-cells he maintained I would see in certain sections of the brains of imbeciles or idiots. It is true that my eyesight is declining, the bitter price of age, but even with the best will in the world I could see nothing but a jumble of disparate cells. He told me then that it was his study of the brains of hens that had convinced him that the fern-cells were the source of happiness.

Upon returning to my room at the asylum that night, I was most perplexed. To say that I gave little credence to Dr. Dansereau's theories would be a euphemism: in fact I gave them none at all. How was one to believe that some vague experiments performed on hens, which are undoubtedly the stupidest animals in creation, could be extended to the human being, who was created in the image and likeness of God? How could anyone conceive that ordinary magnets placed on a patient's skull would effect even a modicum of change in the complex cells of the brain? At that moment I was, without knowing it, blinded by my own theories: for me, heredity and heredity alone determines the configuration of the brain. Until then, that is what I had always believed. Despite the undertaking I had given you, I wanted to advise him on the following day that I would no longer assist him in his research. Only my weakness prevented me from doing so: I envisaged the poor man, alone in his laboratory, so happy to be able at last to talk with someone about his research, and thought I must surely disappoint him should I refuse my support. I realized then that, despite characteristics that have always irritated me, and despite — or perhaps because of — his harebrained ideas, I was very fond of Dr. Dansereau. Therefore I decided to damp my critical spirit and to follow what he was doing, regardless of the consequences. After all, placing magnets on a patient's head did not strike me as a very risky undertaking; perhaps we would arrive at some spectacular discovery. (Are those the true reasons that incited me to open my mind to his theories? I doubt it, and shortly I shall speak with you about the true motives that impelled me then, but I can tell you now that, no matter what they may have been, in the end my decision was a felicitous one.)

The next evening, after our working hours, we joined Oscar Parent in order to begin our experiments. Dr. Dansereau had suggested that we perform our first tests on that patient, and his reasons struck me as convincing. Although no rod exists with which to measure unhappiness, there was no doubt that Oscar Parent was at the time the unhappiest patient in the asylum and, moreover, the only one who was merely unhappy (by that I mean that, aside from his great unhappiness, he did not appear, oddly enough, to be afflicted with any congenital disease or weakness, either physical or moral). In addition, Oscar Parent was a relatively educated man, able to read and write, which would allow us, if necessary, easily to verify the consequences of our treatment on other facets of his personality. As soon as he was made aware of our intentions, the man agreed without conditions to become our guinea pig. He would not regret it.

To avoid arousing Soeur Pudentienne's suspicions, we suggested that Oscar feign a violent headache, then join us in the infirmary. When he went to advise her that he would be absent for some time, we requested the assistance of Nurse Girard: having had the opportunity to work with her on many occasions, I was counting as much on her talent at bandaging as on her exemplary discretion. She agreed to help us and, a few hours later, we were all in the infirmary for our first experiments.

After we had settled Oscar in a bed, we secured a number of magnets to his neck and temples, which we had previously moistened, then waited for an hour. When we removed the magnets, he declared that he had felt nothing particular. While we were somewhat disappointed, none of us, myself above all, had expected quick results. That night we repeated the experiment, changing the number and position of the magnets, but with no more success. It must have been after midnight when we separated, having arranged to meet again at the same time the following day.

All during the next day, each of us pondered what we had done, and when we met again, around seven o'clock, we agreed that we must increase the number of magnets and leave them to act overnight. Here I must pay tribute to Nurse Girard: I should never have thought it possible to keep so many magnets in place with gauze bandages. I must also acknowledge Oscar's patience and courage. Just think of the poor man having to tolerate those dreadful magnets for twelve consecutive nights and never complaining of his discomfort! All he asked was that we place some ferns by his bedside. (It seems that, for some obscure reason, the sight of the plants brings him effective, although temporary, relief.)

I may as well tell you straightway: those twelve nights brought no change to Oscar's state of mind. That splendid fellow has always had great confidence in Dr. Dansereau, confidence verging on veneration, and he did not seem discouraged. I could not say the same of Dr. Dansereau, however: he left us earlier and earlier every evening, and when morning came he would complain of violent headaches. Once again, his sense of failure had taken him onto the slippery slope of his vice. Nature has endowed the doctor with a seething brain, always ready to play with new ideas. Unfortunately, he seems to suffer from a remarkable lack of persistence. It is often thus: I have frequently observed the same phenomenon in individuals who could be described as overly intelligent, who have quantities of good ideas but never bring them to term. Genuine scientific minds, I am convinced, are rather obtuse.

After two weeks of fruitless attempts, he suddenly announced that he was abandoning the experiments with magnets and was going to perform trepanations; since the grape-cells did not want to dissolve, he would root them out surgically. With all the energy I still possess I violently opposed this change in course. What, we were to abandon such promising experiments after only a few weeks! Were we true researchers or merely Sunday tinkerers? And I told him to consider for a moment what you, Soeur Thérèse, would think, reminding him that it was you, through your patience and tenacity, who had created out of nothing an asylum that was the envy of the entire world.

My arguments seemed to sway him. But if they were to be fully effective, they had also to be associated with some new research trails, otherwise the enthusiasm I was striving to re-create would be only temporary. Having none to propose, I suggested, in order to gain some time, that we temporarily abandon our practical trials so as to perfect our theoretical knowledge. After all, we knew nothing about magnetic fields and we had left the university long ago.... He agreed to my suggestion without much enthusiasm, and the next evening, and every night for the next two weeks, we met at his house to study.

After a good meal, each of us would read books borrowed from the asylum library; then, at about ten o'clock, we would gather around a delicious snack which Florence had prepared to discuss our reading. We soon observed that the charge of our little magnets, while probably sufficient to produce an effect through the thin skull of a hen, could not do the same with the skull of a human being, and that we would have to multiply our charges a hundred-, if not a thousand-fold. We could apply the same reasoning to the few drops of water with which the hen's temples had been dampened: if we were respecting relative weights, should we not use quarts of water rather than drops on Oscar? Dr. Dansereau, his enthusiasm restored, wanted to resume the experiments at once, using more powerful magnets, but I tried to curb his alacrity. Night after night, I proposed that we go back to our calculations, read additional treatises on magnetism, and draw up plans for a system that would enable us to fasten such powerful magnets to a patient's skull. I was pleased to tell myself that my action was intended to spare our friend more cruel disappointments, but I know now that, in truth, my motives were not nearly so noble. And now, dear Soeur Thérèse, let me give you my thoughts on the matter.

When I went home in the evening, I often asked myself, before getting into bed, why I was helping Dr. Dansereau with such relish when I gave him no chance whatsoever of succeeding. Although these reasons were certainly important ones, the friendship that unites us and the undertaking I had given you struck me as insufficient. I grasped the true reason on one of those evenings when we had gone back to our interminable calculations. In the space of a mere second I remembered my early years when, as a young student at the university, I would go to prepare for examinations in the company of my classmates. We would spend sleepless nights at the house of one student or another, cramming our books and anatomical drawings, when we could, obviously, have done the same at home. Why did we do this? I realize now that it was mainly to while away our solitude, and because all of us appreciated the discreet presence of our classmates. We sought to multiply and to prolong those moments, and preparing for examinations seemed to us an altogether honourable pretext. For two weeks I had found myself once more in a comparable state of mind, with Oscar, Nurse Girard, and Dr. Dansereau; I was simply trying to make it last. Moreover, in Florence's house I had discovered a kind of family life which I regarded with envy, I who have never known such domestic bliss.

I tell you all this, Soeur Thérèse, not to

evoke your pity but rather to give you a good understanding of my role in the discoveries we made. It could indeed strike you, upon reading my account, that it was because of my own selflessness and tenacity that the experiments ultimately succeeded. You know now that, deep down, I have always acted out of utter selfishness; consequently, it is Dr. Dansereau and no one else who deserves all the credit for our discoveries. Should they one day bring him renown, I would be the happiest of men, nor would I claim any share of it, not even the smallest. The memory of those happy moments will be my sole reward and it will be more than sufficient.

Now, let me resume my story where I left it. . . . After completing our theoretical work, we had to solve certain technical problems. First, we had to find some very powerful magnets whose intensity could be controlled. For that, we consulted the asylum's electrician, who, in exchange for a promise on our part to intercede on his behalf concerning some contract (which has now been done), was willing to make a Williams' coil available to us and to explain how it worked. As soon as we had seen the device, a second problem occurred to us at once: how could we cause such a mass to adhere to a man's skull? We were speaking in Oscar's presence and he told us that, in his youth, he had worked on a farm and had been a skilled harness-maker. If we could procure some straps and harness, he could easily knock together something. In a matter of hours he had fabricated a most ingenious sort of helmet, one that was not especially elegant (when a patient puts it on, it makes him resemble a dog with its muzzle raised) but that proved, with use, to work very well indeed.

Once these problems had been solved, we still had to find a place to perform our experiments that would be safe from indiscreet eyes. This time it was Nurse Girard who found the solution: why not set ourselves up in one of the cells? As we expressed considerable surprise at such an incongruous suggestion, she explained that never as far as she could remember had she seen one of the government-appointed doctors go to the cells. Now she had the enthusiastic agreement of each of us. And so it was in one of those cells where we lock up our most violent lunatics that we set up our Williams' coil and helmet, as well as a barrel that we would substitute for the bathtub (to bring one down from the hydrotherapy room struck us as too risky, to say nothing of the fact that we lacked the strength to do so).

On the night of June 6, we were ready to begin our experiment. First we covered Oscar's body with a thick coating of petroleum jelly, then he slipped into the barrel, which had been filled with warm water to which we had added a few linden-branches. After that, we fastened a rubber sheet around his neck to limit the drop in temperature; then, finally, we fitted the helmet onto his head. As soon as the magnetic field was activated, Oscar, to our great surprise, fell into a deep sleep. His pulse seemed regular, so we decided to let him sleep: after all, the poor man would be marinating in his bath for three days and three nights; we would be well advised to let him sleep to his heart's content. For this first night, Nurse Girard wanted to watch over Oscar, checking his pulse every hour and his blood-pressure and temperature every three hours.

At dawn the next day, when we came to spell her, Oscar was still not awake. His pulse was still slow and even, his temperature and blood-pressure perfectly normal. We were concerned about this lengthy sleep, which seemed very much like a hypnotic trance, even a comatose state. At times his eyelids fluttered slightly, suggesting that he was dreaming; as these dreams, if we were to judge by the faint smile we could see on his lips, seemed very pleasant, we decided to let him sleep. After all, the poor man was so unhappy when awake that three days and three nights of oblivion would surely do him no harm. Should our experiment fail, at least he would have enjoyed a brief respite.

When we met again that evening, however, we had to interrupt his untroubled sleep to feed him and to change his water. And we had great difficulty keeping him half-awake for an hour, in the course of which, moreover, he did not utter a word; no sooner had we reactivated the magnetic field than he lapsed into his deep lethargy again. It was Dr. Dansereau who spent the second night with him. The next morning, nothing had changed. All three of us were very concerned about these unexpected developments, and again we considered breaking off the treatment. After a lengthy discussion, however, we agreed that there was no risk to his physical health and that we should continue at all costs. I must confess, Soeur Thérèse, that on the third night none of us could sleep, neither I, who was on call, nor the two others, who came in frequently to see me. At least Oscar was sleeping enough for the three of us.

On the morning of June 9, unable to wait any longer, we decided to discontinue the treatment. Unable to awaken Oscar, we had to remove him from the barrel by force and lay him on a stretcher; then we took him to the infirmary, where we administered smelling salts. He opened his eyes slowly, looked dully at the three of us, and immediately fell asleep again. After breathing in the salts a second time, he opened his eyes again and asked for something to eat. While he was wolfing down some food without a word to us, we observed his slightest reactions, his slightest moves, to discern any change, but in vain. Sometimes he displayed an idiotic grin and seemed to be altogether absent. As soon as he had finished eating, he fell once more into the arms of Morpheus. Dr. Dansereau was profoundly discouraged: it seemed that his treatment had erased any trace of intelligence along with Oscar's unhappiness. (That had been his greatest fear throughout his experiments.)

It took two full days for Oscar to get his wits back, two days during which our spirits had fallen so low that we scarcely reacted when he told us, on the morning of June 11, that he felt completely cured, he had been certain of it as soon as he awoke, and he had been feigning idiocy until he was quite certain that his cure was permanent. Were we too tired to show that we were pleased? Were we annoyed with him for having led us astray? Were we being wary of premature enthusiasm? I cannot say. Nevertheless, when he noted that we had not reacted to his good news, he repeated again and again that he felt completely cured. Only then did we dare to question him. Was he no longer unhappy? "Not in the least!" Was he happy, then? Was he experiencing a sort of bliss? How would he describe how he felt? "I don't know what happiness is. . . . All I can say is, I'm in a very good mood."

Ten times, a hundred times that day, we returned to see him, and each time he gave the same answers. I don't need to tell you that we spent an excellent day, and an excellent night as well. The day after, we began submitting him to a battery of tests, which he accepted willingly, to measure other aspects of his cerebral activities. As Dr. Dansereau was very concerned about the effects of the treatment on Oscar's intelligence, we started by assigning some mathematical problems, using the questionnaire for an examination that the nuns give to primary-school pupils. Aside from an obscure problem about a bathtub and taps, with which, he admitted, he always had trouble, he performed brilliantly. Then we asked him to write a two-page composition on a subject of his choice. He set to work on this task with alacrity and thirty minutes later handed us five pages on the coming of spring. Both Dr. Dansereau and I judged the content of his essay to be acceptable, the style fair. His vocabulary was reasonably precise and his syntax in keeping with what one could decently expect of a man in his condition, although it betrayed certain lacunae: the poor man seemed quite ignorant of punctuation, and his sentences were inordinately long. But Dr. Dansereau, who had had the opportunity to read his prose before, assured me he had always written in that way.

To measure his memory we asked him to recite his prayers, and he applied himself to that with touching reverence, dedicating the Our Father to Dr. Dansereau, the Credo to your humble servant, the Gloria to Nurse Girard, and to you, Soeur Thérèse, the most beautiful prayer of all, the Hail Mary. Perhaps I should not admit it, but never before have prayers so affected me.

Wishing to leave nothing to chance, we continued to probe his memory, using the appendix to Form C. Oscar remembered perfectly well the names of his parents, his many brothers and sisters, his parish priest, and the principal vicars, even that of the bishop from whom he had received the sacrament of confirmation. His memory therefore seemed to us intact, with one exception: Oscar told us that he no longer had any recollection of Véronique, to whom he had written countless letters, and whom I believed to be the source of his unhappiness.

That one exception is undoubtedly rich in lessons. To tell the truth, we know nothing about how our device works, but the fact that it has obliterated the cause of his unhappiness suggests that the magnetic field acts upon memory, erasing certain unhappy memories and perhaps, who knows? a single, particularly painful one. When our intelligence must reorganize the past, it works in such a way as to cluster memories around some happy event, causing the patient's entire past to appear in a new light. I discussed this with Dr. Dansereau, but he believes that the magnetic field affects the grape-cells and modifies how we perceive things, rather than how we remember them. (Nurse Girard has her own little theory, which I am giving you just for your information. In her opinion, water plays an essential role in the cure: the magnetic field has the effect of temporarily erasing all memory, so that for three days the patient feels as if he is in his mother's womb, from which he finds himself emerging a second time.... Needless to say, we must reject this theory about a second birth until subsequent examinations. It seems quite clearly to have no scientific basis.)

As I write to you now, almost a month has elapsed since Oscar underwent his treatment, and both his behaviour and his mood have remained stable. As a physician, I would not hesitate for a moment recommending that he be released. For the moment, while awaiting your return, to which he looks forward eagerly, he has resumed his activities with Soeur Pudentienne, and has not breathed a word to anyone about his cure.

It is, of course, too soon to draw any final conclusions, and we must beware of making hasty judgements. After all, Dr. Dansereau's method has been successful on just one patient, and our knowledge of the functioning of both the brain and magnetic fields is still so incomplete that we have only a very vague idea of how the mechanism operates ... but still, we've made progress since you left!

I must stop here, although I would rather not. Life goes on, as always there are patients to be cared for ... and the mail must reach its destination. If all goes well, the ship carrying this letter will arrive when your meeting is beginning. As I write these final words, we are preparing to attempt a second experiment, which we shall describe on your return.

May Our Lord watch over you and return you to us in good health. May the Holy Ghost shed His light upon us so that, together, we may find a balm to relieve our poor patients! Pray for us, Soeur Thérèse, and think that perhaps in a few years we shall all be in Paris, listening as Dr. Dansereau presents a paper! The eyes of the entire world then will be turned to your asylum, Soeur Thérèse, just as today the prayers of all the patients and staff are on their way to Our Lord, asking Him to return you safe and sound to our dear Canada.

Lucien Villeneuve, M.D.

14

Upon her return from Europe, Soeur Thérèse was welcomed home with pomp and ceremony. She was driven from the port to the asylum in the magnificent carriage that was usually called into service for the St.-Jean-Baptiste Day parade; a number of villagers had even congregated along the road to wave to her. Florence, however, had chosen to watch the procession from her window, at the same time starting a piece of knitting that didn't require a great deal of concentration. Despite Bernard's repeated invitations, she had refused to attend the reception in Soeur Thérèse's honour. "Being with all those lunatics doesn't appeal to me in the least, I'm simply not in the mood for festivities, so don't keep pestering me." Bernard yielded without asking any questions, but his friend's attitude surprised him. Why was she withdrawing into her shell like this? Why had her expression suddenly clouded over?

Florence was knitting her third row when her fingers began to slow down. Why had the woman come back? Bernard had been a different man over these past three months; the change had been gradual, barely perceptible from one day to the next, but it had been constant. Although he was still far too often lost in thought, he could always find a few moments in the evening to confide his doubts and to enquire about her day's activities. He was beginning to listen, really listen. Associating with Dr. Villeneuve had undoubtedly done him enormous good. That man had the gift of getting Bernard's feet back on the ground. Every time he came over to study, he spoke of his regret at having never married, and his words gave Bernard pause. Would it continue now that *she* was back? Ever since her arrival had been announced, Bernard had again been aloof and dreamy, preoccupied by nothing but *scientific* problems. Could it be that, in the end, science had nothing to do with it? Soeur Thérèse manipulated him like a puppet and, what was worse, he didn't even seem to notice. Lord! Why can't we trust people, not even nuns!

* * *

When Soeur Thérèse had walked through the asylum's iron gate at nightfall, there had been an outburst of joy. The trees were decorated with twelve hundred Chinese lanterns, the buildings decked with three hundred flags and banners. When she alighted from the carriage, the brass band struck up a tune and more than a thousand nervously awaiting patients began to cheer. She had tears in her eyes as she handed round the holy pictures she had brought back from Italy, and so many spontaneously knelt around her that, for a long moment, she couldn't take one step forward. To extricate herself from the human tide, she ordered them to stand up, but with her voice breaking from emotion she couldn't make herself heard. The nuns had to intervene, threatening to deprive the recalcitrant patients of the party that was to follow, so that Soeur Thérèse could make her way to the temporary dais that had been erected in her honour. Over her protests, she had to climb onto it and shake the hand of the Cabinet minister who had come directly from Quebec City for the occasion, the two MPs, the mayor, the curé of Longue-Pointe, and finally the chaplain, before she could have a few words, *sotto voce* — there were many journalists present as well — with Soeur Madeleine-du-Sacré-Coeur, who had kept the asylum running smoothly during her absence.

"What's the meaning of this sideshow, Soeur Madeleine? I thought I'd expressly forbidden. . . ."

"That would have been impossible, Soeur Thérèse, the patients were so excited that we had to keep them busy. They'd have been bitterly disappointed if we hadn't let them celebrate your homecoming."

"That's fine, but what about the politicians and the reporters?"

"They invited themselves, as usual. But sit down, Sister, the entertainment is about to begin."

"How long will it last?"

"A few hours, I'm afraid."

"That's far too long, I have work to do. After an hour I'll pretend to feel faint, and you can take me to my office."

"You can't do that to our poor patients, Soeur Thérèse! Think how happy they are to have you back!"

"All right, very well, but on one condition: I want you to sit next to me, and we can quietly take

221

care of routine business during any lulls in the performance."

"But, Soeur Thérèse, where will we put the minister?"

"If it were up to me, he'd be on the lawn with the megalomaniacs."

Soeur Madeleine finally gave in, but she couldn't bring herself to ask the minister to move, and so she had to stand behind Soeur Thérèse throughout the whole ceremony. And she had to lean towards her very often. . . .

After the appropriate speeches, which were brief — one advantage of an asylum was that the patients who lived there didn't have the vote — the entertainment got under way. First the patients' brass band struck up "God Save the Queen", a fairly easy piece but badly played. There were any number of wrong notes and the tempo began very slowly, then accelerated from one bar to the next, for no apparent reason. After some polite applause, they launched into a spirited rendition of "Vive la Canadienne", the nun who conducted the brass band having finally succeeded, it appeared, in transmitting her enthusiasm to the musicians. During the first pause, Soeur Thérèse beckoned to Soeur Madeleine.

"Tell me, Sister, where are the doctors sitting?"

"They should be in the front rows, Soeur Thérèse, just under the dais."

"I can't see them."

"It's very dark tonight, Sister. I can't see them either."

"Are they seated to the right or the left of the stairs?"

"The right, Soeur Thérèse."

Peering into the darkness, Soeur Thérèse could see nothing but the long black waves formed by hundreds of dark heads slowly swaying to the rhythm of the music. Perhaps her eyes would get used to the darkness. Why had the moon not yet risen?

From his seat in the front row, Dr. Dansereau was trying vainly to attract her attention. Why did her gaze keep sweeping the crowd and never settle on him? She looked very pale.... Was it the lighting? Perhaps the journey had tired her.... Was there any way of sending her a message?

The interpretation of *The Poet and Peasant Overture*, Soeur Thérèse's favourite piece of music, was so fine that a long silence followed its execution. When the musicians began to put away their instruments, the crowd finally emerged from its torpor and started to applaud, quietly at first, then very warmly.

"Tell me, Soeur Madeleine, do you know where Oscar Parent is?"

"I can't say, Soeur Thérèse, but I'm sure he's somewhere in the crowd."

"Have you noticed anything particular about him, Soeur Madeleine?"

"I haven't seen him for some time, but in fact Soeur Pudentienne was telling me just this morning that she could hardly recognize him: he smiles often now, and apparently even makes jokes sometimes. I don't know if his humour is very refined ... but it's remarkable progress all the same. I confess I found it hard to believe her."

"Soeur Madeleine, I'd like him to come to my office as soon as the ceremony is over. Is that understood?"

After the brass band had left, the gathering was treated to a playlet entitled *The Verger, the Horse, and the Priest*. Two rather hefty patients played the role of the horse while another, in priestly raiment and assisted by his verger, vainly tried to mount it: the priest finally succeeded and the steed divided into two "parts" that began to prance around the stage, causing the priest to fall upon his posterior — the high point of the play. With the exception of the chaplain, everyone laughed heartily — including Soeur Thérèse, who, remembering the anecdotes recounted by the old German at the conference, was overcome by giggles, for which she apologized to Soeur Madeleine, pleading the fatigue of her journey. After that, she was unable to ask the slightest question. . . .

Then came some humorous dialogues, followed by a few light-hearted songs. Emilienne Robichaud, a recent arrival at the asylum, had an unexpected success with her rendition of *My Cousin's Wedding*, a song which she had undoubtedly heard many times in her native Acadian village and which she now repeated innocently, with no notion that it had nothing to do with marriage, but rather was filled with racy allusions to almost every edible fruit and all the vegetables in the garden. . . . She probably had no idea why the crowd had laughed so hard, nor why the faces of the nuns had suddenly gone red beneath their wimples. This time it was the Cabinet minister who was unable to repress his laughter. As for Soeur Thérèse, she did not appreciate the ditty at all.

"That's enough. It's late and the patients should have been in bed long ago. Have the performance stopped at once."

"Be patient, Soeur Thérèse, the brass band has prepared two more pieces."

"Tell them to play only one, and have them choose something serious: the patients are overexcited and they'll never get to sleep."

After a consultation between Soeur Madeleine and Soeur Rose-de-la-Trinité, who was conducting the band, they decided to repeat *Poet and Peasant*, playing it very slowly.

Bernard, who had resigned himself to wait until the performance was over, allowed the music to lull him; it had been a magnificent evening, with the leaves shuddering in the cool August breeze while the sky was filled with shooting stars. Briefly, he felt twenty years old again: he imagined himself back in Longueuil, where Viviane's parents were giving a party . . . Viviane at the piano . . . while he stood off to the side, resentful of the crowd that had separated him from his beloved. . . .

At the same moment Soeur Thérèse, on the dais, hidden behind the huge bouquet she had just been given, looked up at the sky, where she too saw the shower of shooting stars: it's summer in Sainte-Hyacinthe . . . the orchestra is playing a slow waltz and she's waiting for Edouard, so distinguished and sensitive, to ask her to dance . . . later that evening they walk in the park . . . he tells her of his religious vocation and says he will enter the seminary in September. . . . She never saw him again.

Bernard was still lost in his dreams when the band finished its piece and, confusing the applause with the sound of the wind in the branches, he took several moments to emerge from his torpor. When he started making his way to the dais, it was too late: all the patients wanted to go there too, so the nuns and the guards had to intervene and stop them. After attempting three times to plough his way through the crowd, only to be driven farther back at every try, he resigned himself to entering the asylum through a concealed door and trying to catch up with Soeur Thérèse inside the building. She for her part had been swept along to the main entrance, after turning several times towards the great black waves that were rippling nearby.

* * *

Once she was inside the asylum she still had to shake a few hands, offer the distinguished visitors a glass of wine, and give the minister a report of her trip to Paris. She was strongly tempted to drive these thieves from the Temple with a whip, but she resisted and instead spoke to Soeur Madeleine.

"I'm not feeling well, you must excuse me for a moment. Have you found Oscar?"

"He should be waiting in your office, Sister."

"Excellent. When you see Dr. Dansereau, please send him to me: I'm afraid I caught cold during the crossing. Please apologize to our guests. . . . "

The other nun had no need to do so. Under
the harsh light of the electric bulbs, everyone had
observed that Soeur Thérèse was disturbingly pale.

Her conversation with Oscar was very brief.

"How do you feel, Oscar?"

"In good spirits, Sister, thanks to Dr.
Dansereau. . . ."

"Say no more, I know all about it. Do you
want me to sign your release?"

"I couldn't ask for more, Sister."

"I'll see to it first thing tomorrow. But before
that, I have a question for you, only one, and I hope
you'll answer it honestly. It's very important for me.
Do you swear that you will, Oscar?"

"It's not good to swear, Sister."

"If I ask you to, Our Lord will understand. Do
you swear?"

"I swear."

"Very well. Tell me, Oscar, are you still afraid
of the devil?"

"More than anything, Sister."

"Very well. That's all I wanted to know.
Come to my office tomorrow morning. Do you
intend to go back to Joliette?"

"No. With your permission, Sister, I'd like to
stay on at the asylum, as an employee. I think Dr.
Dansereau will need my help, and . . . and I'd like to
go on looking after the ferns. I wouldn't ask for any
wages, Sister, only my room and meals."

"All work deserves a salary, Oscar. Tomorrow I'll see what I can do. Please leave the door open
on your way out, Dr. Dansereau shouldn't be long."

* * *

Dr. Dansereau, followed shortly by Dr. Villeneuve, arrived a few moments later. Once the door had been shut, at Soeur Thérèse's urgent request, they finally sat down and had a long, very long conversation.... At first the two doctors tried to interest the nun in the Williams' coils, in the functioning of memory, the temperature of the water, and the fern-cells, but she interrupted them briskly: she had no interest in techniques, she wanted results. Where were they? With a questioning glance at Bernard, Dr. Villeneuve began by listing the patients who had been treated during her absence: Tancrède Tarte, an epileptic in the Saint-Luc ward, Victorine Langevin, a former milliner who suffered from nostalgic hypermania, Clara Dufresne, who was afflicted with religious delirium, and, finally, Eugène Lavallée, a melancholic who also suffered from congenital sexual inversion. Then Bernard interrupted Dr. Villeneuve to say that the results, however, had not been very encouraging, as no change had occurred in their condition.

Dr. Villeneuve hastened to intervene to register his disagreement: perhaps they had not been cured, but at least they were all in good spirits. Between fits, Tancrède was all smiles, and his bouts of violence seemed to have permanently disappeared. The nature of Clara's frenzy had changed: instead of the devil, it was now the Blessed Virgin who appeared every day to deliver messages of hope. As for Victorine, although she still suffered from the same malady, she seemed to have forgotten everything about her unhappy past. Eugène's case was more troublesome: he was still attracted to young men, but now did not experience the slightest guilt.

Bernard spoke up next to explain his disappointment: the patients were in good spirits, perhaps, but they still had not been cured. The mechanism would have to be modified, adapted to each type of sickness, they would have to find the areas of the brain that contained the cells that caused each kind of madness, adapt the magnetic fields . . . everything still had to be done.

Then there began a long dialogue between the two physicians. Dr. Villeneuve repeated that the machine was exceptional, that they had made great strides in mental medicine, that the rest was only a matter of time. Bernard, for his part, was less certain: what was the good of improving an epileptic's spirits if he was still prostrated by fits? Was it morally proper to remove all feeling of guilt from a sexual pervert? If you listened to him, only Oscar, who was "merely" unhappy, had been cured; cases of *pure* unhappiness were so rare that, all things considered, his machine would hardly be of any use.

Soeur Thérèse looked at each of the men in turn. Whenever they finished a sentence they would turn to her, seeking the faintest sign of approval. It was obvious that they were only going over arguments they had already fully discussed during her absence. They were speaking now not to each other, but for her. That is always the case, she had often observed, whenever a conversation takes place in public. And so she let them talk until their arguments had exhausted themselves. They're in good spirits, Dr. Villeneuve repeated, their hallucinations are happy ones now, the megalomaniacs no longer think they're Napoleon Bonaparte, but St. Francis of Assisi! What more could they ask for? We must go further, replied Dr. Dansereau, strip politicians' brains of prejudice, create architects who no longer care only about conventions, poets who no longer are lazy. . . .

Neither man, in fact, said what was on his mind. Why didn't Bernard come right out and say that he was very satisfied with his work, but didn't want to show it too much, and why did he not plead with the other two to shower him with the praise he deserved? And would it not have been to Dr. Villeneuve's advantage to come right out and say that he too had doubts about their experiments, but that basically they didn't matter because he was going along with them out of friendship for Bernard?

As she had expected, the conversation was drawn out for more than an hour. The subject turned, successively and at times cumulatively, to good and evil, which seek each other out like newly separated Siamese twins, to the moral sense, which may be nothing more than an especially perverse form of epilepsy, to remorse, from which the old man with the scythe obviously does not suffer, to the thin layer of tissue paper that separates reason from madness, to God, who enjoys our blunders, to His blindness when innocent children die, to science, which will probably never put an end to war, and to all sorts of other topics that men enjoy bringing up between themselves when they are in a woman's presence.

"What about you, Soeur Thérèse, what do

you think?"

She was so busy observing the dance of words around their heads that she didn't react to Bernard's question. Dr. Villeneuve had to repeat it to get her attention.

"What do I think? Not much, to tell you the truth. But don't worry about me, go on with your conversation."

"I'm afraid it will never be over."

"Why start it over all the time, if that's the case? I'll never understand men. Very well, since you asked my opinion, here it is. The situation is very simple. I'm not a doctor or a theologian and I leave such matters to those who are more competent than I. As directress of this asylum, I believe that Dr. Dansereau's discovery is one of capital importance. The patients aren't cured? What of it! Did anyone expect to find a panacea for diseases of the soul in just a few years? Did you expect that your magnets would wipe out original sin? The patients are in good spirits, you tell me. . . . Perhaps that is a great advance for science, it's not for me to judge. What I can tell you, though, as directress of this asylum, is that I believe we have taken a giant step. Do you realize what enormous sums we must spend every year just to divert our poor fools, or to isolate a patient who screams so shrilly during his night-mares that he wakes up the other patients? Have you thought about how much we would save if we could get along without straitjackets and soothing syrups? Imagine, for a moment, what our asylum would be like if all the patients were to undergo your treat-ment: no more complaints about the quality of the food, or terrors during thunderstorms, or fights in the dormitories.... Think about your own work too, doctors. Would you not be happy to stop spending the better part of your time cleaning the ears of those poor souls who suffer from persecution mania, who think they hear voices? How long would it take, do you think, to treat each of our one thousand two hundred and forty-six patients?"

This time it was the doctors who took a few moments to react. Dr. Dansereau finally replied that, at the rate of three days per patient, on average, it would require a good ten years. That period could be reduced if they used more than one machine, but to do so might arouse the government doctors' suspicions. . . .

Now that the conversation had taken a practical turn, everything was settled in the twinkling of an eye. It was decided to apply the treatment immediately to the greatest number of patients possible, using a single machine, until Dr. Dansereau had published an article declaring to the entire world that the administration of asylums by nuns did not interfere with scientific progress, quite the contrary. They agreed to treat children first, then mothers and wage-earning men, and finally unmarried individuals of both sexes, with erotic monomaniacs and inverts to be treated only in the last instance. Perhaps, in time, the machine would be sophisticated enough not to erase every sign of guilt.

It was almost two a.m. when Dr. Villeneuve, utterly exhausted but overjoyed, left Soeur Thérèse's office, not before advising her to take care of herself: she was very pale. Bernard remained a few minutes longer. The door stayed open. . . . They talked softly about this and that, then they were silent. For a long moment they were quiet and still, savouring their reunion.

* * *

From the fall of 1889 until the early spring of 1890, doctors Dansereau and Villeneuve, assisted by Oscar Parent and Nurse Girard, successfully treated almost fifty patients. If Bernard had started writing his article sooner, they would undoubtedly have been able to treat many more, especially because they had refined their technique: it often took them just a few hours to eliminate any trace of unhappiness. If anyone asked now when his article would be published, he said merely: "I'm working on it." Actually, he had put only a few scattered notes on paper. Fascinated by his experiments again — and therefore relatively sober — he was able, through trial and error, to cure not only nostalgia and violence, but also a few cases of kleptomania, ebrious mania, and circular madness. Because he proceeded through trial and error, and because every night he had to watch over the patients to check the operation of his machine, changing the location of the magnets here and the intensity of the magnetic field there, he had very little time to write.

* * *

Although the effect of a single rotten apple in a basket is known, no one has ever been able to verify what the result would be in the opposite case. None the less, good spirits finally came to affect almost

five per cent of the asylum's inhabitants, a remarkable proportion in any institution.

Numerous foreign delegations visited the
asylum in the course of the year. Reports were
unanimous: Saint-Jean-de-Dieu was flawless, there
was no more modern asylum to be found, and it was
filled with an atmosphere of calm, of *joie de vivre*
even — that was astonishing in such a place, where
moral misery seemed to be taken for granted. This
quality of life was attributable, according to some, to
the exceptional purity of the air at Longue-Pointe,
while others credited the many splendid plants that
adorned the wards, but everyone emphasized as a
primary factor the devotion and self-sacrifice of the
ever-smiling nuns. It was stupefying that so much
had been accomplished with such slender means.
Early in the month of April 1890, Soeur Thérèse
signed a long-term agreement with the government,
to the great despair of Dr. Paquette.

Shortly after the signing of this agreement,
the experiments had to be interrupted for several
days, owing to a deterioration in the health of Soeur
Thérèse. Her temperature rose dangerously, she
complained of pain in her upper chest and difficulty
in breathing. After they had both examined her,
doctors Dansereau and Villeneuve, observing an
inflammation of the pharynx and larynx, bowed to
the evidence: she was suffering from influenza.
Camphor pastilles and infusions of cow-parsnip, an
Indian remedy that was often effective, were prescribed, and she was ordered to stay in bed. She
agreed on one condition: that the doctors take up
their experiments again.

They obeyed, even stepping up their fervour;
at this rate, they would undoubtedly have treated all
the patients by the end of the following year.

15

Tuesday, May 6, 1890, would prove to be a memorable day.

It was cloudy and rather cold for the time of year, although the springtime sun had already begun its work: the snow had long since vanished from the muddy fields and the ploughing was under way, there were leaves on the poplars and hungry bees were limbering up their wings before they frenetically set off in search of flowers that were all too rare. At the asylum, the windows were open wide.

All the patients who were able to work were outside. Wilfrid had started to let his hens go out and he was keeping an anxious eye on his roosters. The thirty-six horses and seventy-four cows now had company: a few days earlier the nuns had bought from neighbouring farmers one hundred and sixty young oxen, five hundred sheep, and a hundred or so pigs, which would be fattened up over the summer and slaughtered at the first snowfall, the meat then stored in barrels.

People were already dreaming of the nights when they would gather on their balconies and listen to the love songs of the frogs that inhabited the many ponds of Montée Saint-Léonard, the men smoking their pipes, the women knitting.

At the asylum, as everywhere else, nature's awakening was felt not only by the animals. The most remarkable change occurred among the nuns, who suddenly grew several inches taller, like ferns slowly unfurling in the sun. Their smiles seemed more radiant, not quite so sad as usual. This minor occurrence, which seemed to be contagious, was enough to make everyone, patients, doctors, and guards alike, feel some additional warmth.

For the patients, at least for those who had not yet undergone Dr. Dansereau's treatment, the coming of spring usually had positive effects: idiots, imbeciles, and lunatics seemed a little more alert, almost more intelligent; in the eyes of those who suffered from melancholia and nostalgia there appeared glimmers of happiness — only fleeting, alas, for the smallest cloud, the briefest rainfall, pulled them even deeper into dejection; as for the ordinary maniacs, their reactions were extreme, depending on the phase they were going through: either it was utter euphoria — when you had to be wary of their effusions — or, more despondent than usual, they wept for days at a time; finally, the hysterics, the erotomaniacs, and those suffering from sexual inversion became so dangerous that they required twice as much attention as usual.

At eleven o'clock, the men's wards were still very calm. The few patients who weren't busy in the fields were smoking their pipes on the balcony, playing cards, or daydreaming and rocking in their chairs while they waited for dinner.

On the women's side, in contrast, everyone was hard at work. Every spring, the woollen blankets and winter clothes had to be stored away in huge trunks. The odour of damp earth came in the windows, mingling with the smell of mothballs, and, as it did every year, this odd mixture provoked some flights of nostalgia: when one of the patients in the Sainte-Marthe ward struck up the first notes of "Un Canadien Errant", all the others took up the refrain with such conviction that soon the women in the next ward were singing along as well. A few moments later, the women in all the wards, except the Sainte-Cécile, were singing the song of the 1837 exiles. The wind helped carry their voices to the men's side, and they too joined in the wonderful concert.

In the Sainte-Cécile ward, the situation was very different. The women who paid forty dollars board a month were exempted from any work that was not in keeping with their rank. The patients had private rooms, with attractive curtains that concealed the bars on the windows, somewhat daintier meals, full decks of cards, a properly tuned piano, a separate parlour for entertaining visitors, and, finally, the right to wear their own clothes on all occasions.

All these little privileges were taken for granted by these society ladies, who, once the shock of internment had passed, were quick to resume their old habits, and, in the end, weren't too disoriented in the asylum: while their servants now wore nuns' habits, in other respects they behaved exactly like their maids. These great ladies never saw the cooks, but they were able to complain about the food through the intermediary of the idiots from the public wards who brought their meals on silver-plated trays. What most of them dared not acknowledge, however, was that they were secretly relieved to be interned: they no longer had to rack their brains to organize ceremonial meals in honour of the bishop, or tolerate the assaults of their wealthy husbands, whom they never saw in any case except on Sundays, or worry about the disastrous scholastic performances of their ungrateful children, who never came to see them.

People coming to this ward were always surprised by the calm, the serenity, by something close to *joie de vivre* which reigned there. The ladies no longer had to vie with one another over the sumptuousness of their living-room decor, the social progress of their husbands, or the provenance of their hats. They were liberated from the frightful demands of the unbridled competition that was the prerogative of their class, and a genuine solidarity had now been woven between them which, far more than material privileges, delayed their recovery. In fact, Soeur Thérèse often worried about the statistics on this group: while the average rate of recovery in the asylum was 83.81 per cent, for patients in the Sainte-Cécile ward it was only 31.27 per cent. But if their privileges were abolished, could one still require their families to pay board, as well as use their visits to remind them discreetly of their charitable duties? Then she would have to be content with the paltry hundred dollars paid annually by the government, which would be of no help either to these ladies or to the other patients. And if they were piled into the public wards, would that not be a dreadful

trauma, even worse than being interned? . . . Very
well, that was the way it was; after all, it was impossible to solve every problem at once. For all these
reasons, Soeur Thérèse had recommended that Dr.
Dansereau treat these patients last.

That morning, the ladies in the Sainte-Cécile
ward were busy assembling boxes of candy which
they would then distribute to the patients in the
public wards in celebration of spring — even here in
the asylum, these ladies had their charitable works
— or feeding the canaries and parakeets in which
they took such pride. They were allowed to keep
their birds with them, certainly the most agreeable
of their privileges: assembled in one ward, the birds
warbled away to their hearts' content, and in spring,
when the windows were opened, their songs wafted
across the lawns, to the delight of strollers. (The
most picturesque bird in the aviary was unquestionably Jocko, a splendid Amazonian parrot with a
highly varied repertoire, who imitated both the
chapel bells and a creaking floor well enough to fool
people, and could respond to prayers with a hoarse
but perfectly understandable "Amen".)

During this time Bernard, Oscar, and Nurse
Girard were adapting their helmet to the head of a
severely deformed hydrocephalic, and getting ready
to put the poor man in the basin. Soeur Pudentienne
was tending the plants, Dr. Villeneuve was resting
in the chapel, and the government doctors were all
in the hydrotherapy room so they could be present
during Angélique's bath. As for Soeur Thérèse, she
was in bed. She had been brought an infusion of
cow-parsnip, and she sipped at it while Soeur

Germaine-de-l'Annonciation, the community's bursar, read her the kitchen's annual financial statement. Dr. Dansereau had advised her to stay in bed, which she did conscientiously, but he had not forbidden her to work. . . . How much was left of the nine hundred pounds of strawberries they had cooked up into jam last summer? Could they take some to town and sell it? What if they were to organize a charity sale? At ten cents a jar, they could cover part of their heating costs: the winter had been harsher then expected. . . .

And so, on that morning of May 6, 1890, there was no hint of the dramatic events that were to follow.

* * *

At about ten minutes after eleven, Idola Bergeron, a poor idiot from a good family, had left the aviary to ask permission of Soeur Henriette-de-l'Immaculée-Conception to get some scissors from her room. Soeur Henriette had raised no objection, for Idola was the most docile and harmless of all the patients in the Sainte-Cécile ward, perhaps in the whole asylum.

Now she went to her third-floor room, closed the door behind her, and shut herself in the closet. The darkness was total; Idola was happy. At last she would be able to strike one of the matches she'd snitched from the kitchen and admire to her heart's content the yellow flame that appeared as if by magic at the tip of the little wooden stick. She cracked a match and the pretty flame sprang up, all yellow at first and surrounded by sparks; then the centre became blue, like a grotto in the middle of the sun, the flame came away from the stick, and there was nothing now except a black hole, and from it burst Lucifer's horns, followed by his forked tail and hoofs. The flame ran slowly down the length of the match and Idola, fearing that the devil would prick her finger, extinguished it, and immediately lit another. What would she see this time? Would the Virgin Mary finally appear to her, as she had so often in the past? Idola struck four matches, but still the Blessed Virgin did not show herself.

When she had only one match left, she hesitated for a long time before lighting it, then suddenly remembered the vigil light she had taken from the chapel: there was hardly any wax left in the bottom of the red container, and the glass was dull ... so it hadn't really been a theft ... no, actually, she had borrowed it to clean it.... The flame was still yellow and blue when you looked at the vigil light from above, and a handsome dark red when you looked through the glass; really, it was superb! The slightest movement was enough to make the flame dance to the right and to the left, and as soon as she stopped moving it, the flame straightened up and pointed towards Heaven. Now Idola had no doubt: the Virgin Mary was going to talk to her.

The apparition soon appeared in the middle of the flame. Idola heard the Blessed Virgin say that she was very pleased with her, very fond of her, and she asked her to feed the fire because it was cold in Heaven. Immediately, Idola added first the six half-consumed matches, then some wads of paper, and finally the lid of a cardboard hat-box. When she saw the smoke spreading through the closet, she tried to smother the fire with her hands, but she only managed to burn herself. Panic-stricken, she sped downstairs to warn Soeur Henriette. When she got to the first landing she changed her mind: she mustn't upset Soeur Henriette ... it would be better to put out the fire herself. She raced back up the stairs, flung open the closet door, and threw in the contents of her chamber-pot, but the closet had become an inferno. It was eleven thirty-five when she sped down the stairs again to look for Soeur Henriette:

"Sister, the Blessed Virgin made me do something foolish in the closet."

Soeur Henriette looked upstairs and noticed the flames that had already started to tear at the wall. She must set off the alarm and evacuate the patients without delay.

* * *

It was very difficult to fight the fire. The flames, driven by the ceiling fans, spread into each of the wards in the women's wing, and the wind, blowing from the northwest, kept drawing them back to the asylum. They were so huge that even the pumps and inside reservoirs couldn't extinguish them, and all thoughts were on saving the patients. Employees, doctors, and nuns all searched for horrified survivors by the light of the flames that were consuming the ceilings. The smoke made rescue work more and more difficult, to say nothing of the fact that they had to overcome the resistance of the patients, who, drawn as by an irresistible force, kept going back to the inferno.

When the firemen arrived from Montreal, the entire women's wing was in flames. In an attempt to save the side occupied by the men, a barrier was erected of religious medals and holy pictures. But then the wind changed abruptly and flames blasted the rest of the building.

At four o'clock that afternoon, all that remained of the building were some charred sections of walls and smoking ruins. Only the safety vault near the front door had escaped disaster. They had just managed to save the laundry and the service buildings.

There were eighty-six victims, nurses and patients. None on the men's side.

* * *

The survivors were grouped together in the yard around Soeur Thérèse, who was perched on top of a cart. While the firemen were finishing their job and a thousand patients, at the request of the directress, recited prayers in chorus, a cold rain began to fall. It had come very late. . . .

Our Father, who art in Heaven, hallowed be Thy name, Thy kingdom come, Thy will be done, on earth as it is in Heaven.... Really and truly, Lord, You don't do things by halves, do You? Why all these trials at the end of my life? If I've sometimes committed the sin of pride, You're quite entitled to punish me, but those poor innocents had nothing to do with it. Why, Lord, why?

Hail Mary, full of grace, the Lord is with you.... And what about you, Blessed Virgin, could you not intercede? Forgive me, I don't know what I'm saying. For the moment I can keep them busy praying, but what will I do after that? A thousand simpletons to be housed, a thousand! Oh, there are a few farms nearby, but not nearly enough for all my lunatics. . . . How much time will I need to rebuild everything?"

By the end of her rosary, Soeur Thérèse had had time to get her wits back and to organize her plan of action. During the crowd's silent prayer, she repeated the words of Job: "The Lord gave and the Lord hath taken away; blessed be the name of the Lord."

"Blessed be the name of the Lord," echoed the crowd.

"And now we must get organized. Soeur Rose-de-la-Trinité, are you there?"

"Yes, Sister," said the nun, detaching herself from the crowd.

"The stable is still intact, I want the fifty most dangerous patients billeted there. The nights are chilly, but they'll have hay to protect them from the cold. Ask Louis Campagna to keep an eye on them. They won't dare try to escape."

"Very well, Sister."

"Soeur Vipérine. Where is Soeur Vipérine?"

"Here, Sister."

"Soeur Vipérine, you will go and examine the laundry. If the building isn't too badly damaged, you should be able to put a hundred women there. Select the ones you don't think would be able to travel. Soeur Jeanne? Bring the women from the Sainte-Cécile ward and take them to the henhouse. Wilfrid, take out your hens, and be careful not to break the eggs, we'll need them. Soeur Huguette, I want you to set out with two hundred women at once: the Jesuits' country house is two leagues away, you can get there in a few hours."

"Wouldn't it be wise to tell the Jesuits first, Soeur Thérèse?"

"So that they can take off? Certainly not. Go, and if they raise any objections, tell them they'll have me to deal with. The rest of you, stay here, I have to talk with the police chief; I'll be back in a moment. Soeur Jeanne, have them pray while they're waiting."

"Soeur Thérèse?"

"What is it, Soeur Huguette?"

"Should I take the parrot?"

"The parrot? What parrot?"

"The one from the Sainte-Cécile ward, Sister. He was saved, miraculously. Should we take him with us?"

"This is *not* the time to worry about a parrot! But then, since you're going to the Jesuits, perhaps it would make sense. . . ."

To see her jump down from the buggy, then walk in the rain through the mud, hiking up her habit to straddle the debris, no one would have thought that, just moments before, the poor old woman had been confined to her bed, gravely ill.

"Chief," she said to the policeman, "tell me, how many men can be piled into a normal-sized haywagon?"

"About twenty, Sister."

"Very well. And how long would it take to get to Verdun?"

"At least five hours, Sister."

"I see. Will you assign a few of your men to borrow some haywagons from the farms at Longue-Pointe? There are three hundred patients to transport, so I'll need fifteen wagons. If they're here within the hour, they can be in Verdun by nightfall. The Protestant asylum is big enough for another three hundred patients, isn't it?"

"But don't you think it would be wise for my men to stay behind, Sister, to protect you?"

"Protect us from what, Chief? Can anything worse happen?"

"What if the madmen tried to escape?"

"They won't. I'll forbid it."

"Very well, whatever you say."

"Send your men for the haywagons at once; I'll assemble the three hundred patients who will be going with you."

Then she went over to Soeur Pauline, who was weeping bitterly.

"Your tears won't do any good, Sister, please get a grip on yourself. When the Lord sends us trials, we must show ourselves to be worthy. Soeur Pauline, I want you to round up three hundred patients, preferably the most violent: we'll send them to the Protestants. . . . If you can find any who are both violent and incontinent, that would be perfect; we've looked after their lunatics long enough, it's their turn now. And stop your crying, at once!"

As she was making her way to Soeur Madeleine, she met Bernard, who was busy with the other doctors setting up a makeshift infirmary in the barn.

"Soeur Thérèse? You should be in bed! Come with me, we'll make a place for you in the barn."

"Not until I've settled all my patients."

"I won't hear of it! If you stay outside in this rain it will kill you!"

"I'm sixty-three years old, Dr. Dansereau, and nothing has killed me yet. I see no reason why it should happen today. That's enough now, you're wasting your time and mine. To work, Dr. Dansereau. Soeur Madeleine? Come here a moment."

"Yes, Sister."

"Soeur Madeleine, you will set out at once with fifty idiots, take them to the curé at Longue-Pointe, and ask him to place them on his parishioners' farms for me. He can keep a few in his presbytery too, there's plenty of room. And tell Soeur Berthe to do the same with fifty healthy men who can walk to Pointe-aux-Trembles. On your way, tell the chief of police to come and see me: we'll have to borrow some omnibuses from Montreal to transport patients to the mother house of the Sisters of Providence. Tell him we'll need at least fifteen, drawn by four horses: they'll have to climb hills. Where are we? You're still there, Dr. Dansereau? I thought I told you to take care of your patients. Since you're there, you could ask your ... let's say your 'fiancée' ... to take in some patients. She has a barn?"

"Yes, Soeur Thérèse."

"Very well, she can take ten. Let her be useful for once."

"Yes, Soeur Thérèse."

"And don't stand there saying, 'Yes, Soeur Thérèse,' it's most annoying."

"Very well, Soeur Thérèse. I just wanted to tell you how much I admire you."

"You've told me. Now get to work."

By half past seven, a certain number of patients had been billeted in various places, while others were *en route* to temporary shelter. A carriage pulled up at full speed, stopping in front of Soeur Thérèse. A very elegant man stepped out.

"I'm delighted to welcome our member of Parliament to Saint-Jean-de-Dieu."

"Poor Soeur Thérèse, what a disaster! I got here as fast as I could. . . ."

"Unfortunately, it's too late, as you can see."

"What can I do, Sister?"

"Do you have a shovel?"

"A shovel? Why?"

"There were some victims and they have to be buried."

"Actually. . . ."

"I understand. Go back to your Parliament, we'll take care of our dead. If you ever meet the premier, tell him for me that, despite the problems we've encountered, we were able to sort matters out by ourselves. And . . . he needn't worry: the asylum will be rebuilt by the end of the summer. I'll see to it myself."

* * *

By half past nine, the last of the injured had been taken away and Bernard could finally go home; he sat in the front of his buggy, along with Dr. Villeneuve — who now had nowhere to live — and they were able to seat six patients in the back. No one said a word during the journey. Oscar Parent, Tancrède Tarte, Edouard Tremblay, and Jacques Linteau followed the buggy on foot.

When they arrived at Florence's house she was waiting for them on the gallery.

"How many are there?"

"Ten, plus Dr. Villeneuve."

"Dr. Villeneuve can have the guest room, and there's room for another four in the house, the beds are ready.... Some will have to sleep in the barn. But come in, I've made a kettle of soup."

While the patients were getting their strength back, Bernard asked Oscar to help him tidy up the barn. When they came out, they dug a trench near the garden. Then, for over an hour, Oscar brought out glass jars, while Bernard proceeded to bury more than two hundred brains.

16

The next day, when Bernard arrived at the asylum
— or what was left of it — he was hardly surprised
to see Soeur Thérèse, followed by a group of men
who were taking notes.

"Gentlemen, we have twelve hundred lunatics to house. Time is short. Stone is out of the
question for the moment; we'll use wood. I've calcu-
lated that with one million, five hundred thousand
feet of boards, we could build fourteen temporary
two-storey pavilions. I've drawn up some very simple plans, based on buildings I saw in Belgium. You
must follow them to the letter; we'll be able to
salvage the planks when the time comes for permanent constructions. The pavilions will be linked by
corridors, so we can make do with just one kitchen
and one dispensary. For heating, I'll need eight
boilers. The pipes will run along the corridors."

"But Sister, aren't you concerned about fire?"

"That's precisely the reason for separate pavilions. If fire should break out in one of them, it will
be more easily contained, so the whole group of
buildings won't burn. In addition, you will cover the
wooden framework with perfectly sealed metal
sheets. That will arm us not only against fire, but
against cold and damp as well. You will paint those

metal sheets red."

"Why red?"

"To capture the imagination: three months from now, when everything is finished, people will be talking about the red pavilions of the Sisters of Providence. They will be the symbol of our efficiency."

"Three months? We can never do that!"

"Of course you can. You will hire two hundred workers, from among the best in Montreal, who will be assisted by every patient who is in any condition to hold a hammer. It is absolutely essential that the work be completed before autumn. I've already ordered the wood and the nails; I want work to begin tomorrow. You have the whole day to find your workers. If you have questions, come to me. I myself shall be here every morning from seven until eleven, and from three to five in the afternoon; I shall supervise the work. And let me warn you, I shall not tolerate laziness or cursing on the job. Now you must excuse me, I have to speak with Dr. Dansereau."

The electrician, the plumber, the carpenter, and the woodworker looked at one another in turn, flabbergasted, and then — unable to think of any response except a shrug — each went his own way, in search of workers to hire. Every man also had in his possession a very complete list of all the materials and tools necessary for the reconstruction, as well as information about the maximum prices to be paid. Because the buildings had been insured for only two thousand dollars, they would have to be thrifty.

"Good morning, Doctor. How are you today?"

"Not as well as you, most assuredly. . . . Where do you get all that energy?"

"From prayer, Doctor, prayer is still the best source of energy on earth. Do you know any other that can cause us to travel millions of miles in an instant? . . . Quite frankly, Doctor — and this is strictly between us — I confess that I've always enjoyed difficult situations. Everything was running too smoothly in the asylum, it was abnormal. The Lord doesn't like it when life is too simple."

"Was it prayer that cured your influenza, too?"

"Don't trust appearances, Doctor. To tell you the truth . . . I feel very feeble . . . I'm just trying not to let it show. If it were otherwise, do you think I'd have told those gentlemen I'd be here only six hours a day? But that's enough about me. What do you intend to do, Dr. Dansereau?"

"Continue to look after my patients."

"But where will you do that?"

"I don't know. . . ."

"I'm always amazed at your inability to make decisions, Doctor. All those who require medical supervision are now at the Notre-Dame hospital, where they'll be well looked after. The others are in Verdun, or with the Jesuits, or on various farms, or at the Hochelaga barracks. . . . Do you propose to travel back and forth between Verdun and Pointe-aux-Trembles?"

"It strikes me as rather difficult, actually."

"Here's what I suggest: you and Dr. Villeneuve can set yourselves up in the asylum barn.

If there's an accident, you'll be on hand to administer first aid to the workers and patients. You will work mornings, and Dr. Villeneuve afternoons."

"And what will we do during the rest of the day?"

"Dr. Villeneuve will rest, he's certainly earned it. Did you know he told me a year ago that he was going to retire? The reason he's stayed on is to help you—at my request, as it happens. As for you, don't even think about your machines for the moment. You'll be able to use your free time to write your article, as quickly as possible; three months from now, when the temporary buildings are inaugurated, I want it not only finished but published. And then we shall announce to the entire world — especially the government doctors — that we've invented a revolutionary treatment. As soon as the temporary pavilions are ready, we'll begin erecting permanent buildings on the hillside. This time, we won't repeat the same mistakes: we'll build separate pavilions, linked by long corridors which will help us cope with the winter, and with large balconies looking out on the gardens. In the central pavilion we'll set up an even more modern hydrotherapy room: every bath will be equipped with a Williams' coil. Tell me, how much do those things cost?"

"I have no idea. You'd have to ask the electrician."

"It never occurred to you to ask the price?"

"No, Sister."

"There's no doubt about it, you continue to amaze me. And while we're on the subject, Doctor, I'd like to ask a question. I hope you won't consider it indiscreet. . . ."

"Go ahead, Sister."

"Tell me, Doctor, so far you've treated more than fifty patients. Were they really all crazy?"

"More or less. We followed your instructions and started with the children, then mothers, and wage-earners with large families."

"Is that all?"

"Yes, that's all. Who else were you thinking of?"

"Yourself, or Dr. Villeneuve. . . ."

"But we aren't sick, Sister!"

"So? You say you spent almost six months working with a machine that had the ability to put one in a perpetually good mood, and it never occurred to you to use it on yourself?"

"It occurred to me, yes, of course it occurred to me, I'd be lying if I said otherwise. Dr. Villeneuve too; we often talked about it. In the beginning, we said we'd have to treat the patients first; on any scale of unhappiness, we weren't the most urgent cases. A few months later, the question came up again. The machine was effective, and Oscar urged us to use it. A few hours' treatment would probably have been enough, it wouldn't have harmed the patients. . . ."

"And?"

"And nothing. We couldn't bring ourselves to do it."

"Why not?"

"To be honest, I can't explain it. Crazy, isn't it?"

"Not at all, Doctor, not at all. The Lord will

remember."

* * *

By May 14 the rubble of the old asylum had been cleared away and construction had begun: both the workers and the patients, who were helping them to the best of their abilities, were impelled by that sense of duty that makes fatigue so soon forgotten. Soeur Thérèse's plans were such a marvel of simplicity that, once the first building had been erected, the others followed almost by themselves. When they got to the fourteenth pavilion, which was exactly like the other thirteen, the crew was working so smoothly that they had completed everything, including the electricity and plumbing, in just three days.

The good humour that prevailed on the site probably accounted for the absence of any tragic accidents. Dr. Dansereau tended some minor cuts and sprains, but he was more likely to be seen wielding a pen than a scalpel. During his free time he would go for a walk, mulling over ideas, then hurry back and record them in his notebooks. In the afternoon he went back to Florence's for a good meal, in the company of Dr. Villeneuve, Oscar Parent, and nine patients; then he would sit at the kitchen table to write a few pages of his article. He resumed his writing after supper, and continued by lamplight until midnight.

Because of the congestion, life at Florence's house had become harder, but everyone was steadfast in the face of adversity and had managed, in the end, to organize themselves fairly well. Florence was very patient with the sick. Usually, that is, because it's true that now and then her mood changed suddenly, usually on a Friday night. To solve this problem it was agreed that, every week, Oscar and Dr. Villeneuve would take a long walk by the river, along with the patients, and stay out until at least eleven o'clock.

By the end of July the work was sufficiently advanced that small groups of patients were being admitted; the last group, from Verdun, arrived on August 10. The next day, the first mass was celebrated in the new asylum. On August 14 Dr. Dansereau consigned a bulky article to the mail and Soeur Thérèse hired an architect, Hippolyte Bergeron, to help her draw up plans for permanent buildings, for she no longer had the strength to do everything by herself.

* * *

A week later Dr. Georges Clément, chief physician at Notre-Dame hospital, professor in the faculty of medicine at the Université de Montréal, and editor of a scientific journal, *La Revue Médicale du Canada Français*, received a heavy parcel, which he opened at once. The first page of the manuscript read: *Some reflections on the use of magnetism in the treatment of mental illnesses at the Saint-Jean-de-Dieu Asylum.* Merely reading the title antagonized Dr. Clément, who harboured numerous prejudices with respect to magnetism, a pseudo-science that inspired so many charlatans. And Bernard Dansereau? He turned the name over in his mind, but it meant nothing to him. As for his rank — "physician" —

that was rather brief. Why, the author wasn't even an alienist! If he made no reference to where he had done his studies, it must mean he hadn't graduated from a European university. The dedication, "To Soeur Thérèse-de-Jésus, Superior of the Saint-Jean-de-Dieu Asylum, to asylum physician Dr. Villeneuve, guard Oscar Parent, Nurse Girard, and Madame Florence Martineau", was highly irritating too. Who had ever heard of cluttering a scientific article with a dedication? And how dare anyone dedicate an article on mental illness to a nun who had spent her life battling the control of asylums by doctors, thereby stalling the inevitable march of progress!

After leafing through the first pages, he was astonished to see that the author had not even taken the trouble to type his paper or to accompany it with any graphics or mathematical formulae. . . . He leafed through the remaining pages, lingering briefly on the crude drawing of a barrel in which had been placed an individual fitted out with a ridiculous helmet . . . then quickly went to the end of the book. Three hundred and thirteen pages! No doubt about it: he had a crank on his hands. He immediately called his secretary.

"Please send the following letter: Université de Montréal, August 20, 1890. Dear Dr. Dansereau, On behalf of *La Revue Médicale du Canada Français*, I acknowledge receipt of your voluminous and no doubt highly interesting contribution to medical science. . . . Unfortunately, however, I regret to inform you that our Fall 1890 issue is already at the printer's and that the one for Spring 1891 is almost complete. . . . Given the extent of your paper, we may perhaps be able to publish it in instalments beginning in the fall of 1891, assuming, of course, that it is accepted by our editorial board. Once the board has met, we shall communicate our decision to you as quickly as possible. . . .' End it with the usual best wishes and so forth, and in the place for the signature give him the full list of my titles: M.D., University of Glasgow, Editor, *La Revue Médicale du Canada Français*, Professor in the faculty of medicine, Université de Montréal, Physician-in-Chief, Hôpital Notre-Dame, Treasurer of the Order of Physicians of the Province of Quebec, and Municipal Councillor."

"Will that be all, Doctor?"

"Yes. . . . By the way, do you think they have the telephone at Longue-Pointe?"

"It's possible, yes."

"If you get a call from this Dr. Dansereau, tell him I'm in conference, or, no, that I'm away. Far, far away. Take this manuscript with you and file it wherever you think appropriate. Perhaps he'll come to pick it up."

* * *

Bernard received the letter five days later and considered it quite satisfactory. Now that his article was in the proper hands, he could go about his business. Soeur Thérèse was not so enthusiastic: the fall of 1891 was a long time away. . . .

On November 1, still without a decision, Bernard telephoned Dr. Clément's office. The other man was away, unfortunately, but he would communicate with Dr. Dansereau upon his return. . . . Three months later, there was still no sign of the professor. Every time Bernard called, the secretary said that her employer was out of town or in conference ... that there was no need for concern ... such delays were normal ... someone would communicate with him as soon as his article had been read.

At the beginning of May, even though he had stepped up the number of calls and letters, his manuscript was returned to him. After lengthy discussions, said the brief note from Dr. Clément enclosed with the parcel, the editorial board had concluded that his article was, unfortunately, much too long for their journal, and they recommended that he address himself to a publisher instead, suggesting the names of several houses that might be interested in such a work.

Not in the least discouraged, but having learned a lesson, Bernard spent the summer recopying his manuscript. As soon as he had finished a copy, he would mail it and commence another.

Bernard was very fond of writing by candlelight, at night, when the rest of the household was asleep. Often he would simply copy out a few chapters word for word, but at other times, stimulated by brandy, he would allow himself to describe the improvements he would make to his machine, to speculate on the role of certain groups of cells, or to write long panegyrics to scientific progress. Carried away by his own prose, he would see the words race from his pen, see veritable orgies of superlatives, see sentences plunge into the twists and turns of endless subordinate clauses, finally taking flight in an irresistible crescendo that carried him along from comma to comma and up to the final exclamation point. Sometimes, at the end of an especially lyrical passage, he was so filled with emotion that he had to stop and dry his eyes. Even though his back ached, his vision blurred, and the rough paper impeded the momentum of his pen, he persisted, happy to have found the ideal laboratory at last.

When midnight struck, he always told himself that it was time to stop work and go to bed . . . as soon as he had finished his chapter. At two a.m. he would still be at his desk, jotting down ideas for future developments. At three he heard the footsteps of Florence, who, still half-asleep, finally persuaded him to go to bed. After he had filed his papers, somewhat reluctantly, he barely had the strength to climb the stairs; as soon as he lay down he sank into a sleep so deep that it was undisturbed by dreams.

* * *

Mornings, he arrived at the asylum early to look after Soeur Thérèse. Alas, there was no longer much he could do, and most often he simply injected into her veins — which were now difficult to find, she was so thin — a few millilitres of laudanum to alleviate her suffering.

"What's in that injection, Doctor? Not opium, I hope."

"Of course not, Soeur Thérèse, just a sedative."

"That's good. I want to have my wits about me when I meet Saint Peter, because I intend to negotiate with him. Once, in a theatre in Paris, I was so badly seated I could only see half the orchestra during the secular concert I was attending. Can you imagine me spending all eternity seeing only half of God?"

"I'm sure you'll be given an excellent seat, Soeur Thérèse."

"You're very kind, Doctor. Do you think I'll meet Saint Joseph?"

"I'm sure of it, Soeur Thérèse."

"I'm very anxious to know what he thinks of my plans. And if I see the Holy Ghost, I shall tell Him about you, Doctor. Have you had any word about your articles?"

"Everything's going very well. I had an interesting offer from a Paris publisher only yesterday. The book should be coming out this fall."

"Will it be translated into other languages?"

"Of course, of course. Into German, English, Spanish. . . ."

"You *are* telling me the truth, aren't you?"

"Nothing but the truth, Soeur Thérèse."

Every morning, they took up the same conversation. Had she forgotten? Was she taken in by his lies? Was she trying to catch him out? He never knew.

One day in November, he told her proudly that the book would be appearing very shortly, and that he would bring it to her so she could touch it. Did she even hear him? For two weeks now she hadn't spoken, and no one knew whether she could still hear. She had long ago been given the last rites, and the nuns watched over her day and night, praying for her soul. Bernard gave her one last injection of laudanum. She did not feel the needle. Her breathing, barely perceptible, now became irregular.

Slowly she sank into dreams: the new permanent building, then the red pavilions of which she had been so proud reappeared in her memory. . . . She saw a fire . . . a celebration in her honour . . . ocean waves . . . a conference in Paris . . . the Notre-Dame basilica where she had stopped for a brief prayer. . . . After that, quick visits to Italy, Belgium, England, Scotland . . . and there was the old asylum, where she stopped in at the rooms to say goodbye to the nuns and the patients. . . . Ah! the ferns and the pianos. . . . Room by room, stone by stone, the building strangely fell away until nothing remained except a fallow field, a vast lot of one hundred and sixty-six *arpents*, purchased in 1868 for three thousand dollars. . . . Soeur Thérèse's heart began to slow down markedly. . . . A carriage was taking her to Valparaiso . . . then a boat to Oregon, where another carriage took her to Vermont, and to the hospital at Hochelaga where she had cared for Irish typhoid victims.

Then she felt her wedding band being removed: was it a dream? reality? What she felt next was very painful. She was no longer called Soeur Thérèse, but Cléophée Têtu, daughter of Jean-François Têtu, a Saint-Hyacinthe notary . . . long winter months in the convent, summers rocking on the big verandah. . . . Little Cléophée walks along a pretty flower-lined road where there are no stones or flies, she crosses meadows, fields of oats . . . then suddenly everything is blurred. All that remain are some childhood odours, vague sensations, then a great and very gentle warmth.... Soon her memories will cease to unfurl and Soeur Thérèse will no longer be of this world.

She is still breathing slowly, very slowly, her nostrils barely quivering, but the brain is extinguished now, it no longer has the strength to command the lungs, which are expelling their last breath of air. Her heart still beats, irregularly. The old pump still puts up a fight, out of habit, but now it sends the brain only black blood, without oxygen. One by one, the brain cells die. Next will come the principal organs, cell by cell....

Soeur Thérèse died on November 22, 1891, at an hour of which no one was certain. In conformity with her last wishes, no autopsy was carried out. Had he been asked to perform it, Bernard would certainly have refused. Still, in the weeks that followed he had trouble chasing from his mind what he might have discovered: a Soeur Thérèse who was younger and even more delicate than Viviane . . . inside, an inextricable network of nerves as solid as wire, which would have broken the scissors . . . under the nerves, neat and tidy little organs, embedded in cases that would open cleanly ... and once the vessels had been removed, a little white skeleton... from which relics could have been made that would have produced energy for centuries and centuries.. .. If only there had been a way to slip a long needle into her skull and remove a few cells and, once they had regenerated, inject them into the brains of neurasthenic patients....

* * *

A few days after Soeur Thérèse's funeral, Bernard was summoned to the office of Soeur Madeleine-du-Sacré-Coeur, who had been named superior of the asylum. She was a strong, decisive woman with a determined jaw and a broad forehead. As soon as he walked into what had been Soeur Thérèse's office, he was struck by the changes she had made. In just a few days she had taken away half the plants, and on the wall she had hung an enormous portrait of Pope Leo XIII. As he took his seat across from the new directress, Bernard could not help seeing her as a usurper.

"God bless you, Dr. Dansereau. Soeur Thérèse spoke very highly of you, and I hope you'll be staying with us for a long time."

"I hope so too, Sister."

"That's the spirit. I've asked you here this morning first of all to tell you that certain things are going to change in the asylum. We owe a great deal to Soeur Thérèse and we shall always revere her memory. However, we have to recognize that times change and that we must adapt to modern life. We stand on the brink of the twentieth century, Doctor. Soeur Thérèse had very great qualities, she was a most talented administrator, but, for reasons I'm unaware of, she seemed to be excessively suspicious of the medical profession, particularly of government-appointed physicians. Dr. Paquette, to whom I spoke just this morning, acknowledges that he suffered considerably because of that almost pathological mistrust. I reassured him. Henceforth, I intend to see to the administration of the asylum, and, as far as treatments are concerned, I shall give the doctors *carte blanche*. Dr. Paquette will have full powers and you, Dr. Dansereau, will be able to work in peace."

"I thank you, Soeur Madeleine, but I must also point out that Soeur Thérèse never prevented me from working: far from it. Did she ever talk to you about the . . . about the asylum trees, or about the ferns?"

"I don't understand what you mean. Does it have anything to do with your experiments? Dr. Paquette has been asking a lot of questions about them, I know he doesn't care for these mysteries. . . . What are these experiments, Doctor?"

"Nothing terribly remarkable: Soeur Thérèse and I shared a great interest in botany, we often used to discuss it. As for the experiments, they were simply some harmless grafts. It was nothing to make a fuss about, and I must say I don't understand why Dr. Paquette is worried. There must be some misunderstanding."

"Very likely. You should discuss it with him as soon as possible. The poor man is terribly worried."

"I'll do that without fail."

"Excellent. While we're on the subject, Dr. Dansereau, had Soeur Thérèse mentioned the new hydrotherapy rooms?"

"Vaguely, yes."

"In that case, perhaps you'll be able to help me with a problem. When Dr. Paquette and I were looking at the plans, we realized that every bathtub was fitted out with a peculiar electrical device. Dr.

Paquette was as surprised as I, and even rather angry because no one had asked his opinion. Have you any idea what it's about, Doctor?"

"No, I can't imagine. A system for heating the water, perhaps?"

"Such a system already exists, there would be no need for another. . . . Very well, since no one seems to know what it is, I shall see that the plans are modified. I'm sad to say this, but during her final days Soeur Thérèse no longer had all her wits about her. Very well, Dr. Dansereau, you may go back to your work."

17

When she was twelve years old, Florence thought there were only three kinds of women in the world: children, nuns, and old ladies. Indeed, marriage seemed to have the peculiar quality of instantly deforming the bodies of young girls. After several pregnancies, faces were furrowed with wrinkles, the skin on the arms became flaccid, the elbows rough and dark, the breasts huge and heavy, the belly covered with stretch marks. Long before entering their fifties, mothers had to wear those long dark dresses that were the only style that seemed to suit them. When Florence married at sixteen, she was certain the same fate awaited her. But her childhood had not been a particularly happy one, so the prospect of such changes did not frighten her: on the contrary, while married women aged in one fell swoop, on the other hand they seemed at the same time to achieve an immutable state wherein age ceased to matter — and that struck her as only fair.

　　After some years of marriage she'd had to revise her notions. While her mind had travelled rapidly from naivety to disenchantment, her body, in contrast, had been very slow to age. Oh, she put on a few pounds, to the delight of her husband, but she still felt young, almost eternal. Pleasantly surprised, she didn't think about it again until her thirtieth birthday, when she discovered that crows' feet had snuck to the corners of her eyes, and that silvery threads were shining in her hair here and there. As she had much better things to do than feel sorry for herself, she merely shrugged her shoulders and moved on to something else.

It was only when her husband died that the years began to show. As the Lord had acted like a particularly considerate thief, the shock of his death had not been too harsh; none the less she was now a *widow*, a word that to Florence, whatever her age and despite the excellent condition of her arteries, was synonymous with being elderly. When she came home from the cemetery she took a long look at herself in the mirror. What the absence of pregnancies had safeguarded until now was shattered: she had just realized that half of her existence was irremediably behind her.

When Bernard had come into her life, she had harboured no illusions. It was neither a second childhood nor a breath of springtime nor a new lease on life. In the early days of their union, she had to admit that she felt herself rejuvenated. It was true that Bernard talked a lot, unlike other men. He paid her compliments, took an interest in her activities, asked her opinion about this and that, and ultimately her own life seemed more interesting to her. But it didn't last long: later, all he talked about was his boring experiments. If you could even call it "talking".... In fact, was he not simply thinking out loud? He had very quickly become a normal man again, and she'd had to learn to be content with a remote presence. The transition had come about quite naturally, however, and it was not all that unpleasant. Her companion's long absences enabled Florence to anticipate his return, which was the best way for her to while away her tedium, and to give meaning to the countless trivial details of her life. Constantly working, at the asylum by day and in his laboratory by night, Bernard was just the man for a woman who liked to wait. At least until the death of Soeur Thérèse, an event that would turn everything upside down.

Nine months had elapsed since she had passed on to the next world, yet it seemed as if her soul had not yet completed its journey to Heaven, for her shadow still hovered over the village of Longue-Pointe.

On the day of Soeur Thérèse's funeral, Florence was surprised that Bernard did not appear particularly upset. During the ceremony she kept watching him from the corner of her eye: although the tributes had been moving and the Mass went on for ever, he held on without flinching, even displaying exemplary dignity as he responded to the numerous litanies in his fine deep voice and delivered a funeral oration of touching sobriety to the packed church. From now on, thought Florence as she looked at him, they would be alone, truly alone. But was that really what she wanted? Rather than seeing Soeur Thérèse as a rival, shouldn't she have been grateful to her for inspiring her fiancé with a little energy, for steering him onto the path of science? Hadn't she, a woman who had never married, instinctively known the proper way to treat a husband? How would he spend his days now that she was gone? Wasn't Florence ashamed of being jealous of a nun for all those years? Contrary to all expectations, it was Florence who shed a few tears.

While Bernard had been able to contain his emotions during the funeral ceremony, the death of Soeur Thérèse would be hard on him in the months to come. Life, which had always struck him as flying past at top speed, suddenly seemed desperately slow. In the morning he ate his breakfast in silence, then went lethargically to work. Now, when he walked past the window, Florence heard him talk to his horse only to grumble; in the evening, as soon as he had set foot in the house, he would pour himself a big brandy, which he drank in silence as he watched the river flow. If he did open his mouth it was invariably to talk about some illness of his: with his heart, it was terribly tiring to climb the asylum stairs. . . . When the mailman brought yet another letter containing a refusal to publish his research, it was even worse: feeling close to death because of his heart, he had to drink several brandies right away to stimulate it.

Although waiting for a man was not unpleasant for Florence, such waiting must not go on for ever. It could last for a day, that was reasonable, but if she had to spend her evenings too hoping he would finally shake off his gloom, it was hardly worth the trouble. She had to do something.

As an expert housekeeper she knew the beneficial effect of a simple spring-cleaning on the mood of a home's inhabitants. When the lunatics who had been billeted with her for a whole summer had gone back to the asylum, she had rearranged her house from top to bottom. With Dr. Villeneuve now occupying the big upstairs bedroom and Oscar settled on the main floor in the little room behind the kitchen — surrounded by people he loved — perhaps Bernard would feel like resuming his experiments. But increasing the number of extinguished lives is no way to build a new one. Dr. Villeneuve, too, had aged considerably since the death of Soeur Thérèse, and he was no longer the charming companion he had been during the months when Saint-Jean-de-Dieu was being rebuilt. Now that he was a pensioner he spent all day reading newspapers, playing solitaire, and complaining about the ravages of time. As for Oscar, his presence hadn't settled anything. He enjoyed his work at the asylum and performed small tasks in the house, but aside from that he was silent. He had tried more than once to raise the two doctors' morale, but as his attempts were fruitless, he discreetly withdrew. He had been quick to realize that there are times when the cheerfulness of others is intolerable.

Florence, after tolerating this situation all summer, now decided to put an end to it. "When I think about it," she told herself, "before Soeur Thérèse died, Bernard spent half his nights writing, then he'd get up the next day in an excellent mood; now he sleeps all night and he's always complaining that he's tired. . . . And Dr. Villeneuve can't read two lines in his newspaper before he starts muttering about his bad eyesight; but not all that long ago he could read pages and pages of treatises on magnetism. . . . No, definitely, idleness is no good for men."

August would soon be over. Then would come the rains, the dark days, the month of the dead, endless winter. She must act as quickly as possible before they got bogged down in their bad mood. Did her doctors need something to keep them busy? Nothing simpler: a kettle, a typewriter, and a talk with Oscar, that was all she required. Old age may be a shipwreck, but no one's obliged to spend all day in the hold, watching the water seep in between the planks.

* * *

Florence had brought Oscar onto the bank of the river, where she thought she could find a quantity of those little pieces of good dry wood that come from the crates that sometimes drop from boats. They were so useful for starting fires. . . .

"Tell me honestly, Oscar, did that machine of yours really work?"

"Of course it worked! If you'd known me before my treatment you wouldn't have any doubts!"

"Were you crazy before?"

"Mostly, I was unhappy. Maybe a little crazy too, but no more than everybody else."

"And now?"

"Now I'm sometimes unhappy for other people, but not for myself."

"Splendid, we're going to get along well. How many patients did you and Bernard and Dr. Villeneuve treat before the fire?"

"Fifty, sixty . . . I don't know."

"And was it successful?"

"It didn't cure their craziness, but at least it

put them in a good mood."

"Why haven't you started again? What's stopping you?"

"It's impossible, at least while Dr. Paquette's the superintendent. You should see how he behaves in the asylum! Ever since Soeur Thérèse passed away, he's always after Dr. Dansereau about something. One day after work we tried to get into the new hydrotherapy room, just to take a look. When Dr. Paquette found out he forbade us to go back. He's in charge now, and he's got Soeur Madeleine eating out of his hand. In Soeur Thérèse's time. . . ."

"But it wasn't Soeur Thérèse who put the patients in the water. Actually, did you need anything besides a bath?"

"Linden blossoms, petroleum jelly, and a helmet."

"What kind of helmet?"

"A leather one. There were magnets inside it, and there was an electric machine."

"Just between us, Oscar, do you think Bernard would go back to his experiments if we got him the equipment he needs?"

"I don't think so."

"Why not? You're living proof that it works, aren't you?"

"I tell him that till I'm blue in the face, but he always says that, in the eyes of science, effectiveness is no proof."

"What does that mean?"

"I don't know, I'm just repeating what he says."

"It's the stupidest thing I've ever heard. And

what if science were to say he's right?"

"He'd go back to his experiments, I know that."

Everything was turning out as she had hoped. Oscar hadn't gathered any kindling for some time. He was looking into the distance, at the river. . . . There was a light in his eyes. . . .

"In that case, Oscar, would you agree to work with him?"

"Nothing would make me happier, but I don't see how you could make it happen."

"Promise not to breathe a word to Bernard and I guarantee he'll be back at his experiments by next week. I'm going to need you. Do you promise?"

"Of course. What do I have to do?"

"First, we must find someone who knows how to type."

"I could ask Soeur Sabithe. She's been working in the admissions office since Soeur Madeleine took over. Perhaps she'd let us use her machine."

When they went back to the house, neither Oscar nor Florence had remembered to bring any wood. Bernard was surprised but said nothing. He just stuck his nose back in his newspaper, letting himself be swept away by a journalist's enthusiastic description — he must be very young! — of the working of the internal combustion engine, and by his attempt to convince readers that carriages would soon be equipped with such engines. Bernard racked his brain in vain, but he didn't see how the invention represented any real progress: who would be so crazy as to talk to an engine?

* * *

Governing means planning in advance. Some months before the death of Soeur Thérèse, Dr. Paquette, taking his cue from his stormy relations with the superior, had set to win over Soeur Madeleine. To do this he had employed a two-step strategy which had often proven beneficial in other circumstances. Starting from the principle that women — for, after all, Soeur Madeleine was *also* a woman — are never interested in mediocre men, it was important first to stir up the nun's admiration. As she had always shown the greatest respect for any form of authority, he had discreetly played his twofold role: that of physician and that of first medical superintendent. It seemed obvious that she would be impressed by a man who personified science and was also an emissary of the civilian authority; that was the indispensable basis on which he would establish a deeper relationship when the time was right.

The second step consisted of capitalizing on another principle, one whereby women's sense of economy renders them intolerant of waste: they would move heaven and earth to remedy what they considered to be a waste of talent. Little by little, then, without ever pushing too hard, he let fall a few remarks that were intended to arouse an outburst of commiseration from the new directress. Soeur Thérèse had always resented his making himself into the government's spokesman, and he could never bring her round to his point of view. Why must it be that, owing to her incomprehension, he was the victim of so much injustice? For two years he had been allotted neither a desk for filing his papers nor the key to the dispensary. When Dr. Howard resigned he had come very close to following suit, but he had stayed on, convinced that in the end Soeur Thérèse would realize that he was devoted to her. In spite of everything, she remained wary of him. Only Dr. Dansereau — undoubtedly an excellent physician, although he had never studied in Paris — was entitled to her favours. He had been allowed to carry out those mysterious experiments of his for a long time, without ever breathing a word to the alienists, even though they would have asked for nothing more than to be of help to him. . . .

Dr. Paquette's tactic had been wonderfully effective. Touched by his misfortunes, and moved by a sort of affectionate pity, Soeur Madeleine promised him her unconditional support: henceforth he alone would be responsible for all medical matters. If he required anything at all, he need only ask for it. Triumphantly, he drew up a long list of regulations aimed at giving the alienists a monopoly on patient care. He had not, however, been able to obtain from her even the slightest pertinent information about Dr. Dansereau's research: Soeur Madeleine knew nothing about it, but she would find out.

Somewhat disappointed, but buoyed by her unconditional support, he continued making inquiries of the nuns. As they were no better informed than their superior, he found himself time and again on the wrong track. By questioning patients, though, he eventually learned that Dr. Dansereau had given several of them lengthy baths. How had he accomplished that? He never used the hydrotherapy room. . . . Would Soeur Thérèse have allowed him to equip a secret room in the old asylum? What kind of treatment was it that had put all the patients in a state of bliss verging on idiocy? And how the devil had the man been able to effect such a radical change in their behaviour?

By following all the signs, he ultimately learned that Nurse Girard had been privy to the experiments. Then he tried to win her over, but the pity gambit had been used on the nurse so often that she could sniff it coming a mile away. However, she resisted the urge to send him packing, and pretended to play along. With Dr. Dansereau's consent, she even confessed to taking part in the experiments, but said she was sworn to secrecy. There was no question of going back on her word. Never before had she been given so much attention by a doctor. Dr. Paquette began by offering her extra days off and a salary increase; then he promised to help her become directress of the nursing school; he offered her the moon . . . and a good part of the solar system. Distractions at the asylum being few, Nurse Girard did not intend to miss such an opportunity for some fun; she wouldn't discourage him from humiliating himself by pleading with her on bended knee, and it was such sweet revenge to watch him languishing for weeks.

But all good things must end, and Nurse Girard, fearing that Dr. Paquette might give up, finally rewarded him with his lump of sugar. Feigning deep moral distress, she confessed that she felt deeply divided: although she couldn't break her promise, neither could she allow the medical superintendent to remain ignorant of such important research. . . . To extricate herself from this dilemma, she had decided to help Dr. Paquette find the answer himself by pointing him in a promising direction: if he went to see Wilfrid in the henhouse, perhaps. . . .

No sooner had she spoken the last words than Dr. Paquette, too worked up even to think about changing to the proper clothes, rushed over to the henhouse. When the door opened he was soaked with rain and his brand-new spats were spattered with mud.

"Dr. Paquette, I presume?"

"Himself. You've been expecting me?"

"Yes. Well actually, no. . . . If you're here to complain about the taste of my chickens, I have to tell you that I'm not responsible for how they're cooked."

"I haven't come here to complain, I want information. May I come in?"

"Out of the question! My hens are asleep. When the sky is overcast they think it's night. In fact, I'd like you to speak quietly, they're light sleepers. What can I do for you?"

"It's been suggested that you could enlighten me about Dr. Dansereau's experiments."

"You want the recipe for happiness?"

"Precisely. Do you have it?"

"Of course I do, I invented it."

"Could you give it to me? I'm the medical superintendent, you see. . . ."

"I'll give it to you anyway. Have you got a pencil?"

"Yes, but I don't have any paper, and even if

I did, it would be all wet. . . . Are you sure I can't come in? It's pouring. . . ."

"Only if you promise not to make any noise."

"I promise."

Dr. Paquette sat at one corner of the table while Wilfrid dictated to him. An hour later, Dr. Paquette had covered the four large sheets of tissue paper that Wilfrid had been kind enough to give him. Later that evening, he spent hours transcribing the recipe onto clean paper: if Wilfrid was to be believed, he would have to decorticate the brains of five hundred hens fed exclusively on the seeds of Indian hemp, and then extract the cells — which would resemble the wings of the Archangel Gabriel — macerate them in brandy, dry them in the sun for six months, and finally reduce them to a fine powder which was to be administered to patients in the form of a beverage composed of one part powder to ten parts water dipped from a stream on Easter morning.

As well as a nasty cold that it took a long time to shake off, Dr. Paquette came away from this day with the very unpleasant sensation that someone had been playing games with him.

* * *

Back at the house, Bernard poured himself a large brandy and glanced abstractedly at the letter that had been left on the kitchen counter. Florence peeled potatoes while Oscar swept the floor; both had their eyes riveted on him. Bernard turned the envelope over and over, a fleeting ray of hope in his eyes, then set it on the counter with a shrug, took a few steps towards his favourite armchair, stopped, seemed to hesitate for a moment, then went back and picked up the letter again. Comfortably ensconced in his chair, he sipped his brandy and lit a cigar before he finally slit the envelope. He slowly unfolded the thin sheet of paper, read a few lines, then dropped the paper on the table beside the ashtray.

"Anything new in the papers, Dr. Villeneuve?"

"Nothing out of the ordinary. There's a lot of talk about the Manitoba school question. . . ."

Florence and Oscar looked at one another, incredulous. She let the two doctors talk for a moment, and while she was setting the table, asked:

"What's new at the hospital, Bernard?"

"Not a thing. A few sprains, and as usual all those ears to clean out."

"And the . . . the letter?"

"What letter?"

"The one you just finished reading. From France?"

"Yes, another publisher."

"And what does he say?"

"I don't know, I haven't read it."

"I had the impression that you'd given it a good look."

"I just skimmed it. I'm getting to know them by heart: 'Dear Dr. Dansereau, We have read your remarkable manuscript with great interest, and we are very pleased to . . .'"

Bernard suddenly dropped his cigar and his glass, picked up the letter, and reread it four times, wide-eyed. Oscar put away his broom, Florence stopped setting out the plates, and Dr. Villeneuve, intrigued by the sudden silence, laid down his newspaper.

"Good news?"

"Yes. A Paris publisher has agreed to bring out my book, though they want me to cut it down considerably. They say the manuscript should be no longer than three hundred pages. . . ."

"What will you do?"

"I'll think it over. . . . What's for supper, Florence? I'm ravenous."

It had been a very long time since Bernard had shown any interest in what was on the menu, or eaten with such gusto. After their meal, Oscar helped Florence with the dishes while the two doctors spent a long time at the table, writing dozens of pages. It was well past midnight when Bernard went to sleep that night. As he was getting into bed, he asked Florence how complicated it would be to have electricity put in the stable.

* * *

Florence went to Soeur Madeleine's office the next morning.

"Sister, I'd like to make a proposal. I live in Longue-Pointe, about a mile from the asylum. When there was a fire two years ago, I took in a dozen patients. Now I was wondering if it might be useful if I were to take in a few more. Some of them are destitute when they leave the asylum; perhaps I could give them a place to stay until they get work or their families pick them up. . . ."

"That's an excellent idea, but I'm afraid I

couldn't offer you any compensation. The government. . . ."

"I wouldn't ask for a thing, Sister."

"Nothing? Forgive my surprise, but I'm not used to such selflessness. Why are you making this offer, madame?"

"Why? Because . . . I have a very big house, you see, and my charitable duties. . . . I was a great admirer of Soeur Thérèse. . . ."

To the great relief of Florence, who had not anticipated the question and didn't know what else to say, Soeur Madeleine stood up and brought the conversation to an end.

"Very well. When would you be ready to begin?"

"Next week, Sister."

"I'm very grateful to you, madame, and I pray that our Lord will give you the reward you deserve."

"You're entirely welcome, Sister."

Florence went home, pleased at the successful outcome of her plan. Still, she was a little concerned: would she find any publishing company that would agree to print just one copy of a book? How much would it cost? It had been easy enough to unseal the publisher's envelope and slip in the letter that Oscar had brought her, but how would she arrange to have the book mailed from Paris?

As she was going to bed that night, she told herself that Bernard, busy setting up his electrical machine in the barn and giving baths to the patients, wouldn't have much time to devote to his manuscript. It would probably take months . . . and she'd have plenty of time ... she must work on problems one by one. For now, he was back in harness: it was all that mattered.

Afterwards, she thought again about her conversation with Soeur Madeleine and imagined the superior praying for her, asking the Lord to reward her for her charitable act.... She felt ashamed: how would the Lord react to unmerited prayers?

18

Dr. Clément was a man of power. He had practised so that for every circumstance, he could adopt an attitude in keeping with his high opinion of himself. When he took a stroll in the company of his wife or some friends, it sometimes happened that he, like the rest of us, would allow his mind to gently wander; worried at being caught in the act of idleness, he would stop abruptly, knitting his brow at regular intervals as though engaged in intense reflection. The effect was magical: his friends and family were sure that his mind was in a perpetual ferment.

He behaved in the same way with his colleagues, and even more with his subordinates. If his secretary unexpectedly entered his office at the university, he was always busy reading, or writing in his notebooks. It would never have occurred to her that her employer's gaze was lost somewhere between two lines, or that he was only doodling in the margin. To dictate routine letters, he would stand at the window, hands behind his back, staring into the distance: perhaps he was uttering banalities ... but it didn't prevent his mind from being busy with some higher task.

One January morning when the secretary brought in his mail, however, she did catch him with his feet on the desk, hands behind his neck, and staring at the ceiling with a satisfied smile on his lips. This was so unusual that she thought he was sick, and so hesitated before she placed some unsealed letters in front of him.

"Your mail, Doctor."

"I beg your pardon?"

"Your mail.... Shall I leave it on your desk?"

"Do that, I'll look at it as soon as I have time. If anyone asks for me, tell them I'm busy."

"Very well, Doctor."

Dr. Clément had every reason to be contented with his lot. Re-elected with a strong majority to the position of municipal councillor, he had attracted the attention of some Liberal Party organizers, who saw him as a choice candidate for the upcoming elections. On the eve of the New Year, 1892, he had been invited to a reception given in Saint-Lin by Wilfrid Laurier. There he had had a lengthy conversation with the opposition leader, and had been won over as much by his elegant manners as by his eloquence: Laurier's reputation as a great orator was not exaggerated. He had talked with Dr. Clément about the concord he wanted to establish between Canada's two founding races, and of his vision of the entire country turned towards material and moral progress. Dr. Clément had delightedly drunk in these words of wisdom, which were tinged with a healthy liberalism, then had admitted to Laurier that he too felt he was a liberal at heart — not in the French manner, which was far too destructive and pagan, but in the British style: he espoused a liberalism wherein change was marked by justice and moderation. Laurier had valued these remarks, and confided that he needed men of his moral fibre on his team; he was even considering offering him a Cabinet position.

Dr. Clément glanced at the mail on his desk, letting his imagination roam for another few moments: he pictured himself in Ottawa, delivering a fiery speech to Parliament; then on a ship to London, where he had been sent on an important diplomatic mission. When he had dreamed his fill, he heaved a long sigh and finally turned his attention to his letters.

After he had filed some of them and wadded the others into balls, he happened upon a short, ten-page article with the strange title: "Magnets and Moods". The alliteration delighted him and he read the covering letter with great interest. The author, one Bernard Dansereau, was submitting a brief résumé of his research with a view to publishing it in *La Revue Médicale du Canada Français* so that his compatriots could learn about his theories before they were published in France.

Bernard Dansereau? The name was vaguely familiar, but he gave it no further thought; if a French publisher had agreed to publish him, it was, beyond any doubt, an article that deserved to appear in his journal. He summoned his secretary and asked her, first, to set aside the necessary pages for the article in the Spring issue, then to try as quickly as possible to reach Dr. Dansereau, who lived in Longue-Pointe, and notify him of the decision.

A few days later, after his lectures at the university, Dr. Clément went to the Club Saint-

Denis to have a drink with some friends: Dr. Gingras, a physician at the Notre-Dame hospital, Dr. Forest, who practised at the Hôtel-Dieu, and Maître Hébert, who was a Crown attorney. As the men were talking medicine, the conversation quite naturally turned to the letter Dr. Clément had recently received.

"Dansereau? The name reminds me of something," said Dr. Gingras. "It was a long time ago, during my university days. . . . Yes, now it's come back: we were classmates, I remember now, I performed my first autopsy with him. Yes, it's something I'll never forget! You all know what the procedure was before the Anatomy Act was voted in. . . . An odd type, something of an idealist, and very interested in the functioning of the brain. But I didn't know he was still doing research, I thought he had a quiet practice in Hochelaga. What does he have to say?"

"From what I can understand, he's been using magnets that, when they're positioned on the skulls of certain lunatics, have the capacity of modifying their moods. He reports a number of experiments that sound conclusive, but I confess I have my doubts: the theoretical base seems very weak. . . . Quite frankly, I suspect the whole thing is a fraud. You remember Lord Durham's experiments on magnetism. . . . I hope it wasn't a mistake to accept his article for publication before I read it."

"But didn't you say he's going to be published in France?"

"Yes, and by a very well-known publisher."

"In that case, there can be no doubt: it must be an important discovery. You were quite right to accept it, I'd have done the same in your place. Now then, how did you and Laurier get along?"

Hébert, the lawyer, who had been listening abstractedly to the conversation, became animated, and the four men said nothing more about medicine all evening.

Memory is unpredictable, and it sometimes happens in spite of ourselves that a conversation not even intended for us will leave its mark. Maître Hébert enjoyed excellent health and so was only remotely interested in medicine. But as the number of educated people was rather limited at the time, he often found himself associating with doctors. Perhaps that explained why his brain was accustomed to recording fragments of medical conversations.

A few weeks after the evening with his friends at the Club Saint-Denis, Maître Hébert was invited to a reception at city hall. As he strolled from group to group, in the hope of finding either an interesting political contact or a pretty woman, he happened to find himself in the presence of Dr. Paquette and a charming companion. Joining their conversation, he learned that Dr. Paquette was an alienist. The lawyer then attempted to make himself interesting by asking the doctor if he knew about the research being done by a Longue-Pointe physician: he had heard that a way had been found to influence the moods of lunatics. . . . Maître Hébert hadn't expected that his innocent remark, which he had proffered only to feed what had been a rather desultory conversation, would provoke such a strong reaction.

"Maître Hébert, your timing couldn't have been better," said Dr. Paquette, drawing the other man aside. "I am the medical director of the asylum at Saint-Jean-de-Dieu, and I'm most interested in anything that has to do with moods. You were saying you'd heard about some research?"

"Vaguely, yes, very vaguely. . . . If you're hoping for a scientific presentation, I'm afraid you'll be disappointed. I'm a lawyer, you see, and. . . ."

"No one's perfect. Where did you hear about this research?"

"The Club Saint-Denis, I believe. Some doctor friends made a brief allusion to the matter. If I remember correctly, it was Dr. Clément who mentioned receiving an article for his journal."

"Do you recall the author's name?"

"I'm sorry, I don't."

"Would it by any chance be Dr. Dansereau?"

"Possibly."

"And what was his article about?"

"Look, I can't tell you much. I repeat, I really don't understand anything about medicine. . . ."

"Forgive me for pestering you with my questions, but that research is very important. Dr. Dansereau is a friend of mine, you see, and he's a trifle secretive. Out of modesty, no doubt, he has never told his colleagues about this publication, and we'd all like to congratulate him. . . . You're sure you don't recall the title of his article?"

"I'm sorry, I don't. But now that I think of it, I believe it had something to do with an electrical machine that was attached to the skulls of lunatics, or something of the sort. . . . You should talk to Dr. Clément: he knows far more about it than I do."

"I shall do so without fail. I'm infinitely grateful to you, Maître Hébert."

Dr. Paquette shook a few more hands, then went directly home. An electrical machine . . . attached to the skulls of lunatics. So that was it. . . . He spent all night making plans, and at nine the next morning he telephoned Dr. Clément.

"Tell me, dear friend, is it true that you've received an article from a certain Dr. Dansereau?"

"Indeed. And it will appear in our next issue."

"Do you still have it ready to hand?"

"No, unfortunately it's already at the printer."

"Is your whole issue complete?"

"Almost. Do you want to submit an article?"

"I'm working on some extremely important research. If my hunch is correct, and I'll be able to verify that in the next few days, I intend to submit an article that will create quite a stir. Would it be too much to ask you to keep aside a few pages for me?"

"Of course, Doctor, of course. We all know the quality of your contributions, and I'm certain the editorial board will agree. But you must move quickly."

"Give me two weeks. You won't regret it. I promise you a bombshell."

* * *

"God bless you, Soeur Jeanne. What's new this morning?"

"God bless you, Dr. Dansereau. It will be a difficult day, I fear: Louis Campagna has already started operating. He's been waiting for you. It's the first of the month, have you forgotten?"

"No, I haven't. I'm a little behind because of the blizzard. How many patients?"

"About fifty."

"Very well. Let's get going. Still no word from Dr. Paquette?"

"No, and it's rather odd. According to Soeur Pudentienne, he's set up some kind of laboratory near the hydrotherapy room. It's full of diabolical machines and you can hear horrible shouting."

"What's he up to?"

"No one knows, he has the only key. He spends the whole day there, with patients. Soeur Pudentienne wanted to put in some ferns, but he had one of those tantrums. . . . It was the first time in the history of the asylum that someone used a potted fern as a projectile. It would be a doctor, of course. . . . But as you know, Soeur Pudentienne has a lively imagination, you can't always take her at her word; only yesterday she was asking where Soeur Thérèse was. I said she was travelling. . . ."

"You said the right thing. God bless you, Soeur Jeanne."

* * *

Louis Campagna was one of the best guards in the asylum, a man of Herculean strength, but extremely gentle with the patients. Before coming to the hospital he had worked as a bricklayer, mason, hotel bouncer, roadworker, tinsmith, and circus strong man. While he had done the work of four and had always been a man of exemplary sobriety, epilepsy had rendered it impossible for him to keep a job for more than a few months. His seizures were infrequent and very mild — most of the time he only had to rest a moment, then he could go back to work — but he inspired such fear in his fellow-workers that at the first sign of a seizure, he was dismissed on the spot.

Since he had been working at the asylum, everyone had found his work quite satisfactory. He was often called on to restrain agitated patients or to break up fights — his mere presence was an immediate deterrent — as well as when teeth were extracted. As this was particularly difficult work, it had long been the custom to group all the dental cases on the same day, usually the first of the month. For that purpose, a basement room near the furnaces had been outfitted with a solid oak armchair with leather straps at the feet and on the armrests. All day long, Louis pulled teeth. Often patients would ask him to extract them all, to end their suffering at one go.

During these operations, Louis was always assisted by a nun who prayed for the patients and comforted them, and by a doctor who was responsible for stopping haemorrhages, removing tooth fragments from gums, tending to infections, and reviving those who fainted. Dr. Villeneuve had performed these tasks until his retirement, when Bernard had taken over and, with Soeur Madeleine's agreement, made the treatment more humane by giving the patients a shot of brandy.

When Bernard walked into the torture room, Louis was washing his hands; the water in the bucket was already pink.

"Morning, Louis. I see you've started."

"Everything's fine, I'm on my fifth. Easy cases. No problem so far, but it won't last. The next one needs all his molars extracted, they're completely rotten. He's tough, but not very brave: fainted before he was even in the room. Soeur Angèle's looking after him."

"Give him a couple of brandies, that should relax him. It's quite normal for him to be scared; put yourself in his place."

"That's just it, Doctor, about being scared, there's something strange going on. . . . Now that we've got a minute, I'd like to have a word with you. It's about Dr. Paquette."

"Don't tell me you've pulled his teeth?"

"No, unfortunately. It's his patients who are scared. I looked after two of them this morning, and they both said the same thing: 'Once Dr. Paquette gets his hands on you, you stop worrying about having teeth pulled.' What's he doing to them?"

"I've no idea."

"It's none of my business, but if I were you I'd make enquiries. What they're telling me isn't normal. If Soeur Thérèse were still here she'd make him stop, that's for sure."

"I'll look into it, I promise. I'll take the names of the patients and I'll question them."

"I wish you would, Doctor. I've got my reputation to maintain."

* * *

It took Bernard and Oscar quite a while to get home that night. It was cold enough to pop nails out of walls, and the roads hadn't been ploughed yet.

294

Three times they had to get out and help the horse free the buggy, which had got stuck in the snow. The poor creature was expending half her energy fighting the cold and she was having trouble breathing; the vapour expelled from her nostrils was transformed immediately into crystals of ice, so they had to do their best to keep her from sweating.

They left the asylum at seven o'clock, and it was past nine when they finally reached the stable. After rubbing down the horse, they went to check on their installations — the tank covered with a rubber sheet, the transformer, the Williams' coil, and the little stove, which they lit at once.

"Too bad we can't treat patients during the winter. . . . And to think that, all this time, Dr. Paquette's electrocuting them."

"What did you say, Oscar?"

"Just what everybody knows: he puts electrical wires on their skulls, then he gives them shocks until they faint. The patients told me."

"Why don't they complain?"

"Because they're afraid to. They'd never say a word to the nuns or the doctors. The worst of it is, it works: the patients will do anything to avoid going back, including getting cured. But he won't be there much longer."

"What do you mean?"

"Do you promise to keep it secret?"

"I promise."

"It was Wilfrid's idea. Dr. Paquette always has food brought to his laboratory. The patients who work in the kitchens are in on the secret: they're going to poison him."

"But that's horrible!"

"Do you think so? I don't."

"Look, Oscar, you know the patients very well. Try to convince them to wait another week. I don't know yet how I'll do it, but I promise he'll stop those experiments."

"That won't be enough. He has to go."

"He will. Give me a week."

"All right. One week."

"Very well, we'd better go in now or Florence will be worried."

* * *

Florence is indeed very worried. She watches Bernard eat in silence. His brow is furrowed and he answers Dr. Villeneuve with monosyllables. Why is he so preoccupied? Perhaps she should wait until tomorrow. Or should she bring it up now? One worry more, or less. . . . She can't decide. . . . After they've eaten, he goes to his rocking-chair, lights a cigar, pours himself a brandy, drains it in one gulp, then pours another, which he sips more slowly.

"Did you go to the post office?"

No going back now. Might as well get to the point.

"Yes. There was something for you, some letters. I imagined your fingers would be frozen when you got home so I slit the envelopes."

"You did the right thing, Florence. Where are they?"

"On the buffet."

He gets to his feet, picks up the stack of letters, starts to read them. The first lie went well,

Florence tells herself, now it's just a question of waiting for the second one. Never has she dried the dishes so slowly. The first letters make him smile, he's smoking a little more calmly. That's a good sign. She congratulates herself for placing the letters of gratitude from former patients on top. There he goes, now he's reading the one from his publisher.... He frowns, rereads it, shrugs. Wait another few moments, then ask casually:

"Anything new?"

"Not much. Thank-you letters from some former patients. I always enjoy getting those ... and one from my French publisher."

"What does he have to say?"

"He's having financial difficulties, so he won't be able to bring out my book this year."

"That's too bad."

"It's not serious. Once my article appears in *La Revue Médicale du Canada Français*.... But there's something bizarre about his letter."

"What's that?"

"The style. From a publisher, it's disappointing."

Florence's shoulders slump and Oscar brings his face closer to his plate. He's red with shame.

* * *

Bernard is in Soeur Madeleine's office by seven o'clock the next morning. He hasn't slept. Dr. Paquette may be a loathsome individual, but to denounce a colleague.... No, he won't be denouncing him, he'll be saving his life. But still. ...

"What can I do for you, Dr. Dansereau?"

"I have to talk to Soeur Madeleine. It's urgent."

"I'm sorry, she's not here, she's in Dr. Paquette's laboratory. She didn't seem in a very good mood."

"Thank you, Sister. May God bless you a thousand times."

"Once is enough, Doctor."

Is it possible she knows already? Bernard races down endless corridors, finally coming to the laboratory. He slows his pace; the door opens a crack; he listens.

"I'm disappointed, Dr. Paquette, really very disappointed. Now you know what you must do."

19

La Revue Médicale du Canada Français was a prestigious journal, unique in French-speaking North
America, but of its two hundred subscribers, most of
them doctors, rare were those who read it, although
this did not detract from its prestige. Quite the
contrary, in fact.

The Spring 1892 issue appeared a few weeks
late. Whether it was glanced at distractedly or put to
sleep on the shelves of university libraries, one thing
is certain: for six months after it was distributed
there was no reaction to the articles it contained. All
that changed in the autumn, when a fierce scientific
debate was waged in every newspaper in the land.

It all began when Dr. Antoine Bussières of the
Hôtel-Dieu de Québec, an eminent member of the
Conservative Party and a fierce proponent of
ultramontanism, read the very first page of the
issue, on which the editor presented a summary of
its contents.

In a mordant style, Dr. Clément drew his
readers' attention to the remarkable contribution by
Dr. Paquette, an alienist at Saint-Jean-de-Dieu, giving particular emphasis to the unsettling circumstances surrounding his departure from the asylum.
Was it not shocking that this eminent specialist in

mental illnesses, who had studied in Paris under the illustrious Dr. Charcot, should be forced into exile in the United States in order to continue his research? Was this not a heavy loss for Canada, where there was such a need for high-quality doctors? Had the time come to reconsider having the asylum run by nuns, who seemed adamantly opposed to scientific research? Did not these deplorable events offer additional proof of the validity of the repeated demands by the many enlightened individuals who insisted that hospital administration be turned over to the government? He concluded his introduction with the hope that Dr. Paquette would be able freely to pursue his research in a country that was not crushed by the weight of obscurantism.

Upon reading this article, Dr. Bussières had leapt from his chair and immediately composed a long reply to be published in *La Vérité*, a newspaper whose self-assigned mandate was the denunciation of Jews, Freemasons, advocates of public schooling, any paintings except those in churches, and the theatre. In an essay studded with quotations from the French ultramontane journalist Louis Veuillot, Dr. Bussières denounced soulless science and expressed his pleasure at the departure of this Dr. Paquette: if he could not accommodate himself to the enlightened administration of some dedicated nuns, let him spread his materialistic venom among the Protestants. Canada had no need of such slimy serpents.

Dr. Clément's reply appeared in *La Patrie*, and the debate in the two newspapers continued for a full year. This controversy over the respective places of science and religion had the secondary effect of putting an end to Dr. Clément's political career: Laurier, who had enough problems with the clergy, swiftly dismissed him. The debate also left in obscurity the nonetheless exceptional contents of the *Revue Médicale*, particularly a most interesting article by a Dr. Mantha from Trois-Rivières, who presented some discoveries on the use of bread-mould in the treatment of infectious diseases, and an article by a Dr. Masse about the use of flax-seeds for treating chronic constipation.

Dr. Paquette's contribution, "On the Use of Electricity in the Treatment of Certain Mental Illnesses", took up almost half the issue: he began with the very modest declaration that his research was opening a new continent to modern science, and that electricity would be to the treatment of mental illness what the discovery of the microscope had been to biology. Next came an account of the spectacular cures of several cases of hypermania and circular madness, followed by some vague theoretical considerations accompanied by mathematical formulae that, while very elegant, were absolutely useless.

Lacking a place to pursue these experiments, he did not continue his research in French Canada. A year later, an English translation of the article appeared in the prestigious *American Review of Medicine*, published at Harvard. The treatment was briefly fashionable in the late nineteenth century; after some deaths from cardiac arrest, it was quickly abandoned. Some fifty years later, the method would be rediscovered and widely used.

Dr. Dansereau's article, "Magnets and Moods", dedicated to the memory of Soeur Thérèse-de-Jésus, appeared at the end of the issue. It went virtually unnoticed. Was that because of his description of the device, which was needlessly complicated, or because of the author's insistence that his machine was meant not to cure but simply to improve the moods of lunatics? ... No one ever knew.

* * *

In the months to come, Bernard received a total of two letters from readers. The first, oddly enough, came from Finland. How had his article reached that far-off country? That would remain a great mystery. ... A Finnish doctor, having learned about his article, had reproduced his machine and experimented with it on a dozen patients, with most satisfactory results.

The second letter came from Montreal: a young student who wished to study medicine and who, as a result, had shown a lively interest in the article told Bernard he had learned from a missionary uncle that the Chinese treated certain maladies by placing needles in the patients' bodies, and that he himself believed it was possible to influence not only moods but also the career choices of newborns by gently massaging specific parts of the body just before the umbilical cord was cut. Bernard was interested in this theory and corresponded with the young student until he had completed his medical studies and become a brilliant obstetrician. The young man was called Lionel Bienvenue: how could one whose very name meant "welcome" fail to believe in predestination?

Although he received only these two letters, Bernard was not overly disappointed. Once the article had been published he considered he had fulfilled his obligations to Soeur Thérèse. He was convinced, moreover, that no matter what circuitous ways it took, science would irrevocably pursue its course. Nor would anything prevent him from continuing his experiments in peace.

While his article had not stirred up the waves he had expected, his treatments, in contrast, had brought an avalanche of grateful letters. A number of his former patients had left the asylum, and he regularly heard from those who knew how to write. He even received letters from Italy. One patient, who had studied musical theory in the asylum's brass band, had learned that he was gifted as a singer, and that had taken him to the Opera in Milan. Another had resumed his career as an architect; he was already drawing up plans for second homes for megalomaniacal millionaires, but wanted to specialize in churches. He sent Bernard a few sketches in which the churches were at once incredibly complicated and very harmonious, adorned with a number of galleries and arcades, with many rose-windows and endless spires. Bernard examined them in the evening, by the fireside, rather as one might gaze at the road-maps for a country one would never visit, simply for the pleasure of an imaginary journey.

Another patient was now exiled in Manitoba, where he had become a farmer and a poet; while he had been unable to find a serious publisher for his first poems, he intended to try to publish a few copies at his own expense. He hadn't set his sights on any literary prizes, knowing in advance that, for some obscure reason, such rewards would always be withheld from cheerful authors. . . . If only a few of his poems could be set to music. . . . Perhaps the songs would become popular and would be sung at weddings and at family get-togethers. . . .

Other patients were now masons or rural mailmen, carters, confectioners, or weavers; a good many of the women were now mothers, while others had joined contemplative orders of nuns.

Every day, Florence went to the village post office for the mail. On her way home, she sorted the letters. At distant intervals there were still some replies from European publishers. These she opened with infinite care — the envelopes could always be useful — read without a hint of remorse, and threw in the fire once she was back at the house. The others she placed on the sideboard, and everyone was eager to hear Bernard read them in the evening, after supper.

* * *

A bathtub, a bed, some electrical wires, and a lie. . . . In the end they had needed very little to rebuild a human life, and to make the heart of time start beating again. . . . Even though the days were growing shorter and the sun paler, and winter stretched out to the end of time, Florence was happy. Slowly she dried the breakfast dishes, alone in her big house at last. On this morning of October 4, 1893, her men had partaken heartily of her pancakes and syrup, then gone off to work: Bernard and Oscar at the asylum, Dr. Villeneuve in the barn. Through the kitchen window she could see him bring in some logs. He would stir up the fire, then spend the rest of the day keeping an eye on poor Pierre-Henri Champagne, whom Bernard had brought home with him the day before. How long would it take to root out his unhappiness? In Dr. Villeneuve's opinion they would have to continue the treatment all day, perhaps even longer. Except for Oscar, he had never seen a man so unhappy. Were they being sensible? Florence didn't like them to extend the treatments for too long. They mustn't forget that these men and women would go back to live in society, perhaps even to their families.

After supper that night, they would wake the patient to ask him some questions (of what earthly use were prayers and multiplication tables?), then they would probably decide to let him go. They would keep him overnight, and the next morning after breakfast Florence would accompany him to the village, where he would board the tram that would take him to Montreal. She would see him off, then go to the post office before returning home. Bernard would bring another patient, and life would go on. They would place the madman or madwoman in the bathtub and spend a good part of the night with him or her. Should she suggest that Bernard slow down a little, take a few days off? At his age, wasn't it time for a rest?

After Florence had put away the dishes, she replaced her ring, which she always took off so the gold wouldn't tarnish, and went to the living room.

No, Bernard shouldn't stop. . . . Idleness was no good for men: Soeur Thérèse had been absolutely right. At one time or other hadn't every mother in the world said, as they watched their children tinkering with something: "At least they aren't getting into mischief"?

Florence smiled, then continued the task she had started the day before: using a pair of surgical scissors, she snipped the withered tips from the ferns that sat in every window of her house.